OTHER MEN'S SINS

A Maxwell Graham Mystery Thriller

Lawrence Falcetano

Other Men's Sins
A Maxwell Graham Mystery Thriller
Copyright © 2020 Lawrence Falcetano

All rights reserved. No part of this publication may be reproduced, distributed, or transmitted in any form or by any means, including photocopying, recording, or other electronic or mechanical methods without prior written permission from the author.

This is a work of fiction. Names, characters, businesses, places, events, and incidents are either the product of the author's imagination or used in a fictitious manner. Any resemblance to actual persons, living or dead, or actual events is purely coincidental.

First Edition

*"Other men's sins are before our eyes,
Our own are behind our backs."*

Seneca—Roman philosopher

To my wife, Susan:

For sorting through the bad to find the good
For making it clear and understood
For sorting through the wrongs to make them
right for walking in the dark to light the light.
The light shines!

Chapter 1

I stepped into the front entrance hall of the rectory, stomping rainwater off my shoes. There were a few plainclothes and uniform police on the scene, and forensics had already arrived. I spotted Chief Briggs standing by the doorway of Father Conlon's office. He had that look on his face that told me it was bad, something different, and something more than the everyday homicides we were accustomed to. I shook off a chill that wiggled up my spine as I started toward him. I walked past him and into the office without saying a word.

A large fluorescent light fixture in the ceiling lit the office bright, despite the gloominess outside. The perimeter walls were covered with polished wood panels, and two overstocked bookshelves stood on either side of a floor-to-ceiling window that looked out onto a flowered courtyard. On a far wall, behind a large mahogany desk, hung a large brass crucifix surrounded by several framed documents attesting to Father Conlon's academic achievements. A large potted plant stood in one corner of the room, while two leather armchairs and a metal file cabinet in an opposite corner made up the rest of the furnishings. My partner, Danny Nolan, was talking to a couple of forensics people and writing in his notepad, while a young detective I didn't know dusted for prints.

On the carpeted floor, next to the desk, lay the body of Father Andrew Conlon. The random holes in his chest and abdomen told me he had been stabbed multiple times; blood from each wound hole had bubbled up like an effervescent brook and trickled down both sides of his white shirt until it pooled onto the maroon carpet; his vacant eyes, in horror and surprise, looked up at the vaulted ceiling. It was tough for me to see my longtime friend and mentor in such a way.

What kind of thing could do this to another human being, I thought, *particularly a holy man?* I had seen lots of murders during my time in the homicide bureau, but none as heinous as this. What motivates a person to commit such butchery?

I looked away as Chief Briggs came up beside me.

"Custodian found him this morning," he said.

"What's the t.o.d.?"

"Between eight p.m. and midnight. The autopsy will tell us more."

Autopsy! Associating that word with Andy Conlon made me queasy.

Two guys from the medical examiner's office came in wheeling a gurney with a body bag on it. They placed Andy Conlon's body into it, zipped the bag close, and began to wheel it out. I walked back into the entrance hall. Briggs followed.

Mike Briggs stood six feet four and cultivated a gray mustache that sat obliquely beneath his beak-like nose and matching head of gray hair. He had the physique of a bodybuilder, and in the twelve years that I'd worked for him, I'd seen him handle himself with the greatest of ease against the largest of thugs. He could be as hard as nails and strictly by the book, but compassionate and understanding, as well. A widower for five years, his daughter and her husband, and his five grandchildren had filled his personal life since the untimely passing of his wife. Briggs ran the detective bureau by his own set of rules. Despite his tough reputation, any cop that worked for him was glad he did. Over the years, I found him to be a good friend when I needed one.

An August rain beat heavily against the stained glass of the rectory window as I opened it a few inches to let in some fresh air. The area was beginning to get stuffy as more people arrived to do their part in the investigation.

"He was like a part of my family," I said.

"I'm sorry," Briggs said. "How long have you known him, Max?"

"Since I was a kid," I said. "He taught me my catechism."

"He doesn't seem old enough."

"He was fresh from the seminary then. Later he married Marlene and me and baptized my daughters."

I looked at Briggs with as much seriousness on my face as I could muster while trying to abate my anger. "I want this one," I said.

"You got it," he said. "The department will give you every resource."

I was thanking Briggs as Detective Nolan walked over to us. He began reading from his notepad. "No sign of forced entry," he said. "His desk is undisturbed, and his wallet is still in his pocket with forty-six dollars in it." "Rules out robbery," Briggs said.

"And B&E," Danny added.

"What does that leave us?" I said.

"A vengeance killing?" Danny said.

"Who takes revenge out on a priest?" Briggs said.

We looked at each other for an answer…nobody had one.

As I watched the ME people push the gurney carrying the Father's body toward the front door, I wondered how I was going to break the news to my ex-wife, Marlene. She'd be more than upset. Andy Conlon hadn't been just a priest to us. He had been a part of the ups and downs of our lives, and a good friend to both of us during our nineteen-year marriage, and a symbol of strength during our divorce proceedings. Our daughters grew to love him almost like a second father. The void would be a great heartache for them as well. I was particularly concerned about my mother. The news of Father Conlon's death would be devastating to her. He had been like another son to her during the years when my brother and I were growing up.

My stomach was feeling queasy again.

"Where's the guy that found him?" I said.

"Garcia's with him," Danny said. "He's about to take him downtown for a statement."

"I want to talk to him first," I said.

Briggs put his big hand on my shoulder; "I've got a meeting," he said. "Anything you need, come see me."

I thanked him again, and he and Danny headed toward the main entrance. Briggs paused to say something quick to Garcia before he and Danny left by the front door. I walked across the vestibule to where Garcia was standing with his arms folded over his chest, looking like he wished he were somewhere else.

Miguel Garcia was a good cop and seasoned veteran in homicide, but Monday mornings were always a tough go for him. He liked to tip his elbow on weekends, and it usually took him at least until midday Monday to get his act together.

A young man in a short-sleeve shirt and work overalls was sitting on a wooden bench behind Garcia. He looked in his mid-twenties, well-groomed and handsome. His blonde hair was neatly cut and styled, and his skin glowed with a healthy tan; beside him on the bench, he laid a leather pouch crammed with hand tools. He was twisting a pair of unsoiled work gloves in his hands, not nervously, but as if to do something to occupy his time while he waited. He didn't present the picture of a custodian but looked to me more like a young lawyer doing weekend work around his own home. When I approached them, Garcia turned to the young man and said, "This is Detective Graham. He needs to ask you a few questions."

The young man looked up at me with a nod and a smile.

Good start, I thought.

"Have you spoken to anyone yet?" I said.

Before he could answer, Garcia said, "Chief wants him in for a statement as soon as you're done. I'll wait by the door."

As Garcia ambled toward the front door, I sat on the bench. The young man placed his work gloves on the bench next to him and slid over a bit to give me room. His demeanor was calm and obliging, and he didn't seem the least bit unsettled by the tragedy he'd discovered less than an hour earlier. Something about that bothered me.

"What's your name?" I said.

"Davy Crockett," he said.

If this guy thought he was being funny, he was about to find my fist in his face. I wasn't in the mood. He saw my look and said, "That's my real name, David Crockett." He removed his driver's license from his wallet and showed it to me without my asking. I looked at it and nodded. He put it away.

"Happens every time," he said.

Okay, I thought, *an easy name to remember.*

"Tell me what happened this morning... Davy."

He inched up toward the front edge of the bench seat and without having to think about it said, "I went to Father Conlon's office around 6:00 a.m. to replace an electrical outlet he had reported to be faulty."

"Are you sure of the time?"

"Yeah."

"How can you be sure?"

"I met Father Faynor on the stairs. He always takes his morning jog at 6:00 a.m."

"Do you usually start work that early?"

"Sometimes, if I got a lot of catching up to do. I live in the third-floor apartment here in the rectory. It makes my job a lot easier."

"No morning traffic to fight," I said.

He missed the levity and continued. "I knew it would be a good time since the Father wouldn't be in his office that early."

"How would you know that?"

"He's rarely in his office before eight in the morning."

"Go on."

"When I walked in—"

"Was the door locked?"

"I have a master key for every room in the rectory and church, but I didn't have to use it."

"So, the door was not locked?"

"Yes, it's weird because Father Conlon always locks his office door at night."

"Does anyone else have a key?"

"Father Faynor. "It's his office."

I nodded. He continued.

When I went in, I saw Father Conlon lying on the floor beside his desk. The reading light on his desk was on, and I could see him. His mouth was open, and his eyes were wide, staring up at the ceiling. I never saw a look like that on anybody.

Crockett's description of what he'd seen made my stomach queasy again, not because of the morbidity of details but because of the personal nature of the crime. It was hard for me to think of Andy Conlon that way.

"What did you do next? "

"I froze for a moment until my mind cleared. Then I ran out and woke up Monsignor Belducci. After I convinced the Monsignor, he wasn't having a nightmare, he called the cops."

"Did you or the Monsignor go back to the office after he notified the police?"

"No way. We waited by the front door of the rectory until they got here."

"While you were in the office, did you see anything unusual, anything out of place or disturbed?"

"Didn't have time. When I saw the body, I got my ass outta there."

"Did you see anyone else around?"

"Just Father Faynor on the stairs."

"Does Father Faynor live in the rectory too?"

"On the second floor like the other priests."

"What was he doing when you saw him?"

"Jogging down the steps, on his way out."

"Did you exchange words?"

"He asked me why I was up so early. I told him I had work to do in Father Conlon's office."

"What did he say?"

"Nothing, he just jogged out the front door."

"Do you have a regular schedule for cleaning the offices?"

"I give all the offices a quick clean daily."

"What's that entail?"

"Emptying trash pails and vacuuming, it's part of my schedule. The heavy cleaning is done when it's needed, you know, washing windows, and furniture polishing and such."

When I got up, he stood with me, picked up his tool pouch, stuffed his gloves into his side pocket, and followed me to the front door where Garcia was waiting.

"How long have you been working here?" I said.

"Almost two years," he said. "Father Conlon helped get me the job."

I would check his credentials later. For now, I had no reason not to believe him. Garcia held the front door open and waited for Crockett. The rain had stopped, and the sun was cooking the blacktop enough to cause steam to rise from it.

"Thanks for your time," I said. "I'll be in touch."

As Crockett walked past Garcia, he said, "Anytime... detective."

I didn't like the way he'd said it.

As I drove back to the precinct, I tried to think of the easiest way for me to break the news to Marlene. I would have to drive to the house in South Jersey and tell her in person, it's not the kind of thing you do over the phone. The girls would be in school, and it would be best if they didn't see Marlene's initial reaction. She could tell them later in the way she thought would be best.

St. Trinity Church in midtown had been our church since Marlene and I married. Although we were both born and cultivated in the New Jersey suburbs, I'd become involved with the church when Father Conlon transferred across the river from St. Michael's. Andy Conlon had been a young priest at St. Michael's when I was a boy. I attended his bible classes and spilled my guts to him in the confessional booth more times than I cared to remember. Although he was ten years my senior, we'd created a bond of friendship and a trust that lasted throughout the years. He married Marlene and me and baptized our girls. It was naturally expected that he'd perform the marriage ceremonies for Christie and Justine when their day came, an expectation that would never be fulfilled. After Marlene and I divorced, I drifted away from the fundamentals of formalized religion and as a result, hadn't seen Andy Conlon in almost a year until that morning.

I parked in my usual spot at the precinct and climbed the stair to the homicide bureau on the second floor. When I walked in, the coolness of the air conditioning felt good against my damp shirt and reminded me of how much I wished the air conditioner in my Chevy Nova was still working. I needed a new ride, but those double child support payments negated that possibility.

I sat down at my desk and rubbed my eyes with the heels of my hands. Monday morning had started like a train wreck, and I was sure the rest of the week wouldn't be better. There would be the unpleasant business of having to break the news to my mother, Marlene, and the kids and Andy's father and sister, and then the anguish of a wake and funeral followed by an investigation into who and why someone would do this to a priest.

When I opened my eyes and looked up, Danny Nolan was walking toward my desk. Under my auspices, Danny had evolved into a good detective and reliable partner. He was single, handsome, smart, and ambitious; his two preoccupations in life were his police career and finding a wife. Although he'd only been in the bureau a few years, his good sense and natural perception for police work made him someone whose judgment I had learned to trust.

"They haven't started the autopsy yet," he said, "but I can give you this much: the weapon of choice wasn't a knife."

"What does that mean?"

"ME says the wounds were punctures, made by something with a smooth shaft rather than a blade."

"Doesn't narrow it down much."

"The holes were clean with no ragged edges—all twenty-two of them."

Queasy again.

"Was a weapon found?"

"Not much of anything found," Danny said, "except prints. They're running them now. When I get the sheets on the autopsy and the prints, I'll get them to you right away." "Thanks," I said.

He sat down in the chair beside my desk, leaned in closer to me, and spoke in a low voice. "If there's anything I can do, Max," he said. "I mean... well, what I'm trying to say, is if you need me, I'm here for you."

"Thanks, Danny boy," I said. "But, right now, what I have to do, I have to do alone. I'm on my way to tell Arthur Conlon, his son—the priest—has been brutally murdered."

Chapter 2

Having to tell Andy Conlon's eighty-five-year-old father, his only son had been murdered, was about as easy as swallowing a mouthful of fishhooks. The elder's reaction was what one might expect: disbelief, then denial, and then devastation. Andy's younger sister, Eileen, became so distraught; the family physician had to be called in to sedate her.

The Colon's lived in an elaborate well-kept Ranch home in an elaborate well-kept neighborhood on Long Island. Arthur Conlon became a widower a few years after he'd retired from his executive position with the Long Island Railroad; his only daughter, Eileen, decided to follow in her brother's footsteps, and become a nun. After spending several years in a convent, she lost the calling when she fell in love with a salesman who eventually left her for another man. Dejected and despondent, she began selling local real estate and lived an almost reclusive lifestyle, remaining unmarried and continuing to live in the same house where she and Andy grew up. I had been distantly acquainted with the Colon's through Andy, attending several family functions over the years with Marlene, and after our divorce, bringing Sandy along to a 60th birthday party for Andy. The Colon's were good people and didn't deserve this tragedy, but then, where is life's justice?

When I got back to the bureau, I spent an hour wrapping up an unrelated case at the top of my caseload. With the events of the morning swimming in my head, I was lucky to get through it without any inaccuracies. Briggs was a stickler for accuracy.

When I finished, I brought my report into Briggs's office and laid it on his desk. When I got back to my desk, Danny Nolan was waiting for me. He was holding a clear plastic evidence bag out in front of him for me to see. There was something blue and shiny inside. I looked closer into the bag and said, "I see a screwdriver."

"A Craftsman Phillips screwdriver, #3 with a six-inch shaft," Danny said. "And the blood on it matches Father Conlon's. No prints on the handle."

I took the plastic bag from Danny and brought it back to my desk. I sat in my chair and looked hard into the bag. "Where was this found?"

"Trash bin behind the rectory," Danny said, "wrapped inside a pair of blood-soaked work overalls. Blood on the overalls is Father Conlon's too."

"Who would leave incriminating evidence so close to the scene of the crime?" I said.

"Somebody's in a big hurry," Danny said.

"Or somebody who wanted this to be found," I said.

"There was a large brass crucifix lying on the carpet by the body," Danny said. "It had a good amount of Father Conlon's blood on the crosspiece. They also found Father Conlon's prints on it, and a second set of unknown prints. We ran the unknown prints through the database but didn't find a match."

I thanked Danny for the info, locked my desk, and looked at my watch. It was 1:00 p.m. and I wanted to get to Marlene's house to break the news to her about Andy before she heard it reported impersonally through the media. I knew the girls would be in school and I'd have to take the chance that she'd be home. She had taken a part-time job in a local dry cleaner, but I couldn't remember which days she worked.

"Get some lunch?" Danny said.

"Can't. I'm on my way to break the news to Marlene."

"Want company for the ride?"

"Thanks, but after that, I'm going to head home and turn in early. We'll see what turns up tomorrow," I said.

I made good time on the Parkway and got to Marlene's house before three. The Volvo was parked in the driveway, which was a good indication she was home. I parked the Chevy behind it and got out. As I started up the walkway, the front door opened, and Marlene appeared behind the screen door looking solemn. She was wearing that look of impending doom, which I had seen on her face so many times in the past. Years of worry and anxiety had made her good at reading my body language, and today she knew I wasn't there with bright news. Despite the adversity of our contentious divorce, Marlene still looked good. Her shoulder-length hair was held back behind her ears by a red headband and her smooth complexion was taut with a healthy glow, attesting to the fact that she hardly ever needed to wear make-up.

My marriage to Marlene crumbled after nineteen years. I guess I was too busy, or too stupid to see it coming. Living with a cop was no picnic for her. There were the years of shift work and weekend work and holiday work that stretched her tolerance to the limit. And she had to endure the daily uncertainty of whether her husband would come home in one piece or come home at all. We had loved each other as much as any married couple could and had produced two beautiful daughters, Christie and Justine. But near the end, the bickering and complaining became too much, and I conceded to the divorce. I couldn't blame her. She had the marriage, and I had the career, and sometimes it's hard to balance both. After a contentious divorce proceeding, we decided to pursue a civil discourse for the sake of our daughters. So far, our relationship had been on an even keel and we were both working to keep it that way. Marlene opened the screen door, let me in, and waited.

"Andy Conlon is dead," I said.

There is never an easy way to say it.

The blood drained from her face, turning it the color of baker's dough. When I saw her lips begin to quiver and her eyes roll up, I reached out quickly and caught her just as her legs gave out from under her. I carried her into the living room and placed her on the sofa. She stirred and came to before I could return from the kitchen with a glass of cold water. I sat on the edge of the sofa beside her.

"Drink this," I said.

She sat up and sipped the drink with shaky hands. "When I saw your face," she said, "I knew something was wrong. I thought of the girls."

I took the glass from her and set it on the coffee table. The color was returning to her face. "Was it an accident?"

"He was murdered," I said.

"Oh, God," she said.

She squeezed her eyes shut, pushing tears out from behind the lids. She dropped her face onto my chest and began to sob. I let her. She continued sobbing for nearly a full minute before she looked up at me and said, "When did it happen?"

"Sometime last night. He was found in his office this morning."

She removed a tissue from the waistband of her sweatpants and wiped it over her face.

"How'd it happen?"

"I think it'd be better if you didn't know the details."

"Why would somebody do this, Max?"

"I intend to find out," I said.

She got up and walked into the kitchen and got herself another drink from the faucet and splashed water over her face.

"How will I tell the girls?" she said.

"I'll tell them if you want," I said, as I walked into the kitchen.

She went to the table and sat. After a moment, she said, "It'll be better if I do it."

I was relieved that she'd said that, but tried not to show it.

"His father and sister will be devastated," she said, "such a close family. It's a blessing his mom's not alive to bear this."

"They're doing the best they can," I said

"You've already told them?"

"I couldn't let a stranger tell them, although it wasn't any easier for them coming from me."

"The wake and funeral will be tough to get through," she said, "especially for the girls."

"I'm sure you'll make them understand," I said.

She looked up at me and said, "But who will make them understand why something like this happens to a man of God?" I had no answer.

I left before the girls got home from school, feeling a bit guilty that I'd left Marlene alone to tell them the sad news, but comforted by the thought that she would do a better job with it than I would.

It was almost 5:00 p.m. by the time I reached central Jersey. I turned off the Parkway and drove directly to my mother's house in Greenridge Borough, which is a small community in north-central New Jersey situated east of Route 78 and nestled comfortably in the shadows of the Watchung Mountains. My mother was still living in the same house where my brother Vinnie and I had grown up. The house was just a short drive from my apartment in Greenridge. I had been lucky enough to get the apartment after my divorce. Marlene and I sold our home, satisfied our debts, and split the profit. Having grown up in Greenridge, it felt only natural to go back there and live the single life again.

When you turned onto Sanford Street, the old colonial-style house was the first you saw. After my father died, my mother lived in the house for a short while with my brother Vinnie. When uncle Carmine passed, my mother's sister, my aunt Theresa, naturally went to live with my mother. That gave Vinnie the chance to move out and head to the South West. He'd always hated the climate in the North East, and when he got a job offer to sell real estate in Arizona, he jumped at it. My mother could never understand why Vinnie would want to leave her, but sometimes mothers have a hard time understanding those things.

I parked in the driveway, turned off the car, and sat for a minute. The house hadn't changed much in fifty years other than the new paint job my mother had applied last year, changing the color from a mundane white to Sandpiper beige. It still had the wrap-around porch with the two-seater swing in front of the big windows. The silver milk can my father had placed next to the front door was still there, although now its finish had weathered to a dull gray. The ancient Oak Tree in the front yard still looked healthy and strong. I remembered the rope my father tied to a limb so my brother Vinnie and I could swing out over the front sidewalk. Even now, I could see the dark abrasions on that limb where the rope had worn away some bark.

I got out and walked up the wooden stairs and rang the front doorbell. My stomach began to feel queasy again. I was afraid of what effect this kind of news might have on my seventy-six-year-old mother.

My mother had kept herself in pretty good shape for a woman in her seventies. She was moderately overweight and still spry on her feet. Her dyed black hair was always neatly kept and looked good against her olive complexion. Although she came from tough Italian stock, news like this is never easy to accept.

When she opened the door, her eyes were already moist. I walked in and put my arms around her. She held me tight and said, "How could this happen, Maxwell?" I walked her to the living room sofa and sat beside her. The television was on and the reporters were telling my mother everything she didn't need to know about the killing of Andy Conlon. I picked up the remote from the coffee table and snapped off the TV. Enough wrong information had already been disseminated through that boob tube, and for my mother to hear more would only add to her grief.

Her eyes were wet and puffy. It was obvious she'd been sobbing for some time. Maybe I should have come here before breaking the news to Marlene.

"It'll be okay, ma," I said.

She kept dabbing her eyes with her white handkerchief and rubbing the gold crucifix around her neck between her thumb and forefinger. I kept patting her back in a meager attempt to comfort her.

"How will I tell your Aunt Theresa when she comes back from the market?" she said.

"The TV said he was—"

"It's true," I said, "We're doing everything to find out who did this, and why."

She leaned her head back on the sofa and closed her eyes. "Santa Lucia, give me strength," she said.

I waited a full thirty seconds before I said, "Would you like me to stay until Aunt Theresa gets home?" No answer.

"I'm just thinking of when your father passed," she said, with her eyes still closed. "The hurt never goes away, and now this."

"Time heals all wounds," I said, then felt stupid for saying it.

I stayed with my mother for more than an hour after I'd convinced her to make coffee. Over a dish of homemade anisette biscotti, we sat at the kitchen table and talked about life and death, family and friends, and joy and sorrow. The conversation bordered on melancholy at times, but she didn't see it that way, and the memories made her feel better. She spoke of Aunts and Uncles, mostly gone now. She mentioned nieces and nephews, married with children of their own. She detailed the births of her own two sons like it happened yesterday, and her face brightened at the memory of the day her grandchildren came into the world. With that thought, she leaned forward and kissed my cheek, as if I were the only one that had anything to do with that. To keep the conversation lively, I let her continue; occasionally adding a quick comment or question, to which I'd already known the answer. The therapy was good for her, and I could see her strength coming back. I knew she would be okay and able to tell Aunt Theresa the news without breaking down again. Before I left, I took her face between my hands and kissed her on her forehead. When she smiled and assured me she'd be okay, I told her I'd call her after work.

Sandy lived in a three-story garden apartment building, just twenty minutes from where I lived, and ten minutes from my mother's house. As a defense attorney, I was sure she'd heard the news by now and was anxious to give me her opinion on the whole mess. In the short time we had been dating, her counsel had been invaluable to me on more than one occasion.

I parked in front of the building and climbed the two sets of stairs to Sandy's second-floor apartment. I walked down the long hallway, and although I had a key, I knocked. Sandy opened the door almost immediately. She was wearing gray sweatpants and a matching sweatshirt and she had nothing on her feet. Her auburn hair was pulled back into a short ponytail. When she saw me, she threw her arms around me, held tight, and kissed me consolingly on the lips. Her display of affection told me she had already heard the news. Behind her on the living room TV, a local channel was broadcasting the events of the murder at St. Trinity Church. I fought off the urge to reach for the remote.

"It's terrible," she said as she closed the door. "I'm so sorry, Lovey."

"It's a shocker," I said.

I went to the fridge and got myself a beer and sat on the sofa to listen to what the reporters had to say. Sandy scrunched up beside me, tucking her bare feet under herself.

Sandy and I had been together for almost a year. We kept running into each other whenever we had mutual court assignments. I was immediately attracted to her. And although our relationship had been strictly professional for a while, I finally worked up enough nerve to strike up a casual conversation with her in the hallway of the courthouse during a brief recess. I was surprised when she responded positively.

Sandra Sullivan grew up in a well-to-do Connecticut family. Her father was a prominent judge and her mother a wealthy homemaker. As an only child, she admits she was obscenely spoiled until her father's untimely death brought a falling out between her and her mother over the distribution of the family estate. Things had soured so badly between them that she viewed it as a blessing when she was accepted into Harvard and was able to live away from home. She was the best thing that happened in my life in a long time and I didn't want to blow the relationship, so I was playing my cards right. I was too blind, selfish, or stupid to see my marriage to Marlene slowly crumbling, and I didn't want anything like that to happen between Sandy and me.

"What kind of person would do a thing like this?" Sandy said.

I took a sip of beer. "The kind of person with a sick motive and no conscience, the world's full of them."

A young woman reporter was standing on the church steps, detailing whatever information had been released to the media, which wasn't much. She was talking fast and using lots of words but not saying anything of importance.

Ratings are everything.

"They don't seem to know much," Sandy said.

"Not much to know right now," I said, "case is too new. It'll hit the fan tomorrow when I start digging. Briggs was understanding enough to give me this one exclusively. The entire department is at my disposal."

"Smart cop, that Briggs," Sandy said.

Chapter 3

I didn't expect to sleep well and didn't. Sandy had made us something to eat, and I left her apartment around eight. When I got to my apartment, I took a shower and got right into bed. Images of Andy Conlon lying on the floor in his office wouldn't leave me. I saw him with my eyes open, and I saw him with my eyes closed. I wondered if that image would ever fade from my memory. When I finally fell asleep, past images rolled through my mind like an old-time movie: Sunday mass, catechism, the dreaded confessional box, my First Holy Communion, confirmation, the marriage ceremony, and the baptisms of my daughters, all with the likeness of Andy Conlon's benevolent face in the midst of it.

I woke up in the morning feeling crappy, started the coffee machine, and took another shower. I wasn't hungry, so I just had coffee. I put on my khaki pants, a tan dress shirt, and a pair of brown casual shoes. I didn't feel like a tie. Although my window air conditioning unit kept my apartment comfortably cool, the morning looked sweltering and that damned unit in the Chevy blew only warm air. I kept promising myself I'd get it fixed, but life kept getting in the way.

Before I left, I called Danny Nolan on my cell. He was already on his way to the precinct. I told him I was heading to the church rectory for interviews and asked him to dig up everything he could on David Crockett.

"Are you kidding?" he said.

I couldn't help smiling. "For real," I said. "He's the church custodian who found Father Conlon yesterday morning. He's currently living in the rectory. I want his history."

"Davy Crockett?" Danny repeated.
"Davy Crockett," I said, "without the coonskin cap."

***

St. Trinity Church is a monolith of stone, concrete, and marble constructed around 1890. It has stood as a symbol of Catholic strength and stability since its construction and has served its parishioners with the reaching hand of God ever since. Its gables and bell tower rise high above the streets of Manhattan and its architectural beauty stands second only to the great St. Patrick's Cathedral on 5th Avenue.

I was lucky enough to find a parking place on the street alongside the rectory, which stands at the rear of the Church and next to the church cemetery. I got out and walked in through a side entrance. Inside, the marble entrance hall was dimly lit, cold and hollow, and smelled faintly of incense. I had to look closely to read the brass-plated directory on the wall to find my way to the Monsignor's office. As I was scanning the list, I heard a voice behind me, "May I help you?" I looked to see a young woman standing in a doorway. She was perhaps, thirty and wholesomely pretty, with short dark hair and wirerimmed glasses.

"I'm here to see Monsignor Belducci," I said.

"Is he expecting you?"

I showed her my ID.

She crossed herself and said, "It's about Father Conlon, isn't it?"

"Yes," I said.

"The Father will be missed," she said. "He was a blessed soul. I'm Sister Mary Margaret. Come with me. I'll see if the Monsignor's available."

I followed her down a marble hallway until we stopped in front of a pair of double doors. A polished brass plate on the gloss mahogany door read: **MONSIGNOR BELDUCCI,** in bold black letters. She paused with her hand on the brass doorknob. "Wait here," she said. Then she opened the door and disappeared inside. In less than a minute, the door opened again. "Go in," she said. She stepped aside to let me pass, and then walked out, closing the door softly behind her.

The office was a large mahogany rectangle. A floor-to-ceiling window looked out onto a courtyard offering a view of a bubbling fountain centered atop a manicured patch of lawn and set amongst a group of statues of holy figures and brightly colored shrubberies. A brass chandelier hung from the center of the ceiling in front of a large mahogany desk and on a pedestal in a far corner, stood a three-foot-high statue of the Virgin Mary in pastel colors. On the wall behind the desk hung a brass crucifix and several framed documents and certificates, neatly arranged. I could see Belducci's name in calligraphy on each one of them.

Monsignor Belducci was a big man, grossly overweight and well into his seventies, with a full head of white hair, flabby jowls, and a huge double chin, no doubt, the product of too much linguini and meatballs. Sitting there behind his desk in his black cassock robe and clerical collar, I couldn't help thinking—at the risk of sacrilege—that he resembled "Jabba the Hut". He looked up at me over the top of his reading glasses and said, "Come in my son." As I walked closer to the desk, I could smell his aftershave, "Old Spice," I think. We shook hands. His grip was weak for a big man.

"I assume you're the detective in charge."

"I am," I said. "Maxwell Graham, Homicide."

"Please sit," he said. He indicated for me to sit in one of the two leather upholstered chairs that were positioned obliquely in front of his desk. I sat. He removed his glasses, closed the folder he'd been reading, and leaned back in his chair, folding his hands comfortably over his ample belly.

"Ugly business," he said. "I hope this thing can be resolved as expeditiously and discreetly as possible."

"We'll do our best," I said.

"We will certainly cooperate in every way," he said. "What is it you'd like to know?"

"Anything you can tell me about Father Conlon, anything that might be helpful? Anything at all that would make some sense out of why this would happen."

The Monsignor leaned forward on his desk, emitted a small burp without excusing himself, and said, "Father Conlon was a fine priest and a fine man. His work here has been exemplary and without reproach. He is loved by many and will be missed by many. That's why none of this makes sense."

"What about his recent personal life, outside the church?"

"The church *was* Father Conlon's life. He spent his free time involved with youth organizations, local boys' clubs, Boy Scouts of America, YMCA. He was a very giving person, which made him a great priest."

"Can you tell me about yesterday morning when the Father was found?"

"I was asleep," he said. "It was very early. I remember being awakened by the sound of my name being called. It was a loud high shrill voice and I remember the urgency in it. As I sat up in bed, my heart pounding, there came a rapping on my door. When I opened the door, young Crockett was waving his arms frantically and shouting that we needed to call the police. 'Father Conlon is dead!' he kept repeating. When I became cognizant enough to collect my thoughts, I hurried to the phone on my bedside table and dialed 911."

"Was anyone else awakened?"

"I didn't see anyone at the time. After Crockett calmed down a bit, we waited by the rectory door for the police to arrive. While we waited, he explained to me what he had seen. I wanted to enter the Father's office to see for myself, but young Crockett said it would best if I didn't."

"What happened after the police arrived?"

"Crockett led them to Father Conlon's office. Before long, more detectives and investigators arrived. I waited in the front vestibule, keeping out of the way, but remaining available. Chief of detectives. I think his name was, Riggs—"

"Chief Briggs," I said.

"Thank you," he said. "He asked us a few questions and said he would need official statements from us. He said someone would be around today. I guess that would be you?"

"Other than the police, did anyone else show up on the scene?"

"The havoc awoke Father Sidletski and Father Romano. Father Faynor showed up a while later. He was returning from his morning run."

"How many priests reside here?"

"There have always been five including myself: Conlon, Sidletski, Romano, and Faynor. Each has his room on the second floor and an office on this floor. The kitchen and bath facilities are shared."

"I'll need a statement from each of them," I said. "You can arrange that with them."

"I would also like to see Father Conlon's room."

"I'll have Sister Mary Margaret show you the way."

He picked up his phone, spoke softly into it, and then hung up.

I stood up and removed my business card from my wallet, wrote my cell phone number on it, and handed it to the Monsignor. "Thank you for your help," I said. "If you need to reach me, that's my number at the precinct and my cell number."

He took the card without looking at it and placed it in the top drawer of his desk. As I turned to leave, he stopped me with: "There *is* one thing, detective. It may not be important, just a personal observation."

"Everything's important in a murder investigation," I said.

"It seems to me; Father Conlon has been a bit out of sorts lately."

"How so?"

"For the past month, he seemed to be somewhat less tolerant of things, easily agitated. I'm a good judge of character traits, as I'm sure you are, and I can tell when something weighs on a person's mind enough to alter his demeanor."

"Had the Father been ill lately?"

"I don't think so, but perhaps I'm making too much of it. It may be of no consequence."

I hadn't seen Andy in almost a year, so I was unable to confirm or refute the Monsignor's assessment. Andy had always had an even personality, and I was sure Belducci could have easily noticed any deviation from it. Andy was the kind of guy who always "had it together". He knew exactly where he wanted to go and exactly how to get there, but he wasn't a robot and just as susceptible to the gamut of human emotions as the rest of us. The Monsignor's comments may have been nothing, but I made a mental note of it. "Did you know Father Conlon well?" I wasn't expecting the question.

"Since I was a boy," I said. "He was a big part of my life."

He made the sign of the cross in the air in front of my face and said, "Then your loss is greater than ours. The Lord will bear your burden with you."

He opened his top desk drawer and removed a metal key ring. I mentally counted at least a dozen keys on it of various sizes. He came around his desk, hooked his arm through mine, and walked with me to the door.

"With the strength of God," he said, "we'll all get through this. I'll be calling the family with words of comfort this morning, and this afternoon we will begin planning for the funeral mass. It will be held in the church. I'll preside over the mass myself. The Father will then be interred in the church cemetery."

When he opened the door, Sister Mary Margaret was waiting for me in the hallway. The Monsignor selected a key from the ring and handed it to her.

"Sister Mary Margaret will show you to Father Conlon's room," he said.

He released my arm and said, "The Lord be with you."

"And also, with you," I said and walked out.

I hadn't used that litany since my church-going days.

On our way up to Andy's room, I questioned Sister Mary Margaret about the keys.

"Monsignor has access to every room in the rectory and church," she said. "It's something few people are aware of—security concerns."

"And you're one of the privileged few."

She smiled. "He keeps the keys locked in his desk and always knows where they are or who has them; he'll be expecting me to return them immediately."

"Of course," I said, "security concerns."

***

Andy's room was in disarray, which was something I hadn't expected to see. He had always been neat and orderly, which was part of his "having it together" attitude. His bed was unmade and the small desk beneath the window was cluttered with papers and folders and books and a laptop that appeared to be in sleep mode. On the floor beside the bed lay a pair of pajamas and a pair of well-worn slippers. A bathrobe had been thrown hastily on the foot of the bed. There was a TV on a stand in one corner and a small bookcase beside that. On the wall above the bookcase were framed photographs of Andy's parents and another of his sister Eileen. On the night table next to the bed there was an opened can of ginger ale and a bag of chips. Besides that lay a gold watch, a gold ring and a pair of reading glasses. The people from forensics hadn't inspected the room yet, so I tried to be as careful as I could.

Using my fingernail, I lifted the lid of the laptop. The screen flickered on almost instantly showing me a travel website. There were scenic views of Arizona and the American southwest and a smaller window showing previously visited sites related to travel. Andy might have been planning a vacation. I closed the lid, and with the same fingernail pulled back the top drawer of the desk. Nothing unusual here: pens, pencils, elastic bands, paper clips, and a package of sugarless chewing gum. I closed the drawer with my hip and moved to the night table. I pulled back the drawer and saw a box of Nyquil, a bottle of aspirin, a string of rosary beads, and a paperback copy of *The Shack*. In the closet hung several vestments and an assortment of lay clothes on plastic hangers. The dresser drawers held underwear, pajamas, and socks. I found nothing that indicated to me that Andy wasn't leading a normal life, other than a degree of untidiness, which he'd probably acquired with age; hardly anything to criticize him for. The Monsignor said Andy had been, "out of sorts" but there was nothing here to corroborate that, other than some cold medicine. I left feeling satisfied that I'd found nothing untoward.

Chapter 4

When I got back to my desk, I called the switchboard at the rectory and got the phone numbers for Fathers Sidletski, Romano, and Faynor. I wanted their insight into Andy's behavior and their take on what happened the morning Andy was found. I phoned Father Faynor first, and he said he'd be glad to speak with me and would be available right after lunch.

As I hung up the phone, I saw the genial but indomitable face of my partner, Danny Nolan, moving toward me. He sat opposite me, flipped open his notepad, and began to read:

"David William Crockett, age, twenty-six years, five feet ten, one hundred and sixty pounds, born in Michigan, the only child of David and Andrea Crockett. The family moved to Connecticut when he was six. He attended a tech school after high school to study carpentry. No military service. No criminal record, never married. He has eight hundred and fifty dollars in a Citibank savings account and two hundred in checking. No inordinate debt. His father died three years ago. His mother lives with his stepfather in their Connecticut home. He's estranged from his mother, never approved of the man she married. After his father died, he moved out of the house, wandered around for a while, and then found his way to the New York metro area. He bounced around for a few years on various construction jobs until he took a steady job at the church as a handyman/custodian, which is his current residence. He's been there for two years." He closed his notepad.

I sat back and took a deep breath. "You're sure you didn't leave anything out?"

"If I did, it's not important."

"So, you're telling me, this guy's clean?"

"As an altar boy—no pun intended."

"What about the overalls and the screwdriver?"

"Too obvious. Being a carpenter doesn't make him a killer, and he's not the only one who wears overalls and has access to a screwdriver. There are service people that go in and out of that church almost daily."

"True," I said, "but someone once taught me to search places that are 'excessively obvious'. There's where you're likely to find what you're looking for."

"What does that mean, 'excessively obvious'?"

"It means you look in places that are right before your eyes, where you wouldn't think to look because you believe it isn't worth looking there. Often, you find what you're looking for. It's a theory that works."

"Oh," Danny said.

I wasn't sure he got it.

I wrote the phone numbers for Father Sidletski and Romano on a piece of paper and asked Danny to conduct the interviews for me. He took the paper and said he would, then went to his desk and picked up his phone. His help would leave me enough time to interview Father Faynor this afternoon and get home in time to make the wake tonight.

I picked up the Daily News from the corner of my desk and opened it to the front page. The headlines blared of the murder at St. Trinity. The narrative was sketchy and the reporting a bit speculative, but this morning, all New Yorkers would learn the details of the atrocity that occurred there. I turned to the obituaries and confirmed when the wake and funeral mass would be. Interment would be in the church cemetery, just as Monsignor Belducci had promised. It was something I wasn't looking forward to.

Father Faynor was a tall man and looked to be in his mid-fifties. His hair was dark without a speck of gray, parted to one side and long enough to cover the tops of his ears. His complexion was ruddy with chiseled features and when he smiled; his teeth shone bright white behind thin lips. He was dressed in jeans and a long sleeve flannel shirt.

We sat at a table in the rectory dining room bathed in the colors of stained glass. He extended his hand, offering a delicate handshake.

"Thank you for seeing me, Father," I said.

"Glad to help," he said.

His voice was deep and monotone and without conviction.

"I won't take up much of your time," I said. "How long have you known Father Conlon?"

"He was here when I arrived, five years ago," he said.

"We hit it off right away. Andy was that kind of person."

"So, you became friendly from the start?"

He smiled and said, "Well, it takes time for people to become close friends, even priests."

"Then it would be safe for me to assume you knew him well enough to see any personality changes in him."

"How do you mean?"

"His general demeanor or any change you might have noticed in his behavior, lately?"

"Andy kept an even personality," he said. "If there were any changes, they would be easy to detect."

"I take it that means you saw none?"

"Changes?"

"In the way, he acted."

"No."

"Can you tell me what you saw the morning the Father was found?"

He shifted his position in his chair, crossed his leg over his knee and thought for a moment before he said, "I was returning from my morning run when I spotted the police and medical people in front of the rectory."

"What time would that have been?"

"After six, I always begin my run at 6:00 a.m. and it invariably takes me thirty minutes."

"What did you do then?"

"I hurried up the steps and into the front vestibule. There were people everywhere in hurried confusion. I spotted Monsignor Belducci standing by the staircase with Father Romano and Father Sidletski. When I approached him, he told me what had happened. I was shocked beyond belief."

"I assume you used the staircase to the front door to begin your morning jog?"

"Of course."

"Then you passed Father Conlon's office that morning?"

"Naturally."

"Did you hear or see anything unusual?"

"It was very early," he said. "Almost everyone was still asleep."

Suddenly his face showed the concern of an afterthought, as he drew his eyebrows together and added, "That is, except for that Crockett."

"The custodian."

"Yes. I passed him on the stairs on my way out." "You mention his name with a hint of disdain," I said.

He uncrossed his legs, leaned forward, and rested his elbows on the table.

"I don't have anything personally against Crockett," he said, "but the boy's an enigma."

"How's so?"

"He's a bit strange. Keeps to himself most of the time, shows up when you least expect him to."

"I don't understand," I said.

"He's everywhere you look, in a dark corner of the church or emerging from the shadows of the rectory or suddenly from behind an opened door, and always at the strangest times."

"Isn't that his job; to be where he's needed? He's the custodian."

"Perhaps," he said, "but I've never been comfortable with him. I don't trust him."

"What has he done to make you feel this way?"

"Nothing definitive," he said, "but there was the time when there was an accusation made concerning missing collection money."

"He was accused of stealing?"

"No, but he was the one under suspicion due to his accessibility." And then he said quickly, "This was all very hush, hush and I'm only telling you this because of your position, you understand."

"The Monsignor doesn't seem to have a problem with Crockett," I said.

"Lord, forgive me," he said, "but the Monsignor is sometimes overly trusting and forgiving to the wrong people. If I were you, I'd keep a wary eye on Crockett."

I didn't find Crockett likable when I interviewed him, but I didn't get the feeling he was predisposed to crime. Danny Nolan did report that Crockett had no criminal record.

Father Faynor's opinion of Crockett could be erroneous, or maybe he just didn't like the guy or maybe there was more to it. Until there was some corroboration, I wouldn't give Faynor's suspicions much credence but, as always, I made a mental note.

Chapter 5

The funeral mass concluded at 10:00 a.m. I attended the service alone. Sandy couldn't attend due to a court commitment. Monsignor Belducci gave a beautiful eulogy followed by a roster of Metro area clergymen and laypeople who knew Andy and felt the need to say nice things about him. I was offered the opportunity to say my piece, but I declined. I knew there would be a shower of accolades for Andy and my personal feelings for him were mine alone. There wasn't an empty pew in the chapel, so I stood at the rear behind a couple of elderly women who cried incessantly into their handkerchiefs. Halfway up the aisle, I spotted Marlene and my daughters, but I thought it best to stay away.

The pallbearers consisted of six young men from various organizations with which the Father had been involved. They carried the bronze casket out the double doors to the small cemetery at the side of the church. The mourners followed in a double line with me taking up the rear. It was hot as usual, but the gentle breeze and the beautiful surroundings of the cemetery made the morning almost peasant, despite the solemn occasion. The procession continued up a grassy slope to the burial site where the casket was placed into position, after which family and friends stood, or sat on folding chairs around it. I kept a distance and watched the proceedings with as much reverence as I could muster. I supposed these practices bring solace to most people, but I've never taken much comfort in looking at a corpse on display, that's why I'd decided not to attend the wake. The good memories of a person live in one's mind forever and to blemish them with the morbidity of these proceedings is a sin in itself.

I stood beneath a huge Sycamore tree and quietly watched and listened. The faces in the crowd were somber and teary-eyed. Every attendant wore black and moved in reverent slow motion, heads hung low, fingers laced together in prayer. Arthur Conlon and his daughter were seated at the head of the casket, looking weak and weary. The pain in their faces made me think of my daughters. I couldn't fathom losing a child that way.

Trying not to think about it, I turned away from the gravesite and walked a few feet into a small clearing. As I did, I spotted Crockett in the distance, half-hidden beneath the overhanging limbs of a Willow Tree. He was leaning against the tree with his hands in the side pockets of his overalls. He was puffing a cigarette that dangled from his lips while he watched the ceremony from beneath the brim of a New York Yankees's cap pulled low over his eyes. He stood motionless and showed about as much emotion as any of the nearby cement statues that dotted the cemetery grounds. I watched him until he snatched the cigarette from his lips, flicked it in a high arc in the direction of the gravesite, and walked casually back to the rectory.

I wondered why he wasn't among the mourners.

After the funeral, I drove back to my apartment, got into my street clothes, and drove to the precinct. There was a note on my desk from Garcia telling me Chief Briggs wanted to see me ASAP. I walked across the room to Briggs's office. He waved me in before I could knock. He was still wearing the black suit he had worn at the funeral, which made his hair and mustache appear more silver than the dull gray they were. He sat in his swivel chair and slid a manila file folder across his desk toward me as I entered.

"Autopsy and fingerprint reports," he said.

He leaned back and waited while I gave the reports a quick read.

"No prints other than the Father's?" I said.

"Not a smudge," Briggs said. "And his prints were found around his desk and on his personal items, just where they should be."

I thought of Crockett's dust cloth gliding over exposed surfaces, obliterating any prints that might have told us a story. *Cleanliness is next to Godliness.*

I turned the page and continued to read.

"According to this, death was the result of asphyxiation due to strangulation."

"And twenty-two puncture wounds, *postmortem*," Briggs said.

"Conlon was strangled to death and then stabbed?"

"That's how the report reads."

"Why would somebody do a thing like that? Dead is dead."

"Sick hatred, uncontrollable rage."

"Could there be an error in the report?"

"Not likely," Briggs said.

I read some more.

"No other marks on the body, other than a large open wound on the back of his head."

"Probably got it when he hit the floor," Briggs said.

I closed the folder and handed it back to Briggs.

"What could a priest do to make someone hate him that much? Andy Conlon certainly wasn't that kind of person."

"People hate for a variety of reasons," Briggs said, "most of the time it's unjustified."

"I get it," I said, "but a priest?"

Briggs didn't answer.

Chapter 6

On Friday morning, I drove out to the Conlon home in my Chevy. I had called Eileen Conlon on Wednesday and planned to interview her. She was more than cooperative, even eager, but told me I'd be unable to talk to her father since he'd been taken to a local hospital and was under a doctor's care. The death of his son was a great blow to him and his eighty-five years, and she didn't want to lose him too. I promised not to take up much of her time.

When I arrived at the house around mid-morning, I drove up the double driveway and parked in front of the two-car garage. The house was a sprawling ranch sided with cedar shakes that had been stained a light brown. White shutters hung on either side of the windows on the street side, and a slate gray roof covered it all nicely. The grounds were immaculately kept. The manicured front yard was lined on either side with evergreen trees and bordered for privacy with flowered rhododendron and closely placed Arborvitae.

I got out and walked up the paved walkway to the front door. I pushed the door button and waited while a melody of soft chimes resounded inside the house. Within a minute, Eileen Conlon answered the door, looking weary. No amount of make-up could hide the evidence of what she'd been through this past week. The paleness of her skin contrasted against her glossy black hair, which she kept pulled away from her face with a white headband. And the excessive amount of red color she'd applied to her full lips didn't do much to improve her appearance. She was wearing black slacks, a white long sleeve blouse, and open-toed bedroom slippers.

"Detective, Graham," she said. "Come in." I stepped into a small entrance hall and then followed her into a large living room. She led me to an oversized, white leather sofa. I sat near enough to her to detect a mixture of expensive perfume and stale cigarette smoke. The room was comfortable, but a bit ornate for my taste. A plush mauve-colored carpet covered the expanse of floor and matching flowered draperies hung from the large windows that were centered in the front wall beside the main entrance door. Several recliners, a mahogany bar covered in white leather, a mahogany coffee table, and a white baby grand piano completed the furnishings. There was a framed photograph of Andy on the piano, arm in arm with his father and sister.

"Thank you for seeing me so soon," I said.

"Although the Lord saw fit to take Andy," she said, "he was all I had left in this life, other than my father. And I fear he won't be with me much longer."

"I'm sorry," I said, not knowing what else to say. "Just a few questions and I'll be on my way."

I waited while she slid a cigarette from a pack on the coffee table, lit it and leaned back against the sofa cushion. She took a long drag and let the smoke out through pursed lips, slowly.

"Is there any reason you can think of why anyone would want to do this to Andy?" I said.

"I can't make sense of it," she said. "My mind's been reeling. Andy wasn't perfect, but he was a good person. You know that as well as anyone."

"Of course," I said. "Is it possible he might have been hiding something? Involved with something or someone that he shouldn't have been involved with?"

"You mean, a woman?" she said.

I didn't answer.

She leaned forward and snuffed out her cigarette in the ashtray on the coffee table, then looked at me with indignation on her face. "The answer to your question is, no. Andy had no past and no secrets, he was exactly what everyone thought he was. What you saw was what you got."

"I'm sorry," I said, "but you've got to understand. I must ask these questions if we what to get anywhere."

She looked suddenly contrite. "Of course, you're right," she said. "I'm being foolish. You were as close to Andy as family. Please, go on."

"Have you noticed any changes in Andy recently, changes in his behavior, moodiness, anything out of the ordinary?"

"No, No," she said, suddenly agitated again as she got up and walked hurriedly to the front window. She stood with her hands on the back of her hips, looking out at the street without saying a word.

I waited.

When she turned around, her eyes were moist with tears. I got up from the sofa and went to her. "Can I get you something?" I said.

She removed a handkerchief from her pocket and began to wipe her eyes. "I'll be all right," she said.

I took my business card from my wallet and handed it to her. "Maybe this is a bad time," I said.

"I'm sorry," she said. "I haven't been much help."

"We'll try again when you're feeling better," I said.

As I turned to the door, she took hold of my arm. "Do you think you can find whoever did this to Andy?" "I'm gonna try my hardest," I said and meant it.

When I got back to my desk in the bureau, Detective Garcia had left a note paper-clipped to my blotter telling me I'd gotten a call from a Martin Bloomhouse of the Youth recreation center in midtown Manhattan and that he'd called concerning Father Conlon. I was to return his call at my earliest convenience. I didn't know Martin Bloomhouse but punched up his number right away.

A deep voice answered the line, identifying its owner as Marty Bloomhouse.

"Detective, Graham," I said, "returning your call."

"Thanks, detective," Bloomhouse said. "I know you're heading the investigation into Father Conlon's murder. I have some information that might be helpful."

I could hear the sense of urgency and concern in his voice.

"You can come by the bureau anytime," I said. "I'm free all afternoon."

There was a short pause. "Can you come to the rec center today? There's someone I'm sure you'll want to meet. Do you know where it is?"

"I'll be there in twenty minutes," I said.

The Youth recreation center was an aging two-story building in lower Manhattan. It consisted of a large gymnasium, a movie theater, several workout rooms, a craft center, and a few administrative offices on the second floor. A fenced-in playground stood against one side of the building. There didn't seem to be a defined main entrance, so I parked in the parking lot and walked to a pair of steel double doors, which opened to the gym. As soon as I stepped through the doors, I was engulfed by the combined odors of sweat and floor varnish, bringing back memories of my high school days when I'd been on the wrestling team. When your face gets that close to the floor, you don't soon forget that smell. It's funny how different smells can trigger different memories.

Other than a few guys shooting hoops to my left, the gym was empty. On the opposite side of the gym, a door opened, and a kid walked across the floor toward me. He was wearing gray sweats and high-top sneakers and a bright red sweatband around his head. He looked to be about eighteen, tall, lean and handsome, and walked with a slight rhythm. When he approached me, he said, "You Detective Graham?"

"I am," I said, with an amiable smile.

He didn't smile back.

"I'll take you to Mr. Bloomhouse's office," he said.

I followed him across the gym, and through the door from which he'd emerged. Although he'd started with a smile, he never spoke another word, but suddenly turned matter of fact and unfriendly. We walked down a short hallway until we reached an open doorway. He pointed through the doorway, then turned and started back down the hallway, leaving me without an introduction. I walked through the doorway.

The office walls were cinderblock painted a dull white, with a paneled drop ceiling and a gloss ceramic floor. It was sparsely furnished with a metal filing cabinet, two wooden chairs, and a large wooden desk. All the furnishings seemed old or secondhand. Behind the desk, Bloomhouse sat with a basketball between his ankles, working a hand pump and breathing heavily. He was short but well-built and had the body of a weightlifter. He wore a sleeveless sweatshirt and the muscles in his arms rippled each time he pushed on the air pump. He worked the pump with perfect rhythm and stopped only occasionally to push back his dark hair whenever it fell over his eyes.

"Take a load off," he said. "I'll be right with you."

I sat in a chair in front of the desk and watched as he continued filling the basketball. When he was finished, he bounced the ball a few times on the floor and then stuffed it into a mesh bag behind his desk with some others. He removed a handkerchief from his back pocket and wiped his face and forehead. "Thanks for coming," he said.

He got up and walked to a small refrigerator in a corner, removed two bottles of Perrier, and brought them back to the desk. He handed me one, sat down and guzzled his before I could say thanks. When he was finished and fully refreshed, he said. "This Father Conlon thing is a terrible business." "The worst kind," I said.

"I mean... a priest. Who would want to hurt a priest?"

"Somebody," I said. "What did you want to see me about?"

"It may be nothing," he said, "But I know how you guys think. Everything means something when you're investigating a crime."

"It does," I said. "What do you have?"

"The kid, Kevin Regan, I want him to tell you." "I don't know him," I said.

"He's a local kid, been involved with the rec center for a couple of years now. He was close to Father Conlon. It may be nothing, but like I said—"

He was interrupted by a knock on the doorframe. Bloomhouse looked over my shoulder and said, "Kevin. Come in." When I turned, I saw a tall kid walking toward me. He was of average weight and built and looked to be about ten years old. There was nothing distinctive about him, except that his hair was bright red and parted neatly to one side, an unusual look for a kid growing up these days.

"This is Detective, Graham," he said. "The one I told you about."

The kid looked me over but didn't say a word.

"I want you to tell him what you told me," Bloomhouse said.

The kid leaned against the desk and pushed his hands down into the front pockets of his jeans. "I don't wanna get in no trouble," he said.

"I explained everything to you," Bloomhouse said. "You want to help Father Conlon, don't you?" The kid nodded.

"Father Conlon and Kevin were very close," Bloomhouse said to me. "You could say the Father took a special interest in him. Ain't that right, Kevin?"

The kid nodded again.

I leaned forward in my seat, closer to him, and said. "There's nothing to be afraid of. Take your time and say what you wanna say."

"Tell him about that day on the playground," Bloomhouse said.

The kid took a moment to gather his thoughts, and then said, "The Father and me was shootin' hoops on the playground."

"When?"

"About a month ago," Bloomhouse added.

"We shoot hoops a lot," the kid said. "The Father was pretty good."

"We took a break and sat on the bench by the fence. Father bought two sodas. It was hot, and we were sweating. I took a long drink, and when I finished I saw him."

"The boy's father," Bloomhouse said.

"That's a problem?"

"His parents are divorced. Kevin lives with his mom."

I looked at Bloomhouse for an explanation. He shook his head. "Go on, Kevin," he said.

"The Father asked him to leave, but he wouldn't. Said the Father had no right keepin' him from his son. The father said it wasn't up to him; it was up to the court. That's when he came inside the gate. The father asked him to leave again, but he started to yell. The Father yelled back, and I thought they were gonna fight 'til, the Father sat down on the bench again."

"Tell Detective Graham what you heard," Bloomhouse said.

"I-I heard him say to the Father, 'I'll kill you if that's what it takes'."

The boy looked embarrassed and lowered his chin to his chest.

Bloomhouse got up quickly, grabbed the bag of balls and walked around the desk with them.

"Thank you, Kevin," he said as he handed the kid the bag. "Take these and give them to Carlos, please. Ask him to put them away."

The kid flung the bag over his shoulder and started to walk toward the door.

"Thanks for the help, Kevin," I said.

Kevin started for the door, then stopped and said, "Is my Dad in trouble?"

"No, he's not," I said.

With that, he turned and disappeared through the doorway without a word.

After Kevin had gone, Bloomhouse walked back behind his desk and sat again.

"What do you know about Kevin's father?" I said.

"Only what I have on file. He's an itinerant carpenter. Works construction jobs wherever he can."

"What's his problem with Father Conlon?"

"He seems to resent Conlon spending so much time with his son. You think there's anything to this, I mean the threat?"

"Maybe," I said. "You said Kevin lives with his mother?"

"Not far from here."

"Got an address?"

Bloomhouse started tapping the keys to a small laptop on the corner of his desk. He read from the screen as he wrote the info on a piece of paper, then slid it across the desk to me.

"Has this guy been around before?" I said.

"Kevin said he's been around a couple of times, but the kid must have gotten scared this time, for him to come to me with it now."

I slid the paper inside my wallet.

"Or scared for Father Conlon," I said.

Chapter 7

"The blood on the overalls matches the blood on the screwdriver, and on the carpet," Danny said, "It's Father Conlon's. Forensics found some body hair on the inside of the overalls. They're checking DNA."

"Let's get DNA samples from Crockett, Faynor, Sidletski, Romano and Belducci," I said.

"Jeeze Max, you wanna ask a Monsignor for his DNA?"

"Why not? Is his DNA different from anyone else's?"

"Maybe more holy," Danny said.

"Take Dawson from forensics," I said, "he'll help you get the samples. I'll see Crockett myself."

I took the paper from my wallet that Bloomhouse had given me and read it again. "Get a rundown on a guy named, Arnold Regan," I said, "R-e-g-a-n, a construction worker. See if you can find out if he's working now and where."

Danny wrote the name down in his notepad and went back to his desk. I called the rectory and got Crockett on the phone. When I told him we needed a DNA sample from him, he wasn't happy and graciously informed me he didn't have to give me one. When I graciously informed him, I could charge him with obstruction of justice. He said, "fuck" softly into the phone and then hung up.

When I arrived at the rectory an hour later, I found Crockett mopping the front hallway. He was pushing around a metal bucket on wheels and moving a mop across the floor from wall to wall like a sailor swabbing a deck. I admired his technique. When he saw me, he stopped working and leaned his mop against a doorframe.

"I don't like this," he said. "Am I a suspect?" "Maybe," I said.
"What do you mean?"
"DNA will tell."
"I told you everything I know."
I removed an evidence bag from my pocket and took out the swab stick from inside it. I held the swab stick up for him to see.
"Open wide," I said.
"Are you kidding?"
"It's S.O.P."
"What the hell's that mean?"
"Standard operating procedure."
"I don't have to do this, ya know."
"Yes, you do."
"What's it gonna prove?"
"Maybe, that you didn't kill Father Conlon."
"This is a bunch o' crap. I cooperated with you guys."
"You think I like doing this?"
I held the swab up and waited for him to open. It reminded me of the hard times I had trying to feed my daughters when they were infants. When he reluctantly opened his mouth, I swiped inside his cheek quickly, then dropped the swab into the evidence bag and sealed the top. I put the bag into my pocket and said, "Nobody is accusing you of anything, but by the way you're acting, you're making yourself look guilty."
He regarded that for a moment and then took a long deep breath. "I been a little uptight lately," he said, "with all that's been goin' on."
"How was Father Conlon's relationship with the other priest in the rectory?" I said.
He removed a pack of cigarettes from the top pocket behind his overalls, lit one and took a long drag.
"The Father got along with everybody," he said, through a cloud of exhaled smoke. "You know what kinda guy he was. He was pretty tight with Father Faynor, I think."
"Why do you think?"

"They seemed to spend a lotta time together, ate lunch together most days. I saw them having a catch on the back lawn a couple of times. Things like that."

"How do *you* get along with Father Faynor?"

He took another drag on his cigarette and said, "Me? I don't think he likes me."

"Because?"

"He's not as friendly, as the others when we talk. Reported me to the Monsignor several times for something I'd done, which upset him. Almost got me fired. He's an asshole." "The man's a priest," I said.

"Sorry," Crockett said, but I don't think he meant it.

"Does he have any reason to dislike you?"

"None that I know of. Maybe he's got issues."

"Why weren't you at Father Conlon's funeral?"

He wasn't expecting that one and hesitated before he answered. "I wanted to attend but changed my mind. I just felt lousy about it."

"But not lousy enough to watch from a distance," I said.

He wasn't expecting that one either. Tossing the remainder of his cigarette into the water bucket, he said, "Father Conlon was a friend of mine, I didn't wanna see him that way." My sentiments exactly.

I was eating lunch with Sandy at Branigan's on West 54th Street. She was working her fork into a Caesar salad, trying unsuccessfully to spear a crouton. After several minutes of watching such a display of inept coordination, I reached into her plate, picked up the crouton, and held it in front of her lips. She accepted it delicately and chewed it like the lady she was.

"I would have gotten it," she said, "if you'd mind your own business."

"The clock was running out," I said. "I couldn't sit here and watch it defeat you."

She washed it down with a drink of Diet Coke and started in on the salad again. I took a bite of my tuna on rye.

Branigan's had been my favorite place to eat and drink for a lot of years. It was the place I took Sandy on our first date. Pete Branigan inherited the place from his father, who had opened it as a local tavern back in the forties. After his father passed, Pete turned it into a legitimate eating establishment. He served breakfast, lunch, and dinner, and, and the bar was always open. The interior carried an Americana motif. The walls were decorated with old photographs and newspapers with famous headlines from a time past: The Hindenburg disaster. The 1929 stock market crash and the 1939 New York World's fair. A banner hung over the front door announcing: **1921, the year the New York Yankees won their first pennant.** Customers loved the nostalgia with a yearning, ostensibly for a more civil time.

Patrons could enjoy their dinner at one of the round tables near the center of the room or choose a private booth along the perimeter walls. The mahogany bar, which ran the length of one wall, was always crowded.

"Any headway on the Andy Conlon case?" Sandy said.

She had caught me with a mouthful of sandwich. I shook my head, "no".

"Suspects?"

I put the rest of my sandwich down on my plate and took a swallow of my beer. It was obvious Sandy wasn't going to let me enjoy my lunch until she got the answers she wanted. Resignedly, I wiped my mouth with my napkin, and said, "Not only do I *not* have a suspect, but I don't have a motive."

"Priests don't get murdered every day," she said. "A case like this bogs down one's sense of logic." "Especially when it's close to home," I said.

She reached out and squeezed my hand.

"I'm sorry," she said.

"They found a pair of overalls and a screwdriver with blood on them in a trash bin behind the rectory. Lab says the blood is Andy's. Forensics found body hairs inside the overalls. I talked Crockett into giving me his DNA. Maybe I'll catch a break there."

"Preliminaries point to Crockett?" Sandy said.

"It's a start," I said. "He found the body, and he has access to every room in the church and rectory, including Father Conlon's. He claims he was friends with Andy, but I couldn't detect any genuine sympathy over the loss." "Establishes very little," she said.

"I know," I said. "And here's one for Sherlock Holmes. The autopsy report says Father Conlon was strangled, then stabbed. Asphyxiation was the official cause of death."

"That's a strange way to kill someone," Sandy said. "Why would anyone do that?"

I shrugged as I picked up my sandwich and took a bite.

"Well, one thing's for sure," she said. "The perp had to be someone who holds a deep hatred for Father Conlon. This was no mob hit, or spontaneous murder. The killer felt they had to use their hands to get satisfaction in taking his life and then took greater satisfaction with every repeated thrust of the murder weapon. That, at least, narrows it down." "To a priest hater?" I said, with a mouthful.

"Or a personal enemy of Andy Conlon's."

"How does a priest engender a personal enemy?" I said.

She began searching through the leaves of her salad for another crouton.

"Why not look for motive and then work from there?" she said.

"Elementary police detection," I said. "Are you offering me advice, counselor?"

"Just trying to be helpful," she said.

I finished my sandwich and drained my beer.

"I have my way," I said.

"You have your way with everything," she said.

"Does that include you?" I said.

She didn't answer but jammed her fork into the salad quickly and successfully speared a crouton.

"Bravo!" I said and clapped my hands.

She held it up for me to see while she poked her tongue out at me.

I loved it when she was silly.

After lunch, I walked Sandy back to the courthouse steps, kissed her on her cheek and told her I'd see her that night. Then I drove back to the bureau. As a rule, I use my Chevy Nova for work. Old habits die hard, but today I was driving a maroon Chevy Impala, one of many the division used for routine undercover work. I had somehow conveniently accepted it during shift transfers and decided to use it to take Sandy to lunch. It had a lot more room than my Nova and eight cylinders of power, but it was basic and nondescript and a bore to drive. I'd get back into my Chevy the first chance I got.

I pulled away from the curb and started down 54th Street. I hadn't driven two blocks when I noticed a dark green Ford pickup following closer to my rear than it should be. It let me get ahead of it a few times, then came up close again, the easiest way to get noticed when you're trying to tail someone, and trying *not* to get noticed. I put more distance between the truck and me so I could read the front license plate through my rear-view mirror. You learn to read a license tag backward easily enough once you've done it enough times. I made a mental note and made a right onto 8th Avenue. The pickup made the right with me. Although the windshield was obliterated by dust and reflections from the sun, I could tell there was a male driver behind the wheel, but I couldn't make out his features.

When I made a right onto West 53rd the truck followed, I was sure this guy was an amateur; but that didn't make him any less threatening. Why was I being followed?

He came up close to me and nearly bumped my rear end, then eased back again. He was starting to piss me off.

I continued down 53rd Street until I pulled to the curb and watched through my side-view mirror as he continued moving with traffic in my direction. He had no choice but to stay in his lane, which meant he would eventually pass directly to my left. As he approached, traffic came to a temporary standstill, which put him directly beside me. His passenger window was in the up position, so I was unable to identify him, even at close range. I could tell by the way he fidgeted in his seat, that he was eager to get on his way. He knew I was on to him and realized he'd become the victim of his own ineptitude. This guy was more of a clown than a threat, so I added insult to injury by simulating a handgun with my index finger and thumb and pointing it out my window at him. When he turned and looked at me, I dropped the hammer just as traffic began to move again. He got the message, hit the accelerator, and with a squeal of his tires, was gone.

I pulled out into traffic again and started back to headquarters. I had this fool's tag number, which meant I could easily identify the truck owner, and maybe who was driving it.

I parked the Impala in a space in front of headquarters and climbed the stairs to the homicide bureau. Danny Nolan was at his desk, talking on his phone. He ended his call just as I passed him and followed me to my desk without a word. He waited for me to sit, then took his notebook from his pocket. When he flipped it open, I knew I was in for a flood of info.

Danny was very efficient.

"Arnold Regan," he said. "Forty-six years of age married to Gwen Radcliff for twelve years. They have one son, Kevin Regan. Divorced a year ago. She got custody. Mental cruelty, according to the divorce decree."

I waited. I knew there'd be more.

"Arrested twice. Once for petty theft and once for Assault and Battery, both charges dropped. Rents an apartment on Rivington Street, not far from where his ex-wife lives. Drives a green Ford 150 pickup, New York registration. He's a carpenter by trade, works whenever he can. He's always broke. Pays out a lot of child support and he likes to drink."

"He working now?"

Danny continued reading without looking up. "A construction site near the Meadowlands in New Jersey. Oslo Construction, here's the address."

He tore off the info from his notepad and handed it to me. I read the plate number Danny had written. It matched the tag on the truck that had been following me.

"I wasn't sure how far back you wanted me to go," Danny said. "That's all I got."

As I said, Danny was very efficient.

I knew then, it was Regan who was following me or someone in Regan's truck. I wanted to know why.

Chapter 8

I retrieved my Chevy Nova from the police lot and left the Impala in its designated spot. Then I drove to the construction site in New Jersey where Regan was currently employed. The Chevy bounced over dusty terrain as I pulled next to a low-level building stacked with dimensional lumber and bundles of rebar. The skeleton of a two-story structure had been completed and a few roofers were laying shingles on the nearly completed roof. Several pieces of heavy equipment were in motion and a few cement trucks were dispensing concrete into a section of foundation. Not far from the work, a piece of land had been set aside for employee parking. I saw several sport vehicles and a half dozen pickup trucks. Parked at the end of the front row, I spotted the green Ford 150 with Regan's license plate on it. I drove to the parking area, parked a few spaces away from Regan's pickup, and waited. No one showed any interest in me or was curious as to who I was or why I was there. My dash clock told me it was three-thirty. I wasn't sure when quitting time was, but I was prepared to wait. While I waited, I worked on a "quarter pounder" with cheese, and a vanilla shake that I had purchased on the way. At a quarter to four, the noise and activity settled down along with the dust. Hardhats came off, and by four o'clock men dispersed from their respective job sites and walked hurriedly to their vehicles, eager to get their hands on a cold beer or a hot wife or girlfriends. Arnie Regan came out the side door of the building carrying a toolbox and headed for his truck. He was tall and slender with shoulder-length hair and a scruff of dark beard, peppered with gray. He wore work boots, jeans, and a gray sweatshirt with the sleeves cut off. I wiped my hands on a handful of napkins as I watched him unlock his driver-side door, place his toolbox into the truck bed, and climb in behind the wheel. I got out and walked up to the pickup as he was cranking down the driver's window. He looked up at me, surprised. I held my ID up for him to see.

"Why were you following me?" I said.

"I don't have to talk to you," he said.

"Talk to me or a judge," I said.

"You can't arrest me. I ain't done nothin'."

"I got a witness says you threatened to kill a priest."

"Bullshit."

"Why were you following me?"

"Why don't you mind your own business?" he said.

"Murder is my business," I said.

"I ain't done nothin'," he repeated.

I removed my handcuffs from my back pocket and held them up for him to see.

"Tell it to a jury," I said.

The sight of steel bracelets impressed upon him the importance of cooperating.

"This sucks," he said. "All I'm tryin' to do is get my kid back."

"By threatening to kill people. That doesn't work."

"That priest…he treated my son like he was his own, made it tougher for me to get closer to him again. I'm sure you know all about it by now."

"I know enough," I said, "except why you were following me."

"When I got the word you went to see Bloomhouse and spoke to my son. I wanted to know why." "When you got the word?" "I have friends," he said.

"Why'd you threaten the priest?"

"I asked him to lighten up on Kevin, give me half a chance to win him back. But he kept blowin' me off. Things got heated that day. I said what I felt at the time."

"And a week later he's found murdered," I said, "doesn't look good for you."

"It was in the heat of anger," he said. "I didn't think it would go any further. But when I learned that Bloomhouse called you, I knew there might be a problem. I followed you, hoping I could talk to you, tell you the truth before things got out of hand. When I lost you in traffic, I knew it would be just a matter of time before you found me."

"Father Conlon wasn't keeping you from your son," I said. "The courts are."

"He was in the way."

"And he's not," I said.

"I don't have to take this," he said. "If you wanna charge me with something, do it."

He leaned over and started the pickup. I reached in and grabbed him by his shirt collar and pulled his head through the window. "Listen you piece of crap," I said. "I don't like your attitude and I don't like you. I'm gonna find out who killed Father Conlon. If you had anything to do with it, you're gonna wish you never met me." I pushed him back into his seat.

He put the truck in reverse and backed away from me in a cloud of dust. As I watched him drive away, I wasn't sure whether to believe him. He had been caught up in a nasty divorce settlement that he had to live with. I was familiar with the scenario. My divorce from Marlene had been, but we'd settled amicably, and I could see my daughters almost anytime I chose, with Marlene's permission. But this guy was no saint. Bloomhouse said when Arnie drank too much, he had hand trouble. Bloomhouse wasn't specific in what he meant, but I could conjure up an ugly image. I couldn't be sympathetic to that under any circumstance.

Kevin Regan lived with his mother in a small apartment above a tailor shop on Orchard Street in the Lower East Side. I found a parking space out front and walked to a red door with the number 14 hand-painted in black. I pushed the door back and found myself at the bottom of a long staircase. I climbed the stairs until I came to a single door in the darkened hallway at the top. I stood for a moment and listened, but heard nothing from the other side. I knocked. In less than a minute, the door opened about six inches and a woman's face peered out at me. I held up my shield. "Detective Graham," I said. "NYPD."

"Has Kevin done something?"

"No," I said. "I'd like to talk to you about your ex-husband."

"I told the police I don't know anything about Arnie's business."

"This is more of a personal nature," I said. "May I come in?"

She thought for a moment, then opened the door and stepped back into a large living room.

"This is starting to become routine," she said, closing the door quickly. "Talking to the police, I mean."

"I'm sorry," I said. "I won't take much of your time."

She was a slender woman with short red hair. Although I guessed her to be in her mid-forties, her complexion was smooth and flawless with just a sprinkle of freckles on her cheeks. Her lips were thin and her teeth straight and white. She was wearing black jeans, a gray sweatshirt, and a pair of gray bedroom slippers. She indicated for me to take a seat on the sofa as she sat opposite me and crossed her legs, almost routinely, as if she'd done this so many times before. From where I sat, the apartment looked clean and well furnished. I could see a small kitchen flooded in sunlight from the front windows and a couple of bedrooms behind me.

"I met Kevin the other day at the Youth Center," I said.

"He's a fine boy."

"Thank you," she said. "I do my best."

"I suppose it's not easy, without—"

"Without a husband," she said, completing my sentence.

"I'm sorry," I said.

"What do you want to know about Arnie?"

"His name came up in an investigation I'm involved with. I was hoping you could give me some insight into his personality and background."

"What kind of investigation?" she said.

I ignored her question and said, "I've discovered your husband has been doing everything he can to get Kevin back with him."

"I have legal custody," she said.

She uncrossed her legs and sat upright before she continued; as if she wanted to be sure I understood everything she was about to say.

"Arnie is his own worst enemy," she said. "Our marriage was a good one until his drinking got out of hand. We loved each other and we both love Kevin," and then she added, "I'm sure he still does."

"Love, Kevin?" I said.

She seemed embarrassed by my question and didn't answer.

I said, "Does your husband have financial problems?"

"He keeps up with his child support," she said, "if that's what you're asking?"

"Is Kevin his biological son?"

"Yes."

"Arnie had a close relationship with Kevin, but his drinking came between them... and me. And four hundred dollars is a lot of money to have to give away every month. Buys a lot of booze."

I was beginning to dislike this guy more and more. "Did he abuse Kevin, physically?"

"No," she said. "But he was scary when he drank too much."

"I know your husband's been arrested more than once. Can you give me the details of the arrests?"

"He got into a bar fight with someone. Hit him over the head with a keg of beer. He thought he killed the guy. When he came home that night, he began packing, said the police were looking for him and he was running away. But before he could leave, the cops were at the door, and they took him. The next day the charges were dropped. I wished they'd have sent him away for a time."

"I apologize," I said. "But was your husband ever been abusive to you?"

I had embarrassed her again, but she offered, "Not physically, at times, verbally."

I stood, and she stood with me.

"Thank you, you've been a big help," I said as we walked toward the door. "I won't take up any more of your time."

"I don't mind," she said. "Like I said, it's getting to be routine."

In the open doorway, I took out my card and wrote my cell phone number on the back and handed it to her.

"If there's anything I can do for you or Kevin," I said, "just call my number." She glanced at the card, then put it in her pocket. "Thank you," she said and closed the door.

I drove back to the precinct feeling empathy for Gwen, Regan and Kevin. Circumstances created through no fault of one person can destroy a marriage. I can attest to that. But in this instance, it was Arnie's behavior that was eroding this marriage. It was obvious he had a bad temper, but could he be provoked enough to kill? No doubt, he'd built a solid dislike for Andy Conlon over time, which might be construed as a motive, but that doesn't make him a murderer. I'd add him to my suspect list and continue digging.

Chapter 9

Danny Nolan was sitting on the edge of my desk, sipping a latte and going over my notes.

I was drinking a black coffee and working on a jelly donut while I waited for his input.

"Regan has a possible motive," he said, "but I don't see one for Crockett."

When I bit into my doughnut, a gob of jelly oozed out from the small hole and fell onto my desktop. I grabbed a napkin and tried to wipe it up, but the paper tore and stuck to the gooey mess. "Damn," I said. "Next time, bring me a bagel." Danny tossed me a handful of napkins. I tried cleaning up the goo by moving the napkins in a circular motion, but it left a sticky film just the same.

"Don't wipe it," Danny said. "Dab it up."

I could tell by the smile on his face, he was enjoying the show.

"Don't tell me how to clean up my own mess," I said. "I've been living alone longer than you have." I dipped a corner of a napkin into my coffee and cleaned up the stickiness as best I could. Then I dried the wet spot with a fresh napkin.

"What did you get from your interviews with Sidletski and Romano?" I said.

"Sidletski is an elderly man," Danny said, "more afraid of the sin that was committed than the crime. He didn't offer much other than a succession of quotes from the New Testament. He claimed he was in his room asleep until he was awakened by the commotion."

I wiped my hands and tossed the used napkin and the rest of my doughnut in the trash basket. I put the top on my coffee cup and dropped that in.

"Did he give you his opinion on Crockett?" I said.

"Indifference, he said he doesn't know him well and hasn't had much contact with him. He suggested I ask Father Faynor. Said he felt Faynor was a close friend to Father Conlon and might know a bit more about Crockett since Conlon helped Crockett get the custodian job at the church."

"Crockett also told me, he and Conlon were close," I said. "And that Father Conlon had gotten him the job at the rectory. At least those two statements agree."

"Father Romano is middle-aged and speaks with a heavy Italian accent. It was tough for me to understand him at times.

You would've had an easier time interviewing him than me." "I don't speak Italian," I said.

"No, but coming from an Italian family, your ear is more in tune with deciphering the words."

"No one in my family speaks Italian much anymore," I said. "My mother and Aunt Theresa used to, but they communicate mostly in English now. If you don't use it, you lose it," I said.

"I still believe you would have had an easier time with him," Danny said.

"Just think of it as a lesson in ethnic vernacular, I said. "I'll round you out as a good investigator."

Danny didn't buy that, and said, "Romano has a strong negative opinion about Crockett. He doesn't trust him."

"Why not?"

"He gave no specific reason but was quick enough to condemn Crockett, which I felt was out of demeanor for a priest. I think he holds an unwarranted dislike for the guy. But there might be more to it."

I remembered Faynor having a similar opinion of Crockett and having nothing to corroborate his feelings, as well. Was this guy inherently unlikable? Or did they know more than they were willing to say?

"How did things go at the Conlon's?" Danny said.

Her father's been hospitalized, but Eileen Conlon is hellbent on finding her brother's killer. She seemed cooperative and eager to help but didn't like it when I asked her some questions about Andy that she felt disparaged his stature. I wanna dig deeper into her recent background. Find out as much as you can about what she's been up to the past years."

"Right on," Danny said.

"Right on?" I said.

Danny gave me a confused look. "What?"

"That saying went out with the seventies," I said.

Danny shrugged, and said, "Guess I heard it on TV."

He started to walk back to his desk, but then turned quickly, set up his shot, and tossed his empty coffee cup in a wide arc into my trash basket. It went in without touching the rim. He looked at me with a big smile.

"Right on," I said.

***

I wanted to search Father Faynor's room at the rectory without his knowledge. Of course, it wasn't the right thing to do without having probable cause to obtain a search warrant. I hoped to get Monsignor Belducci's consent to the search. I'd have to rely on his sense of righteousness and make him understand we were not committing a sin but serving the cause of justice. I wasn't sure what I was looking for or what I would find, but Faynor had gone out of his way to make Crockett look suspicious to me, and I wanted to know why.

When I called Monsignor Belducci, he wasn't receptive to the idea, until I was able to convince him it was an imperative part of the ongoing investigation into Father Conlon's death. Father Faynor would be hearing confessions that afternoon at two o'clock, Belducci said and suggested I come to the rectory then. When I arrived at the Monsignor's office, I could see he wasn't comfortable with my course of action, but gave me the key to Faynor's room just the same. After giving me directions to the room, he went into the church and stood guard, in case Faynor finished confessions earlier than scheduled. Working with a partner of such divine stature assuaged some of my guilt. Father Faynor's room was nearly identical to Andy Conlon's in size and shape. A chest of drawers, a twin bed and night table, and a single desk made up all the furnishings. The windows looked out to the side of the rectory where I could see part of the cemetery. I knew I didn't have much time and began opening drawers from the chest beneath the windows. The drawers held the usual amount of clothing folded neatly in piles. In the closet, a typical priest's wardrobe hung from plastic hangers: several robes and one black suit. A shoe rack on the floor held a pair of black leather dress shoes and a pair of Adidas running shoes. The desk was uncluttered, with a blotter, pencil cup, and several books, but no computer. There was a cellphone on the bedside table. I picked it up and punched up the phone information. I copied the phone's number down on my notepad and put the phone back as I'd found it. There were two drawers in the table. The top drawer held a couple of paperbacks, a package of Band-Aids and an address book. I wished I could read the contents of that book, but knew I didn't have time. The larger bottom drawer was stuffed full of folders and stacks of writing paper. I rummaged through them quickly and lifted the pile of paper away from the bottom of the drawer. When I did, a red and white lettered box the size of a pack of cigarettes caught my eye. When I read the wording on the box, I nearly lost my breath. I replaced the papers and returned the box as I had found it and closed the drawer. Bewildered by my discovery, I left the room asking myself the obvious question: *Why would a priest need a box of condoms?*

Chapter 10

"I've decided to hire a private investigator," Eileen Conlon said. We were standing in her living room in front of the grand piano. She looked more at ease than the last time I had seen her. She wasn't wearing any makeup and looked surprisingly attractive without it. She wore jeans and a flowered blouse, and her hair hung loosely to her shoulders.

Your prerogative, your money," I said.

"I know you're doing everything you can," she said, "but I've been tormented by Andy's death and need to find closure."

My father is hospitalized in ICU," she said. "He may not survive this ordeal."

Of course," I said, trying to show some empathy.

She had phoned me earlier and asked me to stop by to give me this information firsthand. I wasn't surprised. Most people in similar situations do the same thing, some out of frustration and some out of desperation.

"This is his name and info," she said. She handed me a piece of paper with the name, "Martin Denman" written on it.

"He came highly recommended. Perhaps you know him." The name Martin Denman didn't ring a bell.

"He used to work with an agency," she continued, "but now he works alone. He might be of some help to you."

"Maybe," I said. "But if he turns up anything I'd expect him to give it to the police."

"Of course," she said. "I've informed him of your friendship with Andy and your efforts to find Andy's—"

She hesitated and then continued. "He's quite willing to work with you in any way."

I didn't feel comfortable with that. I had all the partners I needed back at headquarters, and other than assistance from Danny Nolan, whom I trusted implicitly, I preferred to find Andy's killer on my own. It wasn't ego or arrogance, I felt I owed it to Andy and his family.

As I slid the piece of paper into my wallet, my eye picked up movement coming from the hallway to my right. When I looked, I saw a guy walking toward us and into the living room. He looked like he'd slept in his clothes. He wore wrinkled jeans and a long sleeve shirt, unbuttoned at the front and hanging out of his waist. He looked to be in his forties with a slender built but with broad shoulders. His dark hair was pulled back tight on his scalp and secured behind his head into a ponytail. As he walked, he drew on a cigarette several times and flicked his ashes into an ashtray that he carried precariously in his left hand. I could see an expression of surprise as Eileen Conlon looked suddenly in that direction and waited for him to enter the living room.

"Oh, Troy," she said, "I didn't know you were up."

As he approached us, he smothered his cigarette in the ashtray and set it on the piano. He reeked of stale smoke and booze and hadn't been close to a razor in days.

"This is Detective, Graham," Eileen Conlon said. "The one I told you about."

"Andy's friend," Troy said.

"I like to think so," I said.

"This is my brother, Troy," Eileen Conlon said.

I had to tighten my jaw muscles, or my jaw would have dropped to the floor. In all the years I'd known Andy Conlon, he had never mentioned to me that he had a brother. It was a revelation that nearly staggered me. I took a deep breath. Troy half-heartily extended his hand. I shook it and said, "Glad to meet you." Troy said nothing

"Troy flew in yesterday from L. A.," Eileen Conlon said. "He didn't attend the funeral but will be here for the rest of the business. Naturally, Troy and I are beneficiaries of Andy's will."

"Naturally," I said.

She pulled a tissue from the box on the piano and began to dab her moist eyes. "Although a sum of money was left to the youth organizations my brother supported and loved, Andy was more than generous to Troy and me."

How much money could Andy possibly have, I thought, a priest living in a rectory with a modest lifestyle? Besides, Eileen and her father were more than comfortable, and whatever inheritance Andy might have left his sister wouldn't have added much to her coffer. Although, Andy's brother looked like he could use a few bucks, if he, indeed, was Andy's brother. There was something about his sudden appearance I didn't like. I made a mental note to check him out.

Troy took a cigarette from a pack in his shirt pocket and fired it up. He placed the spent match in the ashtray, and after a long drag, said, "You think you can find Andy's killer?" His words came out with exhaled smoke and sounded more challenging than concerned.

"I think I can," I said in a blatant, self-assuring way.

"Good cop, bad cop," he said.

"What does that mean?"

"Just that some cops are better at what they do than others," he said.

"Like carpenters or plumbers?" I said.

He smiled, showing neglected teeth as he picked up the ashtray from the piano.

"Good luck," he said sarcastically, then turned and headed back toward the hallway.

I was already beginning to dislike this guy.

After our mystery guest sauntered back to his bedroom, Eileen Conlon and I sat on the sofa. Through a sense of obligation or guilt, she began explaining the history of her *other* brother to me.

"Troy is the youngest of the three of us," she said, "and a bit more cavalier about life. I guess *wild* would be a better adjective. When he was young, he got into trouble regularly and caused my parents' many headaches and sleepless nights.

Troy isn't mean, just different. He never seemed to belong to our family. He never seemed to belong to anyone or anything. I guess you can call him a loner."

"Andy never mentioned to me that he had a brother."

"Troy hasn't been a part of our family for many years, not since he moved to the west coast. It's easy to forget someone when they're no longer a daily part of your life—even a brother."

"You haven't seen nor spoke to him in all those years?"

"We occasionally spoke on the phone and sometimes I'd write to him when he stayed in one place long enough."

"You understand, it was my obligation to notify Troy about Andy's death, and that he'd been named in the will. After all, he *is* Andy's natural brother."

"Of course," I said. "Is there anything else I can do for you?"

"I appreciate all you're doing," she said, as we walked toward the front door. "I hope you'll contact Mr. Denman. He may be of some help."

"If need be," I said.

Back in my car, I called Danny Nolan on my cell phone and asked him to contact Marjorie Palazzo at the probate court. I wanted to get the details of Andy's will without having to go through the hassle and delay of getting a subpoena.

Marjorie Palazzo was a good connection and friend. I had worked with her husband, Jerry, when we were both street cops, until his sudden death of a heart attack, leaving Marjorie and her daughter to fend for themselves. I was married to Marlene at the time. We tried to stay close to Marjorie and offer whatever assistance we could without seeming too charitable. Marjorie survived for a while on the money from the policeman's death benefit fund, and whatever money Jerry had coming from his pension plan. When things began to get tight, she got lucky enough to land her job at the probate court. She was always there for me when I needed her.

I had no reason not to believe Eileen Conlon, but the sudden appearance of the mystery brother was beginning to bother me.

If there was any reason why he was here, other than to collect his booty, I wanted to know what it was.

When I left the Conlon house, it was almost 6:00 p.m. I drove through the Lincoln Tunnel and headed for Greenridge Borough, a small community in North Central New Jersey, where I lived. Traffic was heavy, as it usually was that time of day, and a trip that usually takes me less than an hour took me two. Greenridge sits at the foot of the Watchung Mountains just north of Interstate 78. I spent the first twenty-five years of my life there until I married and moved away. After my divorce, it seemed only natural to go back. Greenridge hadn't changed much during my nineteen-year absence, and I quickly found myself feeling like I had never left.

It was dark when I finally arrived at my apartment at,123 Bigelow Street. The two-story colonial was well kept for its age, painted white with blue shutters, and a wraparound porch on the first floor. Mrs. Jankowski, the widow who lived below me, owned the building. She had rented me the second-floor rooms at a better than fair rate as a favor to my mother, whom she'd befriended during their Friday night Bingo games at St. Michaels's Church. Although, I had a hunch she gave me the rooms because she felt safer with a cop living above her. Nonetheless, she was a decent woman and a good landlady, and I looked out for her.

My apartment was nothing to get excited about. It consisted of a large living room upfront, a small kitchen, a bathroom, and one bedroom at the rear. I kept it modestly furnished to suit my needs, but Sandy had added her personal touch to all the rooms to, "add warmth and ambiance," she'd said.

I used my key to lock both doors of the Chevy, then turned and started down the short distance of the sidewalk toward the front entrance steps. There was no streetlamp close by, and Mrs. Jankowski hadn't turned on the front porch light yet.

As I walked past a low hedgerow, my eye caught movement in the brush to my right. I turned quickly as a dark figure sprang from the hedge and steamrollered me to the pavement. I couldn't see through the darkness, but the guy was big, I could tell by the enormous weight that landed on top of me, probably three hundred pounds. I was unable to move, and I couldn't breathe, until he climbed off me, grabbed me by my shirtfront and lifted me to my feet. When his massive fist crashed into my left cheek, I felt my brains rattle and my knees buckle. I wondered why I didn't go down until I realized he was holding me off the ground by my shirt front. He threw another punch into my midsection, which knocked the breath out of me. I opened my mouth to yell, but nothing came out. I was as helpless as a marionette in this guy's big hands. I could see the murkiness swirling around me as my body melted to the sidewalk. I lay there for a moment, hoping it was over. I knew it wasn't when what felt like a size fourteen boot slammed into my stomach. I tried to curl into a ball, but not before the boot came down again, this time on my ribcage. I lay there unable to move, trying to regain my breathing and hoping this guy wouldn't beat me to death. I squeezed my eyes shut and waited for the next barrage. When it didn't come, I opened my eyes and tried to focus through wet, sticky lashes. Everything was spinning. I held on to a nearby tree and struggled to my feet. I looked around but didn't see anyone.

Conversation over!

The spasms in my stomach wouldn't let me breathe. I took short gasping breaths until I was able to get a steady rhythm going again. I had learned a few things about controlled breathing when I ran tack at college. When my eyes fully focused, I saw that Mrs. Jankowski had turned on the front porch light.

Better late than never.

I pushed away from the tree, took a couple of deep breaths, and waited for my heartbeat to return to near normal. I steadied myself and began to walk toward the front porch. When I reached the bottom step, I grabbed the newel post and crawled up the porch steps one by one. I didn't want to upset Mrs. Jankowski, so I moved quietly through the front alcove and started up the stairs to my apartment. I made it up the first two steps but had to stop for a breather. I only had eighteen more to go. I took hold of the stair rail and pulled myself forward, through the dark hallway, up the steps, one at a time.

When I finally made it to my apartment, I headed straight for the bathroom. I leaned over the sink and splashed oceans of cold water over my face. It hurt like hell, but I knew it would bring me back to life. In the mirror, I could see my left cheek already beginning to swell. My belly ached, and the stabbing pain in my ribs made me wince whenever I moved.

I went into the kitchen, took some ice from the freezer, wrapped it in a towel and pressed it against my cheek. Then I sat down at the kitchen table.

My head was still reeling, and it hurt to think, but I forced myself to make some sense of what had just happened. Had I gotten mugged? No, my gun was still on my hip and my wallet was in my pocket. Was I the target of a vendetta? Somebody from my past that had it in for me; someone I'd sent to prison way back when? The possibilities always existed but didn't seem plausible.

I got up and walked into my bedroom. Struggling through the pain, I stripped off my clothes and flopped down onto my bed in my underwear. I examined my ribs by pressing down gently in various spots. Each time I did, I felt a pinprick of pain. I wasn't sure if any were cracked or broken, but it hurt like Hell. I lay there staring up at the yellowed ceiling, trying to figure out why someone would do this to me. I hadn't been robbed. I had my gun, car keys, and wallet with my money still in it. I figured this incident had everything to do with my investigation into Andy Conlon's murder. Was someone trying to get me to abandon the case? Nobody could be that stupid, I thought, beating up a New York City detective to get him to stop looking into a case. Besides, my assailant hadn't given me any verbal warning. But I thought again and concluded it was a possibility. And if that were the case, who would be desperate enough to try something like that?

It didn't take a middle-aged, slick-minded, experienced, streetwise detective, to know the most logical answer to that question, was—Andy's killer

Chapter 11

"What happened to you?" Danny said. He was staring at my face like he was studying a painting at the Louvre.

"Somebody jumped me."

"You were mugged?"

"No. Somebody jumped me."

"Where'd it happen?"

"Outside my apartment."

"Nice neighborhood. Why would somebody jump you?"

"Don't know."

"Maybe to get you to lay off the Conlon case."

"Maybe."

"Did they say as much?"

"Didn't say a word."

"Well, if that's the case, it never works."

"You know that, and I know that."

"What other reason could somebody have for trying a dumb thing like that?"

"I'm gonna find out," I said.

He held up a manila envelope for me to see. "A copy of Conlon's will from your friend at the probate court, Marjorie... Marjorie, what's her name," he said. "She faxed it this morning."

When he placed it on my deck, I said, "Palazzo."

He said, "Does that mean 'thank you' in Italian?"

I said, "Does *what* mean 'thank you' in Italian?"

"That Italian word you just used."

"Are you kidding?" I said. "That's her last name."

"Oh," he said, moderately embarrassed. "I need a cup of coffee."

Occasionally, Danny wasn't on his game in the morning. I tried to restrain my smile.

While I opened the envelope and read through several sheets of paper, Danny walked to the coffee machine and brought back two cups of coffee. He placed one on my desk in front of me and took a few sips from his while he waited. When I finished reading, I slid the sheets back into the envelope.

"According to his will, Andy Conlon left a fair amount of money to his sister, and a small sum to his estranged brother."

"Why would he leave *anything* to a brother who deserted him and who he hasn't seen in decades?" Danny said.

"Guess you have to have a heart like Andy's to understand that," I said.

I took a sip of coffee. "Let's find out what we can about this guy."

I picked up my desk phone and asked for the Bureau of Vital Statistics in Trenton, New Jersey. Andy Conlon had been born in New Jersey, so it seemed like a good place to find out info on his brother if he was his brother. After a short while, the switchboard connected me; a polite woman's voice picked up the line. I identified myself and told her I needed verification of birth for Troy Conlon. She said she needed to know in which county he'd been born. I told her I didn't know. She said she could look it up but that it would take a few minutes and would I mind waiting. I said I'd wait. When she came back to the phone, she said, "I have that information. Would you like me to fax it to you?"

"No," I said. "Whatever you can give me over the phone."

After she read to me the info she had on record, I thanked her and ended the call. I took another sip of coffee and leaned back in my chair.

"Well?" Danny said.

"Troy Michael Conlon was born in Union County, New Jersey, to Arthur and Mildred Conlon," I said.

"Guess that makes him Father Conlon's brother," Danny said.

"Guess it does," I said. "One question answered."

"You said this guy sounded like he couldn't care if you found his brother's killer?"

"Total apathy," I said.

"Why would he feel that way if Andy is his true brother?"

"He never had a real relationship with his brother," I said.

"And shows up now just for his share of the money?" Danny said.

"Maybe he came here and did his brother in so he could collect his share of the inheritance?" I said.

"How could he be sure he would get any part of an inheritance?" Danny said. "Besides, he'd have to fly here, kill his brother, then fly back to the west coast. Eileen Conlon said she phoned him there to give him the bad news."

"A farfetched, option," I said, "but not impossible. One thing's for sure he's not the one who clobbered me. That guy was huge—gorilla weight."

"When we find motive we'll find our killer," Danny said. "Right now we have three possible suspects: Crockett, Regan, and maybe Troy Conlon."

"And as far as we know none of them has a valid reason for wanting Father Conlon dead," I said.

"Unless we find one," Danny said.

I picked up the envelope with Father Conlon's will inside and locked it in the side drawer of my desk.

"Remind me to send Marjorie Palazzo a box of candy," I said.

"For sure," Danny said.

***

The following morning, I arrived at work earlier than usual. I was at my desk typing my interim report to Chief Briggs when I was interrupted by the presence of someone standing before me. I looked up from my computer screen and saw a guy the size of a small buffalo; his head was as big as an over-inflated basketball and just as round and hairless. The patch of dark hair he wore on his chin got lost in the fold of fat that rippled down from his cheeks. His nose was chiseled square. His eyes looked like two marbles that had been pressed into a ball of soft clay. The three-piece gray suit he wore looked at least one size too small. The vest rode high on his chest like a bib. His gut was big. His arms were bigger. They were so thick; they looked like they should have been where his legs were. He reeked of an overabundance of "Brut" aftershave.

"Detective, Graham?" he said.

I pointed to the nameplate on my desk.

"Martin Denman," he said. "I'm working for Eileen Conlon."

"What can I do for you?" I said.

"I may have information that you might want."

"In regards to?"

"The priest," he said.

I motioned for him to sit. When he did, the chair under him disappeared. I wasn't sure what this guy's game was, but I wanted to hear his story.

"Ms. Conlon said you could be helpful." "I can be, sometimes," I said.

"I thought you could help me find her brother's killer. Maybe we could partner up."

I leaned back in my chair and folded my arms over my chest.

"I can appreciate Eileen Conlon's sense of urgency," I said. "But this is an official police investigation. I'm not obligated to give out information to anyone. Besides, I have plenty of partners. Look around the room."

The bureau looked like the city room of a major newspaper. Phones were ringing, papers were shuffling, and detectives were moving from desk to desk sharing info on cases they were working hard to solve. There was no shortage of crime in the city.

Denman didn't bother to look around the room, but instead, said, "I get it, but I thought there might be some things we can share that could move things along."

I wasn't sure exactly what this guy wanted. I wasn't so sure *he* knew what he wanted. I decided to let him continue.

"How far has your investigation gone?" I said.

"Not far," he said. "Just got the *lowdown* from Ms. Conlon about what happened to her brother."

Lowdown? I guessed it was modern PI jargon.

"What are your intentions?"

"Thought I'd talk to some people that might know something," he said.

"Conduct interviews?"

"Yeah, that's it," he said. "I'm pretty good at tellin' if people are lyin'. Miss Conlon gave me some names."

"You're aware that any information you might ascertain that's relevant to this case has to be reported to the police."

"Oh, sure," he said. "As I said, I'll tell you what I'm doing and you tell me what you're doing."

"That's not the way it works," I said.

This guy didn't have one bit of professionalism about him, no pride or integrity in it strictly for the money. He probably got his PI license off an Internet course, if he had one. But if he should come up with something significant, I wanted to know about it.

I leaned forward on my desk to make sure he understood what I had to say next. "I'll tell you what," I said. "If you find out anything you think I should know, you bring it to me directly. If I have something for you, I'll give it to you."

"Fair enough," he said.

He removed a piece of paper from his inside pocket and began to study it.

"I'm gonna talk to this Crockett guy this afternoon," he said. "Eileen—uh, Miss. Conlon said he's the one who found the body. Can you tell me anything about him?"

"I think you'd be better off finding out yourself," I said. "You know, develop your insight."

He looked perplexed when he said, "Oh yeah...insight."

I had an image of this guy working on Crockett, or Crockett working on him.

He put the paper back into his pocket, stood and extended his hand. When I took it, my hand disappeared inside his. His grip was weak, but his hand was rough. I couldn't help noticing his knuckle were red and there was dirt beneath his fingernails. Not what one would expect from a PI in a three-piece suit.

"Well, I'll go to work," he said. "Thanks."

"Good luck," I said.

Something about this guy didn't smell right. I hadn't asked to see his PI credentials, because I didn't want to blow his cover. I knew he was a phony baloney. What I didn't know was why. I'd have Danny check him out.

The following afternoon, I was in Monsignor Belducci's office watching him eat his lunch. He was seated behind his desk, ostensibly enjoying a cheeseburger, fries, and a Coke and making a mess of himself in the process. The yellow napkin he had tucked between his collar and double chin was grease-stained and mottled with specks of lettuce and bits of onion.

"Sit, my son," he said, through a mouthful.

I remained standing and said, "I didn't mean to drop in on you uninvited and disturb your lunch."

"It's okay," he said. "I grab a bite whenever I can."

When he wiped his fingertips on the end of his napkin bib, it fell out of his collar. He lowered his chins quickly and caught it before it fell to the desk. Reaching up with his clean hand, he attempted to tuck it back under the fleshy folds of his neck. Having a hard time with it, he yanked it away in frustration and tossed it onto his desk.

"What can I do for you, detective?" he said.

"I thought you might supply me with a list of the youth organizations Father Conlon was involved with," I said.

"List? As far as I know, there is no list," he said after emitting a muffled belch, then wiping his mouth with a fresh napkin. "There are just three that I'm aware of."

He leaned back in his chair, took another napkin from the pile on his desk, and wiped his mouth again before he spoke.

"Let me see... there's the Youth Rec Center here in midtown, and the Boy's Club in Queens, and there's the CYO in Brooklyn."

"Is that all?"

"To my knowledge," he said.

"Could there be others you don't know about?"

"I don't think so," he said. "Father Conlon had his hands full and there are only so many hours in the day, or night, for that matter."

"Father Conlon found time in the evenings for these organizations?"

"Oh, yes," he said. "There were always special meetings and award programs. Andy was committed to the kids."

"What are the age requirements for the boys?"

"Eight to eighteen, no other requirements other than a willingness to grow and become a well-rounded, responsible adult. There are no monetary donations requested of the families. Of course, the church contributes annually to their sustainment."

"Admirable," I said.

I made a mental note of the organizations and thanked the Father. He smiled, leaned over his desk, and returned eagerly to his cheeseburger. Before I walked out, he attempted to tuck a fresh napkin under his chins. After having a difficult time, he gave up and went to work on the cheeseburger without it.

The Father would benefit from eating a Caesar Salad and maybe lose a chin—or two.

Chapter 12

I took two aspirin in an attempt to alleviate the pain from the sledgehammer inside my head, pounding my temples. It had been a long day, and I was looking forward to my dinner, a tall glass of red wine, and a good night's sleep.

My desk phone rang. I hesitated. The last thing I wanted was something more to complicate an already hectic day.

I picked it up.

"Homicide," I said, "Detective, Graham."

"This is Sister Mary Margaret," a low voice said.

Five seconds passed before I was able to bring to mind that I had met Sister Mary Margaret at St. Trinity outside of Monsignor Belducci's office. I recalled a charming young lady with short black hair and wire-rim glasses.

"Hello, sister," I said. "What can I do for you?"

"I need to talk to you about something I think is important," she said.

Her voice was soft and low and somewhat reticent.

"This is about what?" I said.

"Father Conlon," she said.

I had no idea what Sister Mary Margaret felt she needed to tell me about Andy Conlon, but I was eager to find out. She was an intricate part of the church and had contact with all the priests daily. Her insight might prove invaluable.

"Would you like to come and see me tomorrow," I said. "Any time in the afternoon would be okay?"

"Oh, no," she said. "Can you come to the rectory tonight? I don't think it should wait."

I looked at the wall clock; It was 5:05 p.m. The aspirin had not yet gone to work on my headache, but headache or not, I needed to accommodate this lady for my benefit, and Andy's.

"I can come over straight away," I said.

"Use the side entrance by Monsignor Belducci's office," she said. "I'll be waiting."

The sun was below the horizon by the time I got to St. Trinity. The church was brightly lit with a warm yellow glow. The rectory was dark but for a few lighted windows on the second floor, and an overhead light at the main entrance. I parked the Chevy in front of the rectory and walked around to the side entrance. I opened the mahogany door and stepped inside. Sister Mary Margaret was waiting for me in the marble hallway.

She was wearing a pair of inordinately loose jeans, a flowered blouse, and a pair of white canvas sneakers, which made her look all the more attractive than when I saw her last; in a wholesome way, of course. She put her index finger to her lips, indicating for me to be quiet, and then used the same finger to direct me to a door across the hall.

When she closed the door behind us, I found myself in a small library. There was a sofa and several leather armchairs arranged in front of a stone fireplace and three walls of shelves packed with books.

"Please sit," she said. She sat in a leather chair. I sat in one opposite her.

"Thank you for coming," she said. "I hope I haven't bothered you for no good reason, but I feel what I have to say is important."

"If you think it's important," I said, "it probably is." She smiled and was glad I'd said that.

"What do you want to tell me?" I said. "And take your time."

She sat up in her chair and laced her fingers together on her lap. "I had come from the cafeteria after having had my lunch and stopped in this very room to fill the rest of my free time reading."

"When was this?" I said.

"This past Saturday," she said.

"Was there anyone else with you?"

"No. I was the only one here."

"Go on," I said.

"I was quietly reading a periodical when I heard, what sounded like a commotion, in the hall outside this door. I stopped reading and listened again. This time I distinctly heard voices being raised, one over the other."

"What kind of voices?"

"Two men, quarreling. It is very unusual to hear any disorder here in the rectory, so I walked to the door so I could hear better. As I listened, the voices became louder and more boisterous."

"Could you hear what was being said?"

"Oh, yes," she said. "There was name calling and even swear words." She crossed herself and continued. "My curiosity got the best of me and I dared to open the door ever so much." She indicated how much she had opened the door by using her thumb and index finger and peering through them with one squinted eye. I got the idea. "And what did you see?" I said.

"I was astonished when I saw Father Faynor, engaged in a verbal altercation with the custodian, Mr. Crockett."

"Did you hear anything specific?" I said. "Why they were arguing?"

"Father Faynor said Mr. Crockett was a worthless bum and didn't deserve to work here, that he couldn't be trusted to mind his own business."

"Why do you think he said that?"

"I don't know, but Mr. Crockett said that Father Faynor should try minding his own business. They called each other names, and the confrontation continued until Mr. Crockett raised the broom he was carrying in the air in front of Father Faynor's face like he was about to strike him."

"Did he hit Father Faynor?"

"No, Father Faynor reached up and grabbed the broom handle and pulled it away from Mr. Crockett and threw it out of his reach."

"Then, what happened?"

"Father Faynor and Mr. Crockett looked at each other, their faces close. I could see the anger in both of them. I thought they were about to engage in a physical altercation, until Mr. Crockett walked over to the broom lying on the floor, picked it up and walked away."

"What happened next?"

"I closed the door."

When I'd interview Crockett, he'd admitted that he and Faynor hadn't gotten along but didn't mention they had nearly engaged in a street brawl. I had taken Crockett's admission as mere animus, but this revelation could upgrade *animus* to *deep hatred.*

"Why did you wait until now to tell me this?" I said.

"I didn't think it any of my business since I had come upon it unwittingly. I know Mr. Crockett is involved, somehow, with the police. I thought what I saw and heard might be helpful."

She sat quietly; her fingers still laced together on her lap. I wasn't sure if she was waiting for my response, or if she had more to say. To abate the awkwardness, I got up from the chair and said, "Is there anything else you want to tell me?"

She stood and said, "I thought it was important."

As we walked out of the library, I said, "It is, and I thank you for your courage."

Before I opened the side door, I said. "I'm sure Mr. Crockett and Father Faynor will settle their differences. Have you mentioned this to anyone else?"

"I've been keeping it inside me, but now I'm glad I've told someone."

"Let's keep this between us," I said.

"And the Lord," she said.

It was dark by the time I got back to my apartment. I skipped dinner and my glass of wine, took two more aspirin, and went to bed. I'd think about Crockett and Faynor tomorrow.

Chapter 13

"No Martin Denman in any PI directory in the Tristate area," Danny said.

"Didn't think so," I said.

"Who is this guy?"

"A phony PI hired by Eileen Conlon. Miss. Conlon wants to keep close tabs on my progress."

"Why hire a phony?"

"I don't know," I said. "Make a left."

We were in an Impala heading for the Boy's Club in Queens. Danny drove. I had phoned the chapter director, Roger Shortman, and set up an interview. When we spoke he sounded reluctant to get involved, but I gave him no choice. He agreed to meet us at two o'clock.

The building that housed the Boy's Club was once a warehouse that had been converted into a recreational center with a set of offices on the second floor. I'd called Shortman from my cell and told him we were outside the building. He told me to come right up. Danny and I went in through the double doors of the main entrance and took the elevator at the rear of the building to Shortman's office. When the elevator doors opened, Shortman was waiting for us.

Shortman wasn't short. He was easily over six feet, probably played basketball. He had the right body for it. His head had been shaved shiny, and his dark skin contrasted with the light gray goatee that adorned his chin. He was wearing dark blue sweatpants and a white tee shirt and high-top basketball shoes.

"Detectives, Graham and Nolan," I said.

"I have a busy day," Shortman said. "Let's get this over with."

We followed him into his office across the hall, which was simple but functional: a large metal desk, a couple of visitor's chairs, a file cabinet, and two large windows that looked out onto a small grassy playing field. Shortman sat behind his desk. Danny and I sat in the chairs.

"Whatta you guys wanna know?" he said.

"Whatever you can tell us about Father Conlon's relationship here at the club," I said.

"He was the kinda guy that worked well with young people."

"How long has he been involved with the club?" Danny said.

"He was here when I got here three years ago."

"So it'd be safe to say he got along with everyone here?" I said.

"Far as I know, everybody loved the guy."

"Did he work with the girls as well as the boys?" Danny said.

"Mostly with the older guys."

"By his own choice?" I said.

"We didn't put restrictions on him. He was a Priest."

"I know," I said, "unselfishly devoted."

Shortman paused while he thought if he wanted to say what he was thinking. When he decided he would, he said, "Maybe too devoted."

This was the first time I had heard anyone say anything remotely negative about Andy Conlon.

"How do you mean?" I said.

Shortman leaned back in his chair and laced his fingers behind his head.

"It's just my opinion, of course, but it's the way he dealt with the young guys, kinda overzealous, the way he did things."

"You said he was devoted," Danny reminded.

Shortman leaned over his desk and folded his arms in front of him.

"Sure, but he acted like he was their personal friend. A mentor should keep himself above the herd. You know, like a good parent. Give love and guidance but stay on a different plane."

"Guess it worked for him," Danny said.

"I guess," Shortman said.

"Course this is all just your opinion," Danny said. "You don't see a real problem here?"

Shortman hesitated a moment, then said, "There were a few boys I thought he was *too* friendly with."

There was an awkward silence in the room while Danny and I tried to digest just what Shortman was getting at.

"I would've handled things differently," Shortman finally said.

We left Shortman and took the ride to the CYO in Brooklyn. It was almost 4:30 by the time we reached Hargrove Street, which is where the CYO building was located. The building was a low-level modern structure surrounded by a newly paved parking lot. A large brass crucifix was situated on the lawn by the front entrance, and the base of the building was meticulously decorated with an abundance of bright flowers and scrubs. The organization's director was Father Marcus. We'd been unable to reach him by phone and were hoping we could catch him this afternoon for an interview.

Danny parked in a visitor space by the front door and we went inside. We found ourselves in a small reception area where there were chairs for waiting and a horseshoe-shaped desk where a pretty young receptionist sat pecking a computer keyboard.

When we approached, she looked up quickly. Her blond hair cascaded softly over her shoulders, and her blue eyes sparkled under the fluorescent lights. Danny spoke first. I knew he would.

"May I help you?" she said.

Danny showed her his bright smile and showed her his bright shield.

"Detective Nolan," he said, "NYPD."

She looked at Danny's smile, then at his shield, and then looked at me.

"I'm with him," I said.

"We'd like to speak with Father Marcus," Danny said.

"Do you have an appointment?"

"No," Danny said. Big smile again.

The girl gave him a half-smile and then picked up a phone. She spoke into it softly and then hung up.

"Follow me," she said as she came out from behind the desk. She was wearing a black dress that stopped several inches above her knees, and black patent leather heels. Her legs were excellent. Danny was unwilling, or unable, to relinquish his vantage point as he followed her with his eyes until I nudged him from his reverie with my elbow.

We followed her across the lobby and down a long corridor until we came to a door at the far end. The girl held up her index finger to indicate, "Just a minute" then went inside. In a few seconds, she was back. She held the door open for us and said, "Father Marcus will see you."

We thanked her and started through the door. Danny gave her another big smile, and she smiled back. I smiled at Father Marcus as we went in.

"Thank you for seeing us, father," I said. "I'm Detective Graham, and this is Detective Nolan."

"I assume this is about Father Conlon," Marcus said as he indicated for us to sit.

We sat in the green leather visitor chairs that faced his desk.

"How may I help?"

"We're trying to get a profile of Father Conlon's relationship here," I said.

"By 'here' you mean here at the center?"

"Yes. How, exactly, was he involved here?"

"The Father was very popular," Marcus said. "He worked mostly with older boys, the ones on the sports teams. Basketball primarily."

"Was there anyone in particular that he was exceptionally close to?" I said.

"You mean like someone he might've had a special interest in?"

I nodded.

Father Marcus thought for a moment before he said, "Maybe, Russell Grayson."

"Tell us about Russell Grayson," Danny said.

"He lives in Brooklyn with his mother. Father died several years ago. He's been a CYO member for about a year. Mother drives him and picks him up, every Tuesday." "How old is Russell?" I said.

"Sixteen or seventeen," Marcus answered. "Shoots a mean hoop."

"What kind of—"

"Why all the questions about Russell?" Marcus interrupted. "Russell's a good boy. He never gets into trouble."

"We're just trying to get a picture here. Every bit helps."

"Well… I don't know what else I can tell you about Father Conlon. He was liked by everyone and committed to the well-being of young people. He'll be missed around here."

Danny and I looked at each other. We'd heard that refrain before.

***

Sandy and I were sitting at my kitchen table enjoying coffee and donuts. I was munching a Boston Cream while she broke small pieces off her butternut crunch and dunked them into her coffee. It had rained all night, but the sun had broken out early and the rays coming through the kitchen window bathed the table in a warm yellow. Sandy looked almost angelic with the sun's rays reflecting off her auburn hair.

"The interviews I've conducted so far have gotten me nowhere," I said. "Everyone agrees that Andy Conlon was an amiable, altruistic father-like figure that devoted himself to the underprivileged."

"Tell me something I don't know," Sandy said. She was holding her coffee cup with both hands and talking to me over the rim in between gentle sips.

"My point," I said.

"There may be something about Andy that you *don't* know that will help you find his killer," Sandy said.

"I've known Andy since I was a kid, and for most of my adult life," I said.

"Yet, you didn't know he had a brother," Sandy said.

"True," I said.

"I wonder what else you might not know about him," she said.

I finished my donut without saying a word and downed the rest of my coffee. Sandy was right. I wondered if there were other aspects of Andy's life I had missed that would help me figure this thing out.

Sandy got up and brought her cup to the kitchen sink and poured the rest of her coffee down the drain. "Andy didn't have an enemy in the world," she said.

I got up and set my empty cup in the sink beside hers, "He had one," I said.

I cleared the kitchen table and then went to the living room and sat on the sofa while Sandy washed the coffee cups. I grabbed the remote and was about to click on the TV to watch the news when my cell phone rang. I picked it up from the coffee table in front of me. "Who is this?" I said.

"It's Gwen Regan," a shaky voice said. "I didn't—you said to call you if I had a problem."

"I did," I said.

"Arnie was here today He'd been drinking and forced his way into my apartment."

Arnie Regan was under a restraining order to stay away from Gwen and Kevin other than during the times the court permitted visitations. He could be in a heap of trouble if Gwen Regan chose to report him. "Was Arnie drunk?"

"Of course," she said.

"Is Kevin okay?"

"Yes, but... Arnie got upset when he learned you had come to see me. He threatened to kill me if I spoke to you again." "A threat like that is not to be taken lightly," I said.

"He was drunk," she said. "He didn't mean it."

"Did you call the police?"

"No. I called you."

"Are you hurt?"

"No, but I'm afraid. He said he'd be back if he found out that I'd spoken to you again. I've never seen him so violent, or so drunk," she said.

"Where is Kevin now?"

"In his room. He was frightened and upset, but I've managed to calm him. He'll be all right."

Sandy came over to the sofa and sat beside me, looking a bit more than curious. I mouthed the words: *Gwen Regan* to her.

"I'll send someone over," I said.

"No, please," she said. "No police."

"But, if he—"

"I'm afraid he'll be back. But I don't want the police involved. I don't know what to do."

"Lock your apartment door and stay with Kevin," I said.

"I can't," she said. "Arnie broke the door lock."

"Then stay by the phone and don't do anything until you hear from me. I don't think he'll be back. He's made his point."

It took an hour and a half for me to get to Arnie Regan's Rivington Street apartment in the Lower East Side. During the ride, I wondered how he'd found out I'd been to see his ex-wife. I parked several doors down and walked to the single door between a butcher shop and a hairdresser. The door was unlocked. Inside an unlit hallway, I found myself at the bottom of a long staircase. A window at the top of the stairs provided the only light. I took the stairs up to a second-floor landing. From there I climbed a second, and then the third flight of stairs until I was on Arnie's floor. There were several doors on the right side of the hallway and a set of dirty windows to my left. I walked by each door until I found Arnie's number. I listened but heard nothing from the other side of the door. I knocked. The silence from inside continued. I knocked again…. Nothing. I turned the knob. The door opened easily. I peered in at a dingy, unkempt living room. Something I'd expected from Arnie. I put my hand on my gun and pushed the door back slowly. I stepped inside, my eyes darting in every direction; sure I'd run into a belligerent Arnie Regan waiting to do me harm.

A sofa stood against a far wall covered with a grimy white bed sheet. In front of it was a coffee table cluttered with crumpled cigarette packs, a large metal ashtray, overloaded with cigarette butts and an assortment of empty beer cans, an old television set, complete with "rabbit ears" sat on top of a bookshelf in one corner. Two front windows let in what light could pass through the grime on the glass. A door in the back wall appeared to lead to a bedroom. I could see a dim light coming from the bathroom door to my left. Before I could close the apartment door, Arnie Regan came out of the bathroom wiping his damp hands on his jeans. He looked like the effects of the alcohol he had drunk were still with him.

"The hell is this?" he said when he saw me. "Get the hell outta here."

He rushed toward the coffee table, picked up the ashtray and came at me with it. I kicked the door closed behind me and reached up and caught his hand as he tried to smash the ashtray against my skull. He dropped the ashtray and followed it to the floor when I brought my knee up between his legs. He squirmed about on the floor, moaning and holding his crotch before he was able to say, "This is illegal. You can't bust in here like this."

"You're right," I said. I took hold of his arm and helped him to his feet. When I was sure he'd regained his balance, I punched him hard on the side of his head. He bounced off the wall and slid back to the floor. He sat there with his legs buckled under him, rubbing the side of his head with one hand while holding his crotch with the other.

"The hell's wrong with you, Graham," he said. "I'll report you for this."

"You better worry about your ex-wife reporting you," I said.

"For what?" he said.

"Threatening her, the way you threatened Father Conlon."

"I ain't done nothin'," he said.

"Except, A&B and disregarding a restraining order, that'll get you time," I said.

He struggled to his feet, hobbled over to the coffee table, and removed a cigarette from a crumpled pack. He lit it with a shaky hand, took a long drag, and let the smoke out easily. "She won't say a word," he said. "She's too afraid." "She wasn't afraid to call me," I said.

"Stay outta this," he said. "It's between me and my wife."

I reached out and grabbed him by his shirtfront." Keep away from her," I said.

"It's none o' your business," he said.

"I'm making it my business," I said. "If she calls me again—"

He twisted himself out of my grip and moved to the front windows.

"Think you can do what ya want because ya carry a badge," he said. "You know where you can put that badge."

He rubbed the side of his head and touched his crotch again.

I walked to the door and opened it. "I'll get your ass for this, Graham."

"Sober up," I said.

Before I could shut the door behind me, I heard him say, "asshole."

When I got back to my car, I called Gwen Regan. I assured her; her ex-husband wouldn't be bothering her any time soon. She asked me what I'd done. I told her I'd employed simple police procedures to convince him it was in his best interest to stay away. She thanked me but didn't sound very reassured. I drove back to my apartment feeling like I hadn't accomplished much. I was sure my meager threats wouldn't keep Arnie Regan away from his ex-wife and kid. Maybe he'd think twice and begin to treat them better.

Chapter 14

It was 5:30 in the morning. The air was cool. I was jogging the path at Oakwood Park. I had been neglecting my usual early morning run since the business with Andy Conlon came into my life. But today I'd decided to loosen up and stretch my lungs with a more than vigorous run around the lake. I had forced myself to get up early, put on my shorts, a pair of running shoes, and my sleeveless sweatshirt, and walk the three blocks to the park. The jog felt good. The crisp morning air burned my lungs and my legs ached a bit, but when I slowed to a more reasonable jogging pace and found my stride, the running came easier. The sun was rising now, slicing obliquely through the trees and reflecting off the still water of the lake. I was the only runner on the path, and other than a few Sunday morning dog walkers; the park was quiet and fresh, as most summer mornings are. It was therapeutic, to say the least.

I was making my second turn around the lake, approaching a small boathouse on my left that had been closed for years. It had been used as a place where young lovers could rent a rowboat to cruise the lake but had since morphed into a dilapidated configuration of wood beams, broken windows, and lath. Weeds surrounding its perimeter had grown to several feet in height in some places, and if they continued to grow unattended would probably conceal the entire structure.

As I passed the boathouse, I wondered why the eyesore hadn't been demolished long ago. It was then that I felt like a truck hit me from behind. I fell to the ground startled and stunned. As the world began to spin, I felt myself being lifted by my shoulders and ankles and carried behind the boathouse into the high weeds. The area was in dark shadow from the surrounding trees. I was unable to see who or what it was that had dragged me there.

A barrage of kicks and punches ensued from every direction. By the number and frequency of blows, I calculated there were, at least, two assailants. There were more kicks than punches, and it wasn't long before they knocked the wind out of me. My chest muscles began to spasm. I couldn't catch my breath. The attack was quick and steady, and I was unable to fight back. All I could do was try to protect myself and hope I wouldn't be beaten to death. I put myself into a fetal position, but that did little good. What felt like heavy construction boots slammed into my stomach and ribcage. I held back my cries of pain, not wanting to give these "son's o' bitches" the satisfaction that they were doing a good job of it.

I awoke to the sounds of summer. I opened my eyes slowly and squinted at the blinding sun. I could hear children laughing and dogs barking. I had no idea how long I'd been out, but during that time, Oakwood Park had come to life. I sat up slowly and leaned against the shed. My head felt light and my body ached whenever I moved. I held on to the shed wall and got to my feet. I looked down at myself. I was mottled with dirt and clumps of grass. I brushed myself off as well as I could, steadied my legs and walked out to the path. A woman pushing a baby stroller passed by me and a young girl on skates neither paid me any attention. With my head spinning, I managed to walk out of the park and trudge the three blocks back to my apartment.

I was doing okay until I reached the front steps of my apartment house. My head began to buzz, and I began to feel lightheaded again. I sat down on the steps and lowered my head between my legs. It seemed to help, so I stood up slowly and felt my equilibrium return. I made it up the front steps to the vestibule. When I pushed open the front door, I saw Mrs. Jankowski, or rather she saw me first.

"Oh, Lord," she said. "What has happened?"

"I'll be okay, Mrs. Jankowski," I said. "I stumbled and fell during my run in the park."

"Looks like you did more than stumble," she said.

She reached under my arms to keep me from collapsing. This woman was smaller than me and half my weight, but she managed to guide me up to my apartment, one step at a time. When we reached the top of the stairs, she struggled to open my door with one hand while continuing to stabilizing me with the other. She led me to my sofa where I immediately collapse onto my back.

"I'll call an ambulance," she said.

"That won't be necessary," I said. "I'll be okay."

She walked to the kitchen and brought back a glass of tap water. The cold water felt good going down, but the muscles in my throat hurt where I had been kicked more than once.

"I'll just call my doctor then," she said.

"I don't need one," I said.

"You look like you do."

"I'll be okay."

"Well, if you have a first aid kit, I'll wash those wounds for you," she said.

"Thank you, but most of that is just mud and dried grass stuck to my skin."

"Then I'll call your mother," she said, "and let her know."

"No, no," I said. "I'm okay."

I sat up and began poking my ribcage and shoulders. "See," I said, "nothing cracked or broken. It looks worse than it is."

"Well... if you think so," she said. "But I think you should call your mother."

"I will," I said.

I stood slowly and walked her to the door. The room went around once and then stopped. I tried not to let it show.

"I'll take a warm shower and climb into bed," I said. "The next time you see me, I'll be as good as new. Thank you for your help."

I smiled to ease her concern.

"If you need me, I'm right downstairs," she said.

"I know," I said. I leaned down and kissed her cheek. I opened the door and she stepped into the hallway. She turned to me and said, "Remember I'm right downstairs."

"I will," I said, "thank you." And I closed the door.

I examined my face in my bathroom mirror. There were no cuts or bruises, but my body had been bombarded unmercifully. Everything hurt from my ankles to my neck. I stripped off my clothes and stood under a warm shower. It hurt to rub soap over myself so I just stood there and let the water soothe my pain. I put on a pair of sweatpants and a tee shirt and got into my fuzzy slipper, then went into the kitchen and made myself a cup of tea. At the table, I collected my thoughts while I sipped my tea. What had happened? I had been attacked twice in the same number of weeks, once by a gorilla and now by at least two assailants. I hadn't been mugged and nothing had been taken from me. There had been no verbal warning and no indication as to why I was being assaulted. And there was nothing to indicate that the attacks were in any way related. But there was no coincidence here. Arnie Regan said he would get even with me. Was this his way of trying to get me to stay out of his life? Or was he trying to get me to halt my investigation into the murder of Father Conlon? He seemed dumb enough to believe he could pull off something like that. Nevertheless, I'd be a fool to think my life was not now in jeopardy. Regan had become a desperate man. There was no telling how far he'd go. I had no choice but to go to him before he came to me.

I walked into my bedroom, took my wallet from my night table drawer, and fished out the phone number Chestnut had given me. I punched up the numbers and waited.

I was tired of getting beat up.

***

Chestnut got his nickname because his skin color resembled the smooth reddish-brown color of a chestnut. He was born in Kingston, Jamaica, the accident of a dope addict mother and a father who abandoned him when he was eight. After a period of running with the wrong crowd, he was saved from the streets by an aunt who raised him until he was of age. He worked a series of menial, low-paying jobs, until he decided to take advantage of his physical attributes, and developed an interest in the martial arts. He spent years studying Karate, to the point that it became a passion. His efforts earned him a black belt, fifth-degree. I knew him as a person of integrity and self-assurance, with an innate understanding of the human spirit. He hated "bad guys" and let them know it. Those who knew him gave him the respect his presence commanded.

Chestnut's nose had been broken more than once so that now, it lay slightly off-kilter on his face. Despite this slight misalignment, it was a good nose, smooth and thin, and situated between a pair of dark, deep-set eyes. His head—for as long as I had known him—had always been shaven as smooth as a baby's butt and maintained with a subdued degree of luster. He towered above my six-foot height by four inches, carrying a solid, well-defined physique, with broad shoulders and a slim waist. I couldn't see a visible ounce of body fat on him.

After closing his unsuccessful karate school on the island, he migrated to the U.S. and found work as a custodian in a midtown hotel. Our paths crossed when he erroneously became a suspect in a case I had been working on, involving the murder of a hotel security guard. In the course of my investigation, I'd discovered he was in this country illegally. Chestnut's cooperation in helping me solve the case was invaluable. My thanks to him was not reporting him to Homeland Security. His gratitude and concern for my welfare never waned. Other than Chestnut's early years, I knew nothing of his current situation, where he lived, or what he did for a living. Although I could have obtained that info anytime by making a few phone calls, I chose not to. Our friendship had survived on confidentiality and his anonymity. It wasn't that Chestnut had anything hide. It had been that way from the beginning, and we both chose to keep it that way. He had helped me out of many tight spots over the years and whenever I called the number he'd given me; he was there for me. I trusted him and could rely on his loyalty and friendship whenever I needed it.

When I opened my apartment door, Chestnut was leaning against the doorframe. He smiled when he saw me and gave me a big hug. I felt like a helpless rag doll in his arms. He was wearing flowered Bermuda shorts, sandals, and a black muscle shirt, the sleeves tight against his rock-solid biceps. He smelled of "bay rum" cologne.

"My mon," he said. "You call. I come."

It was his habit to call me, *my mon.*

"Thanks," I said.

I let him in and closed the door behind us. We walked instinctively to the kitchen table, which had become a ritual whenever Chestnut came to my apartment. He sat and waited while I took down the bottle of rum from the cabinet above the sink. I brought the bottle and two glasses to the table and poured. Chestnut could drink rum like water. He downed the glass without a breath. I poured him another. I sat opposite him and began to sip from my glass.

"What kinda trouble you got, mon?" Chestnut said.

"I think somebody might want to do me harm," I said.

"Kill you?"

"Maybe."

"That's serious, mon," he said. He took another swallow from his glass.

"I didn't take his threat seriously at first but now I think things are getting out of hand. I might have to bulldozer him before he does something really stupid."

"You wanna finish him?" Chestnut said.

"No," I said. "The guy's got an ex-wife and a young son, although he's not much good to either of them. I just wanna convince him to back off, for his own good…or mine."

"Why you need me?"

"He's got friends," I said.

"What kinda friends?"

"The kind that'll beat somebody up just because they're asked to beat somebody up."

"In the name of friendship?"

"In the name of friendship," I said.

"And maybe even kill somebody in the name of friendship," Chestnut said.

"Maybe, even that," I said.

"But you got me," Chestnut said, "in the name of friendship."

"In the name of friendship," I said, and smiled.

He drained his glass again, then slid it across the table. I filled it again.

"Why does he do this?" he said.

I explained to him all the facts I thought he needed to know, so he'd understand why I wanted to do what I wanted to do. When I was through, he said, "You think he killed the priest?"

"I can't prove it," I said.

Chestnut said. "I'll fix him good."

Chestnut had used the term; "fix him" in the past and it had resulted in fixing someone, permanently.

"I don't wanna fix him," I said. "I just wanna teach him a lesson. And keep from getting my head bashed, or worse."

"Maybe I get him to confess," Chestnut said. "Where do we find this guy?"

"I want to catch him in the open space of the construction site where he works," I said.

He finished his drink and then wiped his mouth with the back of his hand.

"You say when," he said.

"Today, before four when they get off work."

"Why that place?" he said.

"He'll probably have his friends with him." "Two birds with a stone," Chestnut said.

"Something like that," I said.

"That's why you got me," he said.

"That's why I got you," I said.

There was a succession of hard raps on my door. When I opened it, Sandy was standing there looking radiant. I was surprised to see her so early in the afternoon. It was her custom to be tied up at her office or in court at that time.

She pushed by me in a huff and made her way to my refrigerator without saying a word. She removed a chilled bottle of Chablis and grabbed a glass from the overhead cabinet and sat at the table. It was evident she was upset, and, or angry. I wasn't sure which. She filled her glass with wine and downed half of it, without coming up for air. Chestnut grimaced at the Chablis and took a drink of his rum. After Sandy drained her glass, she looked across the table at Chestnut and said, "Hello, Chestnut."

Chestnut said, "Hello, Sandra."

Sandy and Chestnut had met previously on many occasions. She had grown to become as good a friend to him as I was. Chestnut, in return, had respected her "womanhood." Their primary connection to me was their mutual interest... my welfare.

I closed the door and said, "Hello, Sandra."

"Hello, yourself," she said and poured herself more wine.

I sat down at the table with her and Chestnut. I knew she was both upset *and* angry.

I wasn't sure what to say. If I offered the right thing, it might calm her, if I said the wrong thing it could set her off even more.

I tried to say the right thing. "Rough day?"

"Rough is not the word," she said. "You've never had a day as I had. That damned prosecutor made me look like a fool in court."

"Part of the game, isn't it?" I said.

"Not the way I play it," she said. "In all my years I've never had a *bitch* treat me like that."

I looked at Chestnut with a "this girl is mad" expression. Chestnut raise his eyebrows and said, "When I get upset, I go to the gym and hit the bag."

"I don't need a bag," Sandy said. "When I get upset, I punch Max around the living room until I feel better."

She tried to conceal the smile that was forming on her lips but couldn't hold back laughing at her own humor. Chestnut offered a big smile, showing her his perfectly place pearly white teeth.

I smiled, too, and leaned over and gave her a gentle kiss on her cheek. She kissed me back.

"Kisses sweeter than wine," I said.

"It's the Chablis," she said.

She got up and went to the fridge and opened it. "How about some lunch?" she said.

She examined the contents and said, "A can of tuna, a jar of pickles, and two six-packs of beer."

"Not what one would call appetizing," I said.

"It's okay," she said. "We'll order from Karcher's Deli. I can put away a pastrami on rye."

I didn't answer.

A dilemma was beginning to form. Chestnut and I needed to leave in time to make it to the construction site before four.

I had always tried not to keep things from Sandy, but she knew inevitably, whenever I hooked up with Chestnut, the situation I was about to undertake could be less than healthy for me. So far, she hadn't mentioned it, but I knew she knew.

I understood her concern. It was the same thing I had gone through with Marlene when we were married; her incessant concern about my safety. Worrying whether her husband would come home injured or come home at all. It was something I tried not to put Sandy through, but it was a part of being a cop.

Sandy closed the fridge and turned to look at Chestnut and me. She finally broke the silence and said, "Whatever it is you two are involved with, I don't want to know."

"You know, Chestnut helps me sometimes with a case," I said.

"I wouldn't want anyone else helping you, *but* him."

"There's nothing to worry about," I said.

"I've heard that before," she said.
"Your man is safe with me," Chestnut said.
"I know," Sandy said, "but it doesn't make me feel much better."
"Chestnut's got my back," I said.
"That's why you got me," Chestnut said.
"That's why I got you," I said.
"In the name of friendship," he said.
"In the name of friendship," I said.
Chestnut smiled.
So did I.
Sandy didn't.

Chapter 15

The Chevy bounced and rattled over the rutted road, kicking up red dust as we drove into the construction site where Regan was working. Chestnut held on to the dash with one hand and cranked up the side window with the other.

"Mon, you need a new ride," he said.

"Can't afford it. I pay out more than I keep."

The construction on the site had advanced noticeably since I'd been here. The skeleton of the two-story structure had been enclosed with corrugated metal and the roof had been completed. A foundation had been dug for a new building beside it, and most of the labor was concentrated there. The usual lineup of cars and trucks was parked where they had been before. I spotted Regan's truck at the end of the row, partially shaded by the overhanging limbs of a half-dead Sycamore tree. I parked about a hundred feet away from the tree and killed the engine.

"That's his truck," I said.

Chestnut looked disinterestedly at Regan's pickup truck, and said, "Where's your man?"

"They quit at four," I said.

My dash clock read 3 p.m. Chestnut looked to see if the dust had settled, then cranked down the side window. We sat quietly for a while, watching the clock, and listening to the roar of heavy equipment in the distance until Chestnut said, "Should have brought coffee and doughnuts with us."

"I'm not hungry," I said.

"Would have made the wait easier."

"It would have," I said.

"Sandra makes great chocolate chip cookies."

"She does."

"Could have brought some cookies."

"Next time."

We sat in silence for almost a full minute, until Chestnut said, "Why we come so early?"

"I don't wanna *miss,* Regan," I said.

Chestnut said, "I *miss* Sandra's chocolate chip cookies."

It was 3:50 when the hum and rumble of the heavy equipment came to a grinding halt. The silence echoed in my ears as I watched the usual drove of workers hurry to their vehicles and start their engine for the ride home. I didn't see Regan. Chestnut and I got out and walked behind the Sycamore and waited. Car and truck engines came to life as we watched vehicle after vehicle parade down the dirt road. Through the dissipating dust, I spotted Regan coming out of the building carrying his lunchbox under his right arm. He was walking with two co-workers in the direction of his pickup. One was taller than Regan and had the body of a weightlifter. He wore jeans, work boots, and a sleeveless red-checkered flannel shirt. His hair was rust red and cut short. The second was smaller, with a wiry body. His arms were thin but muscular and tattooed from wrists to biceps. When he walked, he swung his arms loosely at his side as if they were too much of a burden to carry. He wore dirty overalls and no shirt. His dark hair was cut into a crew cut.

I waited till they got close to Regan's truck, then stepped out from behind the tree. Chestnut stayed where he was. Regan's eyes widened when he saw me.

"Whatta you doing here, Graham?" he said. "I thought you and me were through."

"Not quite," I said as I walked closer to him.

Regan tossed his lunchbox through the open window of the driver's door and reached for the door handle. When he pulled the door open a few inches, I slammed it shut with my hip.

"You're history to me," he said. "I got nothin' to say to you."

"You'll have a lot to say before we're through," I said.

From the corner of my eye, I saw big red step closer to me. When I turned my head to face him, he brought his face close to mine and looked threateningly into my eyes. "Who is this guy, Arnie?" he said.

"A pimple on my ass," Arnie said.

"I smell cop," big red said.

Crew cut moved in closer and stepped behind me. I turned my body so all three of them were in my view.

"Are these the guys you hired to work me over?" I said to Regan.

"You're talking shit again, Graham."

"Why would you do that, Arnie, to get me to lay off the Conlon case? What's your connection to that?"

"Don't know what you're talking about."

"Yes, you do," I said.

Big red put his hand on my shoulder.

I said, "Take your hand off my shoulder."

Big red said, "Make me."

I made him.

I grabbed his forearm and bent my body forward, causing his wrist to bend backward. He let out a cry of pain. I bent his wrist back even further. He went down on his knees in agony. While he was down there, I slammed my knee into his chest. He grabbed his chest and fell over on his side.

Crew cut took a step forward. "You're in no position to be tough," he said. "Three of us an' just one o' you."

Chestnut's timing was impeccable. He stepped out from behind the tree, looking like the Colossus of Rhodes; his hands on his hips, his legs spread shoulder width.

The three of them shot a look in his direction, surprised by his unexpected appearance. Chestnut gave them his big smile and said, "One and one make two, two against three, easy odds."

That's when crew cut got brave and sucker punched me in the gut, knocking me against the cab. Chestnut sprang over the truck bed in warp speed and hit Regan and crew cut with his full body weight, knocking them to the ground. Big red was attempting to get back on his feet until I hit him with an uppercut to his mid-section. When he dropped his hands, I finished him with a right to his jaw and a left to his nose. I heard his nose crack as blood spurted onto his chin.

"Man, you broke my nose," he said.

He melted to the ground and stayed there. When I looked up, Chestnut was tangled between Regan, and crew cut. Crew cut reached into Regan's truck bed and grab a lug wrench. He came at Chestnut swinging. Chestnut ducked the first swing and dodged the next, then let loose with a roundhouse kick that almost sent crew cut into the ionosphere.

I heard a low moan at my feet and looked down. Big red was coming around. I pressed my foot down on the side of his head and kept it there. Wisely, he chose not to resist, although, I don't think he was able. Crew cut raised himself onto one elbow, looking like he didn't know what day it was, and tried to focus on Regan. That's when Regan decided to play the hero. He charged Chestnut, wrapped his arms around Chestnut's waist, and slammed him against the truck body. Chestnut grabbed Regan by the back of his shirt and the seat of his pants and lifted him into the air above his head. He held him there for a few seconds, then spun him around and dropped him into the truck bed. The truck bounced and rattled when Regan's body slammed onto the bed floor.

"Quick and easy," Chestnut said. "That's why you got me."

"That's why I got you," I said.

I took my foot off big red's head. He wasn't going anywhere. He looked like he was in la-la land. I walked to the tailgate of the truck and opened it. I grabbed Regan's ankles and dragged him over the tailgate and pulled him up into a sitting position.

"Are these the guys that jumped me?" I said.

When he didn't answer, I pulled him off the tailgate and stood him on the ground in front of me. Chestnut reached out and grabbed a handful of Regan's shirtfront and moved in close to him. I stepped back and let Chestnut do what I knew he would. He slapped the left side of Regan's face hard with his open hand

and then slapped the right side with the back of his hand. "Are these the guys?" he said. Regan didn't answer, so Chestnut repeated his slap dance a second time. Regan's cheeks began to swell and his eyeballs rolled around like they were loose in their sockets.

"Better tell him, Regan, before he gets mad," I said.

"Okay, Okay," Regan said. "I paid 'em."

"You *paid* these guys, to work me over?"

Regan didn't answer.

"Don't clam up, Regan," I said. "You're trying his patience."

"It was a chance for me to make easy money."

"Somebody gave you money to hire these thugs?"

"Three hundred bucks," he said. "But I'd a done it without the money if I had the balls."

"So you paid these monkeys to do it for you."

"Yeah, I got the satisfaction *and* the money."

"One time wasn't enough?"

"Whattaya talking about?"

"I was jumped outside my apartment," I said.

"Don't know nothin' about that."

"Don't lie to me, Regan," I said. "I don't like to be lied to."

"It was a one-time thing."

"Your boys were the ones that worked me over in the park?"

"That's all I know," he said.

"Who hired *you*?"

He didn't answer.

"Who hired you?' I repeated, louder this time.

When he wouldn't talk, I took hold of his hair and yanked his head back. I felt the anger well inside me. I had had enough of this guy and didn't care what I had to do to get answers.

"I'll ask you one more time," I said, "then I'm gonna hurt you."

I pulled his head back hard until the skin on the front of his neck went taut. Chestnut released his hold on Regan's shirt and stepped back.

"Give me a name," I said.

Regan squeezed his eyes shut tight and shook his head in a futile attempt to free himself.

"A name," I said again. I yanked his head back even further. I was beginning to feel uncomfortable watching the skin on the front of Regan's neck stretch smooth. His veins looked like rubber bands about to snap as I applied more pressure.

He was having a tough time breathing. His face changed from a mottled pink to a shade of crimson. He was trying to say something, so I let up on the pressure a bit. He gasped a few times, and then through quivering lips, tried to speak. We waited until he let out a burst of breath and followed it with the whispered name—"Crockett."

Chapter 16

I was on my way to the Church, mulling over all that Regan had told me and wondering why Crockett would want to have someone work me over. I had gotten everything I could from Regan. He'd said he knew Crockett from having worked with him on several construction jobs, and they had become drinking buddies and garnered a modest friendship. He claimed Crockett offered him three hundred dollars to rough me up, no questions asked. He swore he didn't know Crockett's motive and didn't care since it was easy money and he'd feel good, he said, knowing he'd gotten somebody to "kick my ass." When it came down to it, Regan was a loudmouth weasel with no guts. I should have busted his nose before I let him go, so he'd remember me for a long time.

I parked in front of the church, climbed the stairs, and went in through the front entrance on the chance that I'd find Crockett working in the chapel. I walked through the second set of doors and stood quietly in the back of the chapel. I dipped my fingers in the holy water to my right and blessed myself with the sign of the cross.

It seems my hypocrisy is boundless.

The chapel was dim, save for the rays of colored daylight filtering through the stained glass windows. The pews were empty, and the alter was serene, with the delicate glow of candle flames flickering in the soft shadows. I looked around but didn't see anyone. I walked behind the last row of pews and started up the side of the chapel toward the alter. When I had passed a dozen or more pews, I heard a sound from beside the altar. Up ahead, I saw Crockett emerging from the shadows of an open archway.

He was doing a balancing act with a wet mop, a broom, and a metal pail as he walked toward the altar. When he saw me, he dropped his tools like they were on fire, and ran back through the archway. "Crockett," I shouted. I bolted up the aisle and hurried through the archway which opened to a dimly lit hallway that ran behind the alter. I could hear Crockett rushing down the stairs at the end of the hallway. I said, "Crockett don't make things worse for yourself." But my words only echoed back to me in the hollow space. I followed Crockett down the stairs, tripping over the first step, and almost killing myself. They descended into a large basement room with several ground-level windows on one side, offering the only light. Crockett was opening a door at the far end of the room when I reached the bottom. He hurried through the doorway and let the door slam behind him. When I reached the door, I opened it quickly but didn't see Crockett, just a narrow hallway with another set of stairs leading back up to the other side of the alter. I could hear his running footfalls in the ceiling above me. I took the steps two at a time and made it up to the chapel in time to see a door leading to the outside closing gently. I pushed the brass bar and opened the door and stood in the doorway looking out over the side yard cemetery where we had buried Father Conlon a short time ago. My eyes scanned the trees and myriad headstones, but I didn't see Crockett. I let the door close behind me and walked out onto the grassy landscape. I passed gravesite after gravesite in what I knew was a futile attempt at spotting Crockett. He was young and quick and could have escaped in any direction. Deciding not to waste any more time, I walked back to the rectory to find Monsignor Belducci.

"I don't understand," the Monsignor said. "Why would he run?"

"Establishes an admission of guilt," I said.

"Guilty of what? How could he leave his job, his belonging? I don't think he'll be back," I said.

"Does this have to do with Father Conlon?"

"Probably," I said.

"In what way?"

"I'm not sure," I said.

The Monsignor walked back behind his desk and sat down in his chair with a heavy *thud*. He snatched a tissue from a box on his desk and dabbed it gently over his face and forehead.

"I'll need to see his room," I said.

The Monsignor hesitated and said, "Don't we need a warrant. I don't want the church complicit in breaking the law."

"I'm trying to find Father Conlon's killer," I said.

The Monsignor opened his desk drawer and removed his key ring. "I don't understand all this, detective," he said as he slid the keys across the desk to me.

I stood and waited for Sister Mary Margaret to show up and escort me to Crockett's room, until the Monsignor said, "It's the only room on the third floor, the largest of the keys," then he lowered his head into his hands and said no more. I thanked him and left.

Crockett's room was a mess. Although there was a clothes hamper under a large window, most of his dirty laundry had been thrown into a pile beside it. The bed was unmade and the night table was littered with soda cans, a half-empty bag of chips, and an ashtray overflowing with cigarette butts. The onslaught of stale smoke and musty clothes was not easy to take. I walked to the window and opened it a few inches.

I started with the top drawer of the dresser. It held half a dozen whitey-tighties, several pairs of balled-up sports socks, and a pile of neatly folded white tee shirts. A bulge in the pile of shirts caught my eye. When I pulled back the top shirt, I discovered a Beretta 9mm handgun with a fully loaded clip lying next to it. I took out my cell phone and turned the gun over, using one of the tee shirts, I took a photo of the serial number. Then I replaced the top tee shirt and closed the drawer. I moved on to the next drawer. It was empty. The bottom drawer revealed a single pair of faded jeans tossed in haphazardly. In the closet, there were more empty hangers than clothes. A red flannel shirt hung on a hook behind the door and a heavy down jacket hung from a wooden hanger. On the floor of the closet, there were two pairs of work boots, a pair of black leather dress shoes, and a pair of worn high-top sneakers. The night table had two drawers. I pulled open the larger bottom, but it was empty. The top drawer was so cluttered I had to pull on it using considerable strength. Some of its contents spilled out onto the floor; empty cigarette packs, some loser lottery tickets, and several books of matches. I rummaged around what was left in the drawer, pushing my way through a dozen or so pencils and several black felt markers. I slid out a rolled-up issue of a men's health magazine and tossed it onto the bed. Beneath that, I saw what appeared to be a hard-covered journal or photo album. I lifted it out carefully and opened it. There were lined pages for writing, but no words had been written on them. The back pages felt bulkier; when I turned to them I found two photographs taped randomly to the pages. There was a photo of a young boy on a bicycle that could have been Crockett, and another showing a bungalow-style home with family members enjoying a summer outing. I continued through the other photos until I came upon one of a sandy beach situated at the rear of the house. When I flipped over the last page, a small photo taped to the bottom caught my eye and sent my heart pounding. On that same beach, stretched out in a double hammock, was Davy Crockett, a broad grin on his face and a cool drink in his hand. Lying beside him in an eye-catching white string bikini, smiling shamelessly into the camera—was Eileen Conlon!

***

Danny Nolan was standing in front of my desk giving me the bad news I half expected. "No DNA matches from the overalls. Crockett's clean and everyone else we tested."

He dropped the report on my desk. I gave it a quick look, then slid it into my top drawer.

"Why do you think Crockett's running?" I said.

"Regan dropped a dime. Told him you knew what was up."

"Why would Crockett hire Regan to rough me up?"

"Maybe he didn't. Maybe Regan made the whole thing up."

"Why would he do that?"

"Take the heat off himself."

"Regan had to know I'd eventually confront Crockett about it. It doesn't make sense. Crockett's hiding more than just his involvement with Regan. He ran because he was afraid I'd found out too much of something. He's scared, but not because of a possible lie Regan told about him. What's Crockett afraid I might have discovered?"

"Maybe he thinks his DNA matched, and you were at the church to arrest him."

"Too many maybes," I said.

I took out my cell phone and wrote down the serial number from the photo I had taken of the 9mm I had found in Crockett's room. I handed it to Danny.

"I found this in Crockett's drawer," I said. "Check the serial number, it might lead to somewhere."

"No stone unturned," Danny said.

"You got it," I said.

I took my wallet out of my pocket and removed the photographs I had taken from Crockett's room. "Here's another stone to turn over," I said. I slid the photos across the desk to Danny. He picked them up and looked at them.

"That's our boy," I said. "And the squeeze next to him is—hold on to your hat—Eileen Conlon."

Danny's eyes widened. "The former nun?"

"In the flesh," I said. "No pun intended."

"How long ago was this picture taken?" Danny said, without taking his eyes off the photo.

"I'm guessing it's fairly recent. Crockett doesn't look any different."

"No doubt, it was taken after she lost the calling."

"I guess," I said.

He slid the photos back to me. "Well, if it wasn't... there's more of *Sister Hyde* in her than there is of *Sister Jekyll*," he said.

Danny had a way with metaphor.

I locked the photos in the top drawer of my desk and said, "Let's pay Miss. Conlon a visit."

Traffic was light on the LIE. The Chevy had no problem cruising without stop-and-go traffic, and we made good time. I was hoping to catch Eileen Conlon at home, so I took a chance by not announcing our visit.

I parked the Chevy in the driveway of the Conlon house and we walked up the walkway. Danny pressed the doorbell. In less than a minute, Troy Conlon opened the door. Although it was close to noon, he looked like he'd just climbed out of bed. He was wearing black gym shorts and a wrinkled white tee shirt. His feet were bare. His hair was disheveled, and he looked like he hadn't held a razor in a couple of days. A cigarette dangled from his lips. He spoke through a veil of recently exhaled smoke. "Whattaya want, Graham?"

"We'd like to speak with your sister," I said

She's not here."

"Do you know when she'll be back?"

"No. She was gone when I woke up. You can wait if ya want."

He turned disinterestedly and walked back into the living room, without closing the door behind him. Danny turned to me with a scowl. I gave him a "why not" look and we went in.

We followed Troy Conlon through the living room and into the kitchen where a coffee maker had been dripping fresh coffee.

It smelled good. He didn't offer us any, but took three cups from the cupboard and put them on the table beside a pitcher of cream and a container of sugar.

"Have you found my brother's murderer?" he said.

"Not yet," I said bluntly.

"Maybe you're not trying hard enough," he said.

"Maybe if you lose the attitude, you might be of some help to us," Danny said.

I could tell Danny was annoyed with this guy from the get-go.

When the coffee had finished brewing, Troy lifted the carafe from the coffee maker and brought it to the table. He filled the cups and then brought them back to the machine.

"What makes you think I can help?" he said. "I've been away for years." He sat at the table, crushed out his cigarette in an ashtray, and began fixing his coffee. Danny and I sat opposite him. I poured cream into my coffee and took a sip. It was good. Danny ignored his.

"You could tell us something about your sister," Danny said.

"Guess you didn't hear me," he said. "I've been away."

"You've had contact with your sister from time to time," I said. "She told us so."

Troy Conlon took a slow drink from his cup, while he thought about how much he wanted to say to us.

"Why the special interest in Eileen," he finally said. "Is she a suspect?" He'd asked seriously, expecting an answer.

"We're trying to get a big picture," I said, "standard procedure for a homicide case."

He seemed to accept that, took another drink, and said, "Whattaya wanna know?"

"Anything about your sister that might be relevant," I said.

"Relevant to what?" he said. "She leads a dull life. She was a nun, for Chrissake, until she fell for that loser, Crockett. She thought she was in love with him until she couldn't take his carousing and excessive drinking any longer, so she broke it off. He hurt her bad, screwed her mind up, turned her into a reclusive old maid type."

"She told you all that?"

"She poured her heart out to me, once in a letter. Ya think that's the kinda stuff she would have told Andy. Isn't that what priests do, listen to other people's problems."

"More or less," I said.

"Why *didn't* she tell this to your brother?" Danny said.

"Andy knew what was happening in Eileen's life. She couldn't keep it from him or my father or anyone else, for that matter. But he couldn't understand her feelings for Crockett.

He never approved of her seeing him, and he told Crockett as such. Crockett blamed my brother for their breakup." "Not very perceptive for a priest," Danny said.

"She said she could never open up to him, couldn't confess her feelings or sins to her brother."

"Did she ever mention seeing anyone else after Crockett, another boyfriend?"

"Boyfriend? She lives like an old maid. Never does anything or goes anywhere that might be considered a good time. Believe me, she has since, had no interest in boyfriends. Her only friend now is God,"

I fought off the urge to show him the recent photo of his sister and Davy Crockett frolicking at the beach in their blissful reunion. It was obvious Eileen Conlon had been selective in telling her brother about her life. I was sure he was telling us the truth, and he believed whatever stories his sister had been telling him. I was satisfied he had no info that would help me find Andy's killer. I left my card on the table and asked him to have his sister call me when she could.

"That guy's an asshole," Danny said on our ride back to Manhattan. "I'll bet he knows more than he's telling us."

"He doesn't know a thing," I said.

"Why would you think that?"

"Because he's an asshole," I said.

Danny looked at me and let it go.

Chapter 17

The Marlboro Street fair, in Manhattan, began at 10:00 a.m. Sandy slept over on Saturday night and we had gotten up early to have breakfast and drive into the city to enjoy the fair. It was a beautiful Sunday morning. The day was bright, and the weather was warmer than usual for September. I stood by the front window and looked out while Sandy started breakfast behind me.

"Pancakes or eggs?" she said.

"Oatmeal," I said, without turning.

"Plain or flavored?"

"Maple and brown sugar," I said.

"Instant or regular?"

"Instant," I said.

"Hot or cold?"

Sandy was playing me. When I turned, she was leaning against my kitchen counter with a big smile, waving a metal spatula in the air in front of her. "Well, I need to be sure of what you want to eat," she said.

I rushed to her and lifted her onto the counter. "The only thing I want to eat is you," I said. I pushed my face against her neck and pretended to chomp on her milky white skin.

"Stop it," she said. "You know I'm ticklish." She saved herself from being completely devoured by clobbering me on my head with the spatula. When I lifted her back to the floor, she put her arms around me and gave me a long wet kiss. I returned the pleasure. When our lips parted, we were both breathing heavily. I scooped her into my arms and carried her into the bedroom.

"I want to make breakfast," she said, giggling and kicking her legs in a faux protest. "I'm hungry."

"So am I," I said.

We made love for more than an hour. When we were through, we had both worked up an appetite for a large breakfast. We showered together, dressed and decided there wasn't enough time for a home breakfast so we drove three blocks to a nearby MacDonald's. Sandy had pancakes and bacon and I ordered two sausage croissants, potatoes, and a large juice. We both had coffee. A half-hour later we were on the highway heading toward the city—satisfied in more ways than one.

The city had closed off four cross streets that intersected with Marlboro Street. Both sides of Marlboro Street were lined with a choice of food and dessert vendors from every ethnicity as well as tented cabanas, offering sales of jewelry, books, posters, children's toys, and anything and everything one might want to spend their money on to ensure a fun day. Sounds blasted from speakers mounted on buildings at various locations playing Rock and country music. There were games and children's rides, and three ponies within a small corral where one could ride twice around for only "two tickets". Young couples strolled hand-in-hand, while seasoned parents grabbed for their children, in a futile attempt at curbing their exuberances as they ran excitedly in circles.

Despite the tumult of noise and confusion, I was having a good time, knowing Sandy was enjoying herself. She was wearing her fashionable jeans with her white sketcher sneakers. A white satin shirt was covered by her honey tan corduroy jacket. The morning sun highlighted her auburn hair, making it appear almost red; a white satin ribbon secured it into a ponytail.

We walked, hand-in-hand down one side of Marlboro Street and up the other, stopping occasionally at places that either interested Sandy or me. We bought snow cones, fennel bread, cotton candy, and chocolate-dipped ice cream. Sandy stopped at a vendor and purchased a photo of Albert Einstein in an armchair; smoking a pipe. A bit further down the street, she saw a ring toss game and wanted to try her skill. If one could keep three rings out of six tries on the wooden pegs, one would get the pick of the booth for a prize. I bought two tickets for her to play twice. On her second try, she placed three rings on three pegs—a winner!

She chose, for her prize, a silver chain with an attached medallion, engraved with a red heart. She reached up and hung it around my neck. "Now I can lead you everywhere," she said.

"The bonds of love," I said.

We laughed and she kissed my cheek.

We were enjoying each other's company and the perfect afternoon… until I spotted the stranger.

I had noticed him several times as the afternoon progressed but hadn't mentioned it to Sandy. Each time he was watching us from a furtive place. At first, I thought it might be a coincidence, but he reappeared too many times in too many places and every time, his eyes were directed at us.

Each time I looked at him, he was looking at us.

I couldn't identify him from the distance he kept, but I could tell he was big, fat big, not muscle big, and wearing dark clothes and a wide brim hat, which he wore low over his forehead partially concealing his face. Sandy wasn't aware we were being followed, so I conducted myself in my usual manner. We continued through the street fair, laughing, joking, and having a general good time. Sandy wanted to ride the carousel, so I bought two tickets and we rode double on a spotted pony. All the while, I watched fatso with a keen eye, while he kept a keen eye on us.

When we walked, he walked. When we stopped, he stopped.

The guy was beginning to get on my nerves.

The perimeter of the street fair ended abruptly at the grounds of a branch library amid a park-like setting. I bought two bottles of spring water and Sandy and I sat on a bench to give our legs a break. A half-block away, the street fair continued. Thru the thinning crowd, I saw fatso leaning against a corner building, his eyes were on us again.

Sandy said, "I think someone is following us."
She was more perceptive than I gave her credit for.
"I know," I said. "He's been eyeing us since we got here."
"What does he want?"
"Don't know."
"I'm scared."
"Don't be," I said. "I don't know what his intentions are, but he won't try anything in this environment."

I took Sandy's water bottle and mine, and tossed them into a nearby trashcan, then took Sandy's arm and led her to the front door of the Library. Inside, the sounds of the street fair were muted, but present. Other than a few patrons exploring the bookshelves, and two clerks at the checkout counter, the place was empty. I led Sandy to a row of books arranged on the floor-to-ceiling shelves in the main reading room. We stood between the shelves and waited. Sandy hooked her arm in mine and pressed herself close to me. My eyes were on the front door.

It didn't take long for fatso to make his appearance. He opened the door and walked in like he was a local borrower. He looked about the place quickly, hoping he hadn't lost us. I waited to see what his next move would be. I was hoping not to make a scene, but that depended on fatso's intentions.

When he walked to a small reading table closer to us, I prodded Sandy to move along the shelving further away from him. I could feel her hand trembling on my arm.

"Why is he following us?" Sandy said.

I put my finger to my lips, indicating for her to be quiet.

Fatso picked up a magazine from a nearby shelf and flip a few pages; his eyes scanned the library over the top edge of the page as he made a cursory search for us. Although the library was well lit, I was still unable to see his face

He dropped the magazine on the table and moved between a set of shelves adjacent to where we were standing.

We were no more than four feet to his right. If he'd looked in our direction, he would have seen us through the empty spaces on the bookshelf. Sandy pressed herself closer to me. I hoped he couldn't hear her labored breathing.

"What if he has a gun?" Sandy whispered.

I put my fingers to my lips again as I guided her toward the end of the shelves by the rear wall. Fatso stepped up his pace and moved between the shelving in our direction.

I noticed a single exit door in the sidewall nearby. If the door wasn't locked, it was a chance to make a quick quiet getaway. If it was, we'd have no recourse but to rush out through the front door, which would cause a commotion in the library.

With Sandy in front of me, we moved along the rear wall toward the door. Before we reached the door, I glanced back and saw fatso step out from between the shelves. He looked eagerly in our direction. When he thought I had spotted him, he quickly pulled his head in behind the shelves in a childish display of cat and mouse. Through the shelves, I watched him crane his neck in every direction; he appeared to be disoriented, not sure of himself. If he was trying to conceal the fact that he was following us, he wasn't doing a very good job of it. I guided Sandy between two nearby shelves. We stood quietly. I wasn't sure if he had seen us but wasn't taking the chance. While he was preoccupied, we moved to the exit door.

I pushed the crossbar on the door. It didn't budge.

When I looked back, fatso was moving along the rear wall in our direction. Sandy saw him too. I could see the fear and urgency in her face as I struggled with the crossbar.

Using both hands, I pushed against the bar again. I didn't know what fatso would do, if, and when he reached us, but I was fearful for Sandy.

I had to get the door open—now!

I slammed my entire body weight against it... once... twice until it finally snapped free with a metallic click. When the door opened, we rushed outside, letting the door slam shut behind us. As we walked around to the front of the building, I looked back but didn't see fatso exit the door. We crossed the street at a brisk pace where it was easy to blend in with the street fair patrons.

We concealed ourselves behind a large tree and watched for fatso to emerge from the library. He wasn't very good at what he was trying to do and was probably still inside searching for us. If Sandy hadn't been with me, I would have confronted him and found out what his game was.

When he didn't show, I said, "Let walk back to the car."

We started back through the crowd to where I had parked the Chevy. I kept a keen eye out for this guy's reappearance, but he never showed himself again. The entire way, Sandy wouldn't let go of my arm.

When we got to the Chevy, I found a wrinkled sheet of paper wedged under the windshield wiper with a handwritten scrawl on it. When I pulled it from beneath the wiper and read it, Sandy said, "What does it say?"

"Give up the Conlon case," I said.

This was the third time someone had tried to scare me off the Conlon case. Only this time, Sandy was scared.

I didn't like it when Sandy was scared

Chapter 18

Danny and I had been on the road less than ten minutes when I noticed a black SUV following close behind us. I looked through the rearview mirror and recognized Martin Denman, the phony PI who was working for Eileen Conlon. Any real PI would have enough skill to trail someone without giving himself away. It's easy to keep a distance and not be noticed without losing your subject. It's not brain surgery. This guy was beginning to annoy me. It was time to get him out of my hair. But not before I found out what his game was.

Danny noticed my preoccupation with the rearview mirror. Before he could ask, I answered him. "That phony PI Eileen Conlon hired is following us."

Danny glanced at the side-view mirror. "The black SUV?" he said.

"We'll take him for a little ride and then find out what he knows."

I made a sharp turn off the main street onto the secondary roads. The SUV turned the corner quickly, squealing its tires— *another giveaway*. I drove down several tree-lined streets with the SUV close behind. I made a left, and another left, and then another left, which took us full circle and back to the street where we'd started. The SUV stayed close, only dropping back occasionally. You would think this guy would have enough sense to realize he had been made and was being played with.

Danny was more than amused. So was I.

"Is this guy kidding?" Danny said. "What's he up to?"

"I told you, he works for Eileen Conlon."

To my left, I spotted a little league field with a game in progress. There was a small diamond, and two sets of bleachers crowded with parents and enthusiastic fans. I pulled to the curb and parked. Denman drove the SUV past and parked at the curb a half block in front of us.

"This guy's a clown," Danny said.

"Yeah," I said. "Let's see how funny he can be."

I left Danny in the Chevy and walked out to the bleachers and pretended to watch the game. I made small talk with one of the spectators as I watched Denman get out of his car and walk through a small gate at the far end of the field. He was wearing a black suit with a black knit shirt beneath it. I wondered if he carried a gun under that jacket. He leaned against the fence and folded his arms as he watched the game and *me*. I let him bake for a while in the hot sun inside that black suit, and then I walked away from the bleachers along a narrow path on the side of the first baseline toward a small wooded area away from the game. Denman pushed away from the fence and followed me. I watched him until he walked behind the bleachers, and then I ducked behind a grouping of trees. When he emerged from behind the bleachers, I could see the concern on his face. The great detective had lost his tail. He continued walking in my direction, looking left and right and shielding his eyes from the sun with his hand as he looked across the open field. I took my gun from my hip, then crouched down and waited for him to get close. When he was close enough, I stepped out onto the path, my gun at my side. He stopped and stood perfectly still when he saw my gun.

"Step into my office," I said. I gestured with a nod of my head toward the stand of trees.

He began to put his hands up.

"Keep 'em down," I said.

I followed him into the trees where we couldn't be seen and put my gun against his flabby belly.

"What is this?" he said.

"You tell me," I said. I reached out with my left hand and searched for a weapon behind his jacket. He wasn't carrying.

"Why are you tailing me?"

He stood quietly, searching for something to say. Sweat began to bead on his forehead and trickle down the sides of his fat face.

"I want the truth," I said. "I know you're not a PI."

"I—I was supposed to follow you," he said, at last. "Find out what you were doing."

"You mean, find out how much I'd learned about the Conlon case and report back to Eileen Conlon."

"It's legal," he said.

"Lots of things are legal," I said, "doesn't mean they're moral."

He didn't say a word until I pushed my gun deeper into his flab.

"You're right," he said quickly.

"Why is she so concerned about what I know?" I said.

"She said she'd pay me five hundred dollars to keep an eye on you for a couple of weeks, tell her anything I found out."

"And you lied to me when you told me she hired you to help her find her brother's killer?"

"Yes," he said.

"I don't like being lied to," I said.

He saw the indignation in my face, looked down at my left hand, then jerked his fat head back several inches in anticipation of a left hook.

"Is Martin Denman your real name?"

"Yes."

"How do you know Eileen Conlon?"

"I used to sell real estate. I'm currently out of work."

"So you took her job offer."

"A man's gotta eat," he said.

"Did it ever occur to you that you might be taking on too much? That you might get yourself killed?"

I raised my gun to his face and waved it under his nose.

He looked sacred.

"I don't carry a gun," he said. "I don't even own one."

"Risky," I said. "You have to play this game with a gun."

"I won't need one after today," he said. "I'm through with Eileen Conlon. She can keep her hundred bucks."

"You risked your life for a hundred dollars?"

"A hundred upfront and four more when the job is done. But it doesn't matter, now. I swear you won't see me again."

This guy was such a pathetic loser I was beginning to feel sorry for him—until I remembered the merciless onslaught of kicks and punches he'd given me that night in front of my apartment.

"Why'd you jump me outside my apartment?"

He looked surprised when I said it, then contrite when he said, "I was just supposed to scare you. She said she'd pay me an extra hundred."

"Scare me from what?" I said.

"I don't know," he said. "It was a stupid thing to do, but the money looked good. I didn't mean to come down on you so hard."

"That was the only part of the job you did well."

"It doesn't take many brains to beat up on somebody," he said.

"Were you the one following me at the street fair yesterday?"

He nodded.

"What did you expect to find me doing there, except having a good time?"

He shrugged.

This guy had no idea what he was doing when it came to PI work. He was a potbelly buffoon hired by Eileen Conlon. She sure didn't get her money's worth. She wanted to know what I knew before anyone else did. The question was... why?

He looked relieved when he saw me put my gun back in its holster. That's when I hit him with the left hook he had anticipated earlier. He grabbed his jaw and staggered back against a tree. I knew enough to stay away from his marshmallow belly, so I hit him in the jaw again, this time with a right and another left. His eyeballs rolled upward in their sockets. He looked like he was bird-watching. I hit him one more time, just for good measure. That's when he slid down the tree and went to sleep.

Payback's a bitch!

Back at the Chevy, Danny said, "Did he tell you anything?"

"Yeah," I said. "He's retiring from detective work."

***

When we got back to headquarters, I went immediately to see Briggs. I updated him on Davy Crockett and Eileen Conlon. Briggs put an APB out for Crockett. He asked me what my intentions were at this point. I told him I wanted to confront Eileen Conlon as soon as possible, and maybe, through her, I'd find out where Crockett was hiding and why he was running. If she was uncooperative or evasive, I could always lay the photograph on her. She'd have no choice but to come clean.

The wonders of photography.

I thanked Briggs and headed for the CYO in Brooklyn. I wanted to talk with Russell Grayson, the kid whose name Father Marcus had brought to our attention.

At the CYO building, I stopped in to see Father Marcus. He told me Grayson was on the playground at the rear of the building. I thanked him and drove around the block and parked at the curb next to an outdoor basketball court that was surrounded by a rusted ten-foot-high chain-link fence. There were a dozen kids shooting hoops and sitting on a metal bench waiting their turn. I recognized Grayson by Father Marcus' description. He possessed an excellent basketball player's physique, standing a couple of inches over six feet with thin arms and a pair of slender but muscular legs. His feet looked bigger than they should be, but that might've also been an asset. His hair was a deep brown and cropped close to his head. I got out of the Chevy, walked through the opened gate, and leaned against the fence. I watched Grayson dribble, shoot and move around the court with the gracefulness of a ballerina. He received the ball, dribbled down the court, then spun on his heels and sunk the ball from side court without the ball touching the basket rim. I was impressed.

I liked to think it was Andy Conlon who honed Grayson's skills on the court, but I couldn't know for sure.

After several minutes of enjoying the exhibition, I was suddenly surprised when I saw the basketball coming toward me in the direction of the opened gate. It bounced a few feet in front of me, leaving me no choice but to reach out and grab it. When I turned back, Grayson was standing in front of me with his arms extended. "Thanks, mister," he said. I hesitated before giving him the ball. "Can I speak to you for a minute, Russell?" I said.

"How you know my name?"

I tossed the ball back to him and took out my shield and ID. "I understand you were close friends with Father Conlon," I said. He bounced the ball a couple of times on the blacktop in front of him, ostensibly giving himself time to think about whether he wanted to talk to me or not. Then he turned and fired the ball back to one of his teammates.

"Can we walk a little way down the fence line, away from the noise?" I said.

He followed me through the gate and out to the sidewalk. We stopped about fifty feet away from the ongoing game. Grayson leaned against the fence while we spoke.

"Father Marcus said you and Father Conlon were friends," I said.

"Father Conlon was the best," he said.

"He bent down and tied his sneaker lace, giving himself time to think about how much he wanted to say. When he leaned against the fence again, he was silent.

"I'm not just a cop on a murder investigation," I said. "Father Conlon was a close friend of mine too."

Grayson thought about that for a few moments, and then said, "He was like the father I never had."

"I believe that," I said.

"He did things for me."

"What kind of things?"

"He helped me with my game, made me a better player."

"I can tell. What else?"

"He taught me things."

"Like what?"

"Things about getting along with people. Things about the Bible."

"Did you ever spend time with the Father outside of the CYO building?"

"Once he took a bunch of us for burgers after we won a game. He used the CYO van."

"Have you ever been anywhere with him alone?"

He shook his head.

"Did Father Conlon treat you any differently than he did the other boys? Make you feel special in any way?"

"He treated everybody the same. We were all special to him. He said we were his flock."

I was getting the same answers I had gotten from all the other interviews I had taken. I was glad everybody loved Andy Conlon, but it wasn't helping me find his killer.

I thanked the Greyson kid and slipped him a five before I left. He took it without hesitation and thanked me. He seemed like a decent kid. I hoped the streets wouldn't change that.

I left the playground and drove to the Church Rectory. I was hoping to persuade Monsignor Belducci to let me take a second look at Crockett's room. The condition of his room might give me a clue as to why he ran. If he had been planning it all along, he would have taken time to pack his essentials for a quick getaway when the time was right.

The Monsignor shook his head and did not comment on Crockett when he handed me the key. I thanked him and climbed the stairs to the third floor.

The room looked untouched from the first time I'd seen it. I wasn't sure what I was looking for; maybe something I overlooked. Crockett's dirty clothes were still piled on the floor, and the bed was still unmade. I went immediately to the closet and opened the door. The red flannel shirt was hanging on the hook on the back of the door as it had been, and the down jacket was still on the wooden hanger. The work boots, dress shoes, and high-top sneakers hadn't been disturbed. I pulled back the dresser drawers, giving each a cursory look. Before I closed the top drawer, I instinctively flipped back the top tee shirt from the pile where I had earlier found Crockett's gun.

The gun wasn't there!

Chapter 19

I was in Father Sidletski's office by eight the next morning. The father had called me the night before, insisting that I come by to see him. He claimed he had important information pertinent to the Father Conlon case.

Sidledski looked older than the other priests who lived in the rectory. I guessed he was pushing eighty. He was short and weighed more than he should for his height. His hair was peppered gray and neatly parted to one side. The thick rimless glasses he wore sat comfortably on his wide nose.

His office was much like Father Conlon's but smaller and less ornate. A large desk, a pair of visitor chairs, and a metal file cabinet completed the furnishings. Two double-hung windows let in plenty of light from the street side of the building where the sound of children playing filtered in from the outside.

"Please, sit," the Father said, gesturing for me to take a chair.

As I sat, he lowered himself into a high-back chair behind his desk.

"Thank you for coming," he said.

He pulled a tissue from the box on his desk, leaned back in his chair, and took his time wiping his face and forehead. When he was through, he carefully placed the tissue in a nearby wastebasket, squared his blotter evenly on his desktop, and slid three pencils back into the top drawer of his desk. His senseless fidgeting told me he was not comfortable with what he was about to tell me and was searching hard to find a place to begin. I thought I'd help him alone.

"On the phone, you said you had information pertinent to Father Conlon's case."

I waited.

When he was ready, he sat back in his chair, laced his fingers together across his ample belly, and looked directly at me. "I've been struggling lately with the laws of the church and the laws of man," he said. "An exercise that has cost me more than a few night's sleep."

A silence fell between us while I let him arrange his thoughts.

"In all my years of divine service, I have never been burdened with a situation such as I have been presented. I have always been mindful to keep a person's relationship with the Lord a private and personal matter. Confession is between God and his brethren."

He took another tissue from the box, wiped his face again, and continued. "But occasionally—in the interest of spiritual and social justice—man's laws can supersede the laws of the church. I have, therefore, with guidance from the Lord, summoned you here today to tell you what I know."

I sat quietly and let him continue.

"This has not been easy for me, detective," he said. "But I have assuaged all guilt and believe I am doing the right thing. However, before I continue, you must assure me that the information I am about to disclose will not be passed to anyone other than those who need to know."

"If it's important to the case," I said, "I assure you it will be kept confidential and used with discretion."

He took a few seconds to think about that, and then moved forward in his chair, put his elbows on his desk, and leaned closer to me. "I have information," he said, "the contents of which I will impart to you. I only hope it is relative enough to help find Father Conlon's killer."

He made the sign of the cross, took a deep breath, and continued. "There had been a relationship between Father Conlon and Father Faynor, which is, let us say, contrary to the laws of God. A behavior which is against what the bible teaches us."

Was I hearing him, right? Was he saying what I thought he was saying? Was this something I could believe and accept about Andy Conlon? My mind struggled with incredulity and denial.

"Father," I said. I stood up and took a deep breath. "I want to be sure I understand you."

"I'm telling you exactly what you heard me say," the Father said.

No way. I wasn't buying it. I'd known Andy Conlon for a long time.

I turned and walked to the window. I was visibly shaken and hoped the Father couldn't tell, but he probably could. I looked out the window trying to digest what I had just heard, letting the unexpectedness of the idea seep into my brain for processing.

On a patch of blacktop below the window, several boys were shooting hoops into a basket rim, missing a net. They looked to be fifteen or sixteen, but their ability on the court was impressive just the same. They dribbled and took foul line shots with the same admirable skill as I had seen in the Grayson kid. I wondered if Andy Conlon had been a part of polishing their skills as well.

Behind me, the father was silent.

I walked back to my chair and sat. It was my turn to use a tissue. I blotted my forehead a couple of times, then tossed the tissue into the wastebasket.

"I can understand how difficult it must be for you to accept what I've told you."

"I've known Father Conlon for most of my life," I said.

"He was almost like a second father to me."

"'Hate the sin, not the sinner'," the father said.

"How do you believe this information will help the investigation?" I said.

"I thought it might provide another perspective, somewhere else to look. My conscience told me the right thing to do was to inform you of what I'd learned."

"We need to be sure," I said. "An allegation like this can be explosive if it can't be substantiated."

"It is the truth, detective," the Father said. "Last week, I heard Father Faynor's confession. The revelation was in his own words."

I sat there not knowing what to say, listening to the rhythm of the basketball bouncing outside the window.

***

"A priest can't come out of the closet," Danny said. "Not if he wants to remain a priest."

I was sitting at my desk. Danny was sitting at his, with his chair turned to face me. I lowered my head into my hands and rubbed my temples.

"I can't believe it," I said. "I *won't* until I can prove it."

"And how would you do that," Danny said, "Confront Faynor?"

Danny was right. The situation was awkward.

"It's a hard pill to swallow," Danny said. "But if you accept it and work on that premise as the Father said, it might put a new perspective on the case."

"Let's keep this revelation between us," I said, "until we can corroborate it."

"Sure," Danny said.

"This opens a whole new can of worms," I said. "If Father Conlon and Father Faynor were a couple, what other things might we find about Andy Conlon by digging deeper? What about all those young boys he associated himself with?"

Danny got up from his chair and came over and sat in my visitor's chair.

"You're creating a scenario that may not exist," he said.

"It's a habit I need to break."

"Let's concentrate on finding a motive," he said, "looking for the person who had a reason to kill the Father."

"What about unrequited love? What about a jealous lover? They're possible motives, heterosexual or not, those emotions exist just the same."

"True," Danny said. "And if they are motive, we'll eventually find out."

He walked back to his desk, came back with a single sheet of paper, and handed it to me. "The serial number on Crockett's gun tells us it was purchased legally in Ohio four years ago, but not by Crockett. It was later reported stolen but never recovered."

"How'd it get into Crockett's possession?" I said.

"With no history trail, it's of no value to us." Danny said; "unless Crockett can shed some light on it."

"Troy Conlon called me this morning," I said. "He hasn't seen his sister in two days and nights. He seemed to be concerned."

"You think she's with Crockett?"

"Maybe," I said.

He picked up the photographs of Crockett and Eileen Conlon that had been lying on my desk and studied them.

"We know she's been less than truthful with us," I said. "We know she's had some kind of relation with Crockett in the past. The photo attests to that. She may believe he killed her brother."

"Why would she run with him?" Danny said. "She knows Crockett is the one that found her brother's body. But why would she think he killed him?"

"She knows he was killed with a screwdriver and she's aware that the overalls were found in the nearby dumpster. It was all in the papers in detail."

"What would she think was his motive?"

"Don't know. Maybe she thinks she's in love with him. Even though she may believe he killed her brother, she remains with him out of some kind of morbid affection. It's twisted logic, but love does strange things to people."

"Sorta like a Bonnie & Clyde scenario," Danny said. "In that respect, it makes sense, but he's her brother. How could she justify being with that guy?"

"Maybe she's got her own idea. Maybe she's playing Crockett until the time is right when she can get her revenge for what he did."

"A remote possibility," Danny said, "but that's a lot of maybes."

"We need to locate him, or her, or both of them, if they're together. We don't have anything substantial to charge either of them, but if we can get something out of them, we may have our answers. Crockett's not running for nothing."

Danny walked back to his desk with one of the photographs and took out a small magnifying glass from his top drawer. He studied the photo through the glass for several minutes, then walked back to my desk. He handed me the photo and the glass. "Look in the background," he said. "It's fuzzy and small but you can make out a number on the mailbox on the post by the front walk."

I put the glass to the photo and squinted my eyes to focus on a closer look. Danny was right. On the mailbox, I could make out three black numbers that looked like "728". Just below the letters there appeared what looked like a street name. The first four letters, B-e-r-m were visible, but the remaining ones had been obliterated. Below the letters was the pay-off; clear and crisp were the zip code numbers.

Chapter 20

Danny matched the zip code with the letters we had and came up with the street name we needed. The next morning we were on the parkway heading south toward Ocean Grove, a resort community at the Jersey shore. It was a beautiful day, crisp and clear, with a warm temperature and low humidity, perfect beach weather. I let Danny drive while I took in the scenery. He liked driving those big unmarked Chevy Impalas that were a part of the squad motor pool.

We took exit 100B, then headed east on route 33, which took us into Ocean Grove. We drove beautiful tree-lined streets surrounded by elegant Victorian homes until we came to the shore area. The house we were looking for was a seasonal rental. Records showed the Crockett's had rented the house in previous years until they purchased it as a summer retreat. It's a place Crockett, no doubt, spent a lot of summers. It made sense that he would seek refuge there.

We were looking for the number, 728 Bermuda Drive. While Danny drove, I looked at the photograph to help identify the house when we came upon it. The houses in this area were a bit smaller than what we had seen, with the ocean and a stretch of sandy beach at the rear of each house. We turned onto Bermuda Drive, which was a narrow two-lane road. The houses here were further apart, separated by empty sandlots and parcels of high grass. We continued for a mile or so, taking several turns in the road. At the last turn, the house appeared on our right. I recognized it by the photo and the mailbox out front. We were about a block away.

"There it is," I said.

Danny pulled the Impala to the curb and cut the engine.

"How do you want to work this?"

"Not sure," I said. "We can't rush the house."

"We can ring the front doorbell," Danny said. "Maybe he'll invite us in."

Danny can be resourceful and clever at times. I gave him a look. He smiled at me. I didn't smile back.

I got out of the Impala and stood on the sidewalk. Danny got out on his side and came around and stood next to me. We looked down the block at the house. It wasn't much larger than a bungalow, almost rustic with lots of wood siding. There was a white SUV parked in the driveway beside a four-foot-high stockade fence, which ran down both sides of the house toward the rear. The ocean met a private beach at the rear of the house.

"Follow my lead," I said to Danny.

We began to walk down the sidewalk toward the house. The neighborhood was quiet, deserted. When we approached the house, I crouched low along the stockade fence and followed it along the side of the house. Danny was close behind. As we got closer to the rear of the house, we could hear muted music and lapping waves on the shoreline. There was a wooden gate that partitioned the rear yard from the rest of the grounds. We looked over it, cautiously. On the beach was a round table with an umbrella stuck in the middle of it. A charcoal grill, several lounge chairs, a stand-alone hammock, and a portable well-stocked bar. Crockett was at the grill cleaning the cooking grates with a long handle wire brush while listening to a portable radio that was balanced in the sand at his feet. He was wearing shorts, a tee-shirt and white sneakers. Eileen Conlon was sitting beside him in a lounge chair, looking like a Hollywood starlet in her one-piece bathing suit, wide brim straw hat, and sunglasses. She was reading a book. Crockett spotted us quickly. I wasn't sure how he would react, but I didn't have to wait long. He threw the long handle brush at us and dashed across the sand around the side of the house. "Don't make things worse for yourself, Crockett," I shouted.

Danny moved to Eileen Conlon and made sure she stayed where she was. I hurried after Crockett, slipping a few times on the loose sand. As I turned the rear corner of the house, I saw Crockett enter the house through the side screen door. I wasn't sure what he was up to, so I removed my gun from its holster and released the safety. I moved along the house toward the screen door. I listened but heard nothing. When I looked through the screen, I could see only dim light and shadows.

I pulled the door open slowly. I swore silently to myself as the springs in the hinges squealed and moaned, announcing my presence. I stepped into a small entranceway. Several steps were leading up to a kitchen. I climbed them carefully, pushed back a second door, and walked into the kitchen. The house smelled of stale smoke, beer, and a general uncleanness. The house was silent. Outside, I could hear the ocean waves and the portable radio playing a country song.

I walked into the kitchen and looked out a small window into the rear yard. Danny was standing beside Eileen Conlon. She seemed undisturbed by our presence as she sat in her lounge chair casually drawing on a cigarette.

I moved out of the kitchen and stepped into a larger living room. I didn't see or hear Crockett anywhere. I hoped he wasn't dumb enough to try to jump me, forcing me into a struggle or forcing me to use my gun.

As I moved toward the front door, I heard the sudden rumbling of an engine from the front of the house. I opened the door in time to see Crockett straddling a motorcycle. The bike spewed dust and smoke as it bounced and fishtailed while Crockett tried to maneuver it onto the open road. I holstered my gun and ran down the front stairs. Crockett was about to make good his getaway, until I kicked hard at the rear wheel of the bike, knocking it and him to the ground. With its gears still engaged; the bike spun in circles beside him, its rear-wheel spitting dust and dirt in every direction. Crockett scampered to his feet, but I steamrollered him and knocked him back down. I was able to put my knee down on his chest. The bike was idling and spewing blue smoke in our faces. It was tough to breathe. I coughed a few times and squeezed my burning eyes shut. Crockett saw his chance, pushed me off, and jumped back on the bike. He revved the engine, popped a small "wheelie" and jumped the curb into the street. I sat on the ground mad and defeated, rubbing my burning eyes and watching him disappear down the street in a trail of blue smoke.

Danny came running around the house, gun drawn.

"Take it easy," I said. "He's gone."

"What happened?"

"He disappeared in a cloud of smoke and a mighty, 'Hi Ho Silver,'" I said.

Danny looked down the street in time to see Crockett disappear around a corner.

I got up and dusted myself off. We walked back to the side of the house, where I stopped at a garden hose. I soaked my handkerchief and wiped my eyes and face to alleviate the burning.

At the rear of the house, Eileen Conlon was still sitting in the lounge chair where we had left her. The portable radio was playing a classic country tune. I stood in front of her, reached down and clicked it off. I wanted answers. Now that she was out of her pious element, I'd push her hard to see want I could come up with. I was sure she knew more than she was willing to reveal.

She sat composed, not the least bit flustered or bewildered by what she had just witnessed. She had removed her sunglasses and hat and was still smoking her cigarette. Her hair was pulled back into a ponytail and she had covered her shoulders with a beach towel.

"What happened to you?" she said.

"Your boyfriend was uncooperative."

"He's not my boyfriend," she said. "Am I under arrest?"

"Have you done something that you should be arrested for?" I said.

She drew hard on her cigarette and let the smoke out slowly. When the smoke cleared, she began to offer information before I'd had a chance to ask for any.

"You want to know about David and me," she said. "And why I'm here."

I waited while she dropped her cigarette in the sand and crushed it under her foot.

"We became friends… acquaintances some time ago," she said. "I met him when I visited my brother at the church."

"This was after you left the service of the church?" Danny said.

"Of course," she said. "I would not offend the Lord with what he might construe as insolent behavior."

"How long have you been dating him?" Danny said.

"We're not dating," she said. "We're just friends."

"Seems like more than 'just friends', spending time alone with him at his home," I said.

"He invited me here for the day. I thought it was a way for me to relax, getaway. I've been so upset," she said, "with all that's happened. I lost my father recently. The death of my brother was too much for him."

"I'm sorry," I said.

"Your brother's concerned for you. He said he hasn't heard from you in several days," Danny said.

"I don't answer to Troy," she said. "He's a 'come and go brother' and I don't consider him a part of my life. As soon as the estate is settled and he gets his money, he'll be gone again."

"How much do you know about Crockett?" I said.

"No more than he has told me," she said.

"Tell us about it," I said.

"Just a scanty description of his early life," she said. "How he came to work at the church. It was my brother that helped him obtain the job there. He and David had mutual respect. David told me he thought Andy was a good guy."

She picked up her hat from her lap, and placed it on her head, and slid her sunglasses over her eyes. "Why did David run?" she said.

"We were hoping that was something you could tell us," I said.

"I have no idea. Is he in trouble?"

"He might be a suspect in the murder of your brother."

"Mother of God," she said and crossed herself.

She got up and let the beach towel slip from her shoulders, then turned and walked out toward the water. I watched her walk away, leaving a trail of footprints in the sand behind her until she stopped at the water's edge where the sand was smooth and undisturbed. In the setting sun, she appeared as a silhouette, a lonely figure looking out at the lonely sea.

She stood staring at the horizon, until she lifted her eyes to the Heavens, perhaps in prayer, perhaps in a self-indulgent moment of solitude, designed to elicit sympathy from Danny and me. When she walked back to us, she seemed visibly disturbed. She removed her sunglasses, picked up the towel and wiped her moist eyes, then draped it across her shoulders again. I wasn't convinced her distress was genuine.

"I think you should contact your brother," I said. "Do you need a ride home?"

"I have my car," she said. "I'll change, lock up the house and leave."

"If you hear from Crockett, let us know," I said.

"You'd be smart to terminate your friendship with him, for your own good," Danny said.

"I've been too hasty," she said. "My imprudence may have violated God's law."

"Your imprudence may have violated man's law," Danny said.

Chapter 21

It was Tuesday morning. I was sitting at my desk going over my notes on the Father Conlon case. It had been a week since Danny and I had had our unexpected encounter with Crockett and Eileen Conlon at the Jersey shore. The statewide APB had, thus far, proved fruitless. There had been no sign of Crockett.

My phone rang.

"Detective, Graham," I said. It was Monsignor Belducci.

"Good morning, Monsignor."

"I'm afraid it's not," he said. "There has been a terrible tragedy." The monsignor paused before he said, "Father Faynor has been murdered."

I sat for a moment letting the monsignor's words sink into my brain. As dreadful as the news was, my emotions remained stable. It's not that I was callous or uncaring; but after having spent twelve years as a homicide detective, I learned quickly, the dark recesses of the human mind and its evil capabilities. I wasn't surprised by the degree of malevolence a human being can engender. When one confronts death and murder daily, the only way to deal with it is objectively.

Andy Conlon's murder had hit me hard because of the personal association he had had with me and my family throughout the years. Although I'd endured the heartache and grief over the loss of a good friend, those painful emotions, in and of themselves, provided comfort by reassuring me of my humanity.

"When did it happen?" I said.

"I believe sometime, last night. When he didn't report for his mass this morning, I sent Father Sidletski to his room. He found Father Faynor there. I thought you should know."

"Are there police on the scene?" I said.

"Many," he said.

"I'll be right there," I said.

There were squad cars and an ambulance at the side door of the rectory when I arrived. I didn't know the officer at the door, so I flashed my shield as I passed him and headed up to the second floor where the priest's quarters were. The hallway outside Father Faynor's room was crowded with the usual technicians: fingerprints, forensics, and photos. I worked my way through the suits until I saw Chief Briggs and Detective Garcia standing at the center of Father Faynor's room. Beside them, Father Faynor lay face down on the carpeted floor. He was wearing jeans and a white tee shirt. He wore no shoes or socks. His tee-shirt was saturated with dark red blood. Protruding just below his left shoulder was what looked to me, to be a screwdriver buried deep to the handle. *Things were starting to look familiar.* I walked over to Briggs and Garcia. "This is starting to look like a sick habit," I said.

"What comes to my mind first," Briggs said, "is what's the connection between the murders of these two priests?"

I knew of one connection between these two priests but wasn't about to disclose that information just yet. There was no such thing as coincidence, here. There had to be a motive, a reason that connected the two deaths. I had no intention of telling Briggs what Father Sidletski had revealed to me about Andy Conlon. I was still having a hard time accepting it myself. If Briggs knew I was holding pertinent information about a case, he'd have my head.

"If we find that out," I said. "We'll have a motive. When we have a motive, we'll have our man."

"The press has been having a field day with Father Conlon's murder," Garcia said. "The story's been in the papers almost every day since it happened. The public wants answers."

"We'll keep this one undercover for as long as we can," Briggs said. "But it won't be easy. Did you see any media people outside when you came in, Max?" he said.

"No," I said.

"It won't be long before they're all over like maggots," Garcia said.

Briggs said to Garcia: "Let's clear away some unnecessary vehicles and secure the scene, tamp things down a bit. And tell them to turn off those damned lights. I'll take care of it from my office if there's any media follow-up." Garcia nodded and walked out.

"Max, my office," Briggs said.

***

"The screwdriver indicates the same MO unless somebody's trying to deceive us," I said, "or send us a message."

"It's too blatant, too deliberate," Briggs said. "These two murders are tied together just by the same type of weapon used. Why a screwdriver, why not a knife, or a pair of scissors?"

"The killer might be trying to mislead us, send us looking in the wrong direction," I said.

Briggs removed his suit jacket and placed it on the back of his chair. He sat down at his desk and began rubbing his eyes with the palms of his hands. When he looked back up at me, his eyes were moist. He looked tired. "The Mayor's on my ass, Max," he said. "Whattaya got?"

"Not much," I said. "Other than Crockett, who's on the run. And we're not sure he's guilty of anything, right now. DNA from the hairs found inside the overalls doesn't match his DNA."

"Then, why the hell is he running?"

"Maybe he *did* kill Father Conlon, and he believes his DNA will prove his guilt."

"Does he have motive?"

"None that I could find. He told me he got along well with Father Conlon. Father got him the custodian job at the church. And he's friendly with Father Conlon's sister, Eileen. We traced Crockett to a shore house in New Jersey. Eileen Conlon was there with him. When Danny and I came upon them, they were basking in the sun like a couple of honeymooners. When

Crockett saw us, he panicked and made a run for it. He took off on a motorcycle."

"In what way is this woman involved with Crockett?"

"She said she was there just for the day as per his invite, needed to get away from all the stress. She claims he had always been nice to her, and she saw no reason for not accepting his invitation. She denies having an affair with him. She says she made a mistake by being there that day, regretted that she may have offended the Lord. She's very pious."

"What are your thoughts on this new murder?" Briggs said.

"Crockett can't be in two places at once, unless he doubled back, unseen, to murder Father Faynor. He knows the church and rectory very well, and he has keys to almost every door, but it would be really stupid and risky for him. He didn't get along with Faynor, but I don't think he hated Faynor to the degree he would commit murder. Hatred can be a motive for murder, but I don't think it applies here."

Briggs removed a manila folder from his top drawer and slid out several papers. He began reading the preliminary report that I'd submitted to him regularly concerning the Conlon case. He paused to read the last page.

"Troy Conlon," he said.

"Father Conlon and Eileen Conlon's itinerant brother left the family a while ago. Never been a part of it. Father Conlon left him a small inheritance. He showed up recently to collect it. According to Eileen Conlon, as soon as he gets his money, he'll be gone."

"Motive?"

"Maybe."

"What do you mean?"

"He could have orchestrated his brother's death to gain his inheritance."

"How could he be sure he'd receive any inheritance?"

"I've been confronted with that question before," I said.

Briggs furrowed his brow. "Not an impossibility," he said. "When, exactly did he arrive on the east coast?"

"Eileen Conlon notified him of the Father's death. I'm sure he hurried here for his money. I'll get the exact date of his arrival from the airline's manifest."

Briggs read further down the page. "What about this Regan?"

"He's got an ex-wife and one young son, Kevin, a good kid. I met him at the midtown Youth Center where he spends a good amount of time. Father Conlon took Kevin under his wing, so to speak. He and Kevin became buddies. Kevin's father resented Father Conlon's close relationship with his son, felt he was impeding his efforts to get his son back. There were several heated exchanges and a threat."

"What kind of threat?"

"Regan said he would kill Father Conlon if he didn't stay away from his son."

"And you know this, how?"

"Kevin Regan told me. He'd heard them arguing in the playground."

"Can we rely on a kid's word?"

"I eventually caught up with Arnie Regan and confronted him with it. He admitted saying it, but only in the heat of anger."

"Possible motive," Briggs said.

"He was also dumb enough to hire several 'mouth breathers' to work me over. But here's the kicker. It wasn't his idea. Regan admitted to me, Crockett had paid him two hundred dollars to rough me up, scare me into dropping the Conlon case."

"Do you believe him?"

"He resisted my questioning. but my interrogation method was very persuasive. "I'm sure he didn't lie."

Chief Briggs hadn't been very successful at keeping the Faynor murder out of the media. By the end of the day on Wednesday, the entire city had exploded with the news that a second priest at St. Trinity had been brutally murdered.

Briggs called a press conference for 9:00 a.m. the following morning. He wanted me to be a part of it. I hated those things and wasn't very good at engaging the press, but Briggs gave

OTHER MEN'S SINS

me no choice. The public wanted answers, and it was within his purview to calm the populace.

The next morning, we met on the steps of the church rectory. The morning was crisp and clear. Police barricades cordoned off the front of the steps, and shortly before nine, there were already many journalists and media people gathered behind it. At precisely 9:00 a.m. Briggs stepped up to the podium. I stood behind him and to his left. Danny Nolan stood next to me. The department PR person was there, as were a couple of top brass from other precincts.

"Before I begin," Briggs said, "I want to say I will discuss this case on a need-to-know basis. The public has a right to be informed and the department will release information we feel is pertinent, but will in no way jeopardize the ongoing investigation. You all know, by now, what the current situation is, so, in the interest of expediting things, I will begin by taking your questions."

This ignited a rush of waving arms and chaotic shouting. Briggs pointed to a young woman near the front row.

"It seems that your department is at an impasse with this investigation," she said. "Can you give us any news that might mitigate the public's concern and offer hope that whoever committed these crimes will eventually be caught?"

"This department is not at an impasse," Briggs said. "Our investigators have uncovered several avenues of pursuit, many of which, have proven to be fruitful."

"Can you be more specific?" someone shouted.

Briggs looked at me. I knew he wanted me to answer that one. I walked up to the podium. "I'm Detective, Graham from Homicide," I said. "We have several names on our suspect list, which we are pursuing. There is nothing conclusive at this time, only possibilities."

"Based on what?" a voice shouted.

"Based on suspicious behavior and conjecture," I said. "However, crimes aren't solved with conjecture. There needs to be motive beyond a reasonable doubt."

A reporter in the back of the crowd raised his hand. I called on him.

"When do you expect to have something viable?" he said.

"We hope to tie up loose ends soon," I said.

A younger reporter in the front row asked, "Other than the fact that the two victims were priests, are these two murders related or coincidental?"

"There is nothing coincident about them," I said. "We believe, at this time, the two murders were committed by the same person."

"What about a copycat killing?" someone said.

"A highly improbable possibility," I said, "given the nature of the crimes. People don't kill for no reason, other than those with deranged minds, but the suggestion has been explored."

I'd had enough and walked away from the podium. Briggs stepped up again just as someone shouted, "Is the public at large in any danger?"

"We have no reason to believe these are indiscriminate killings," he said. "There is a definite motive and reason behind them."

"Have you established motive?" a voice said.

Briggs simply said, "No."

An older reporter wearing a wide-rim hat and sporting a full beard moved forward in the crowd and said, "Murders occur every day, especially in this city. But it's not every day that a priest gets murdered. Due to the esoteric nature of these crimes, shouldn't your department be handling them in a special way other than standard operating procedure?"

"A crime is a crime," Briggs said. "Each case is handled according to its particulars. Our department uses state-of-the-art procedures and forensics, which have proven to be positive."

"Then why is it taking so long to find the killers?" another voice said.

Briggs didn't like the question. I could see it in his face. He leaned in closer to the mic and said, "Investigating a crime, especially one as heinous as this, takes its own time. It's like building a wall, one brick at a time until it's completed. Clues are put together, one at a time, until a picture emerges, much like a puzzle. Some crimes are solved quicker than others, some take longer due to the particulars of the crime. Therefore, there is no such thing as, taking too long to solve a crime. This department works as diligently and expeditiously as the circumstances allow."

I knew Briggs had had enough when he said, "Thank you all for coming. We will keep you all abreast of the investigation as is appropriate." He turned away from the podium and walked back into the church. The rest of us followed as the crowd shouted more questions in a chorus of noise and confusion.

Briggs had answered their questions as candidly as he could. There was a certain amount of information that he could not, or would not release, and more than a few questions he could not answer honestly. When the conference was over, the press wasn't happy. They never were.

***

The next morning, Danny and I were in Chief Briggs' office sitting in his visitor chairs. There were several newspapers piled on his desk. Briggs picked up the top newspaper and scanned the headline. He didn't look happy. He picked up the second paper and perused the article on the front page with the same look. The third one also failed to put a smile on his face. He held it up for us to see. The headline read: "**Cops baffled by priest's murders**." Briggs said, "Did I give any indication to the press that we were baffled by these crimes?"

"I didn't hear that," Danny said.

"Neither did they," Briggs said, "but they printed that bullshit, anyway."

He tossed the newspaper down on his desk and said, "Bastards think we're magicians, pull a criminal out of a hat and put him in jail."

"That's today's journalism," Danny said.

"Nothing we say or do makes them happy," Briggs said. "They should be working with us not against us."

"Crime sells newspapers," I said. "The longer they keep a story going, the more papers they sell. It doesn't matter to them if they're peddling the truth or not."

"Let's keep our investigation as tight as we can," Briggs said. "I don't want it complicated by bogus headlines."

He picked up the three newspapers and dropped them into the wastebasket beside his desk. "I wouldn't wipe my ass with them," he said.

He leaned back in his chair and stroked his mustache. "I'm getting calls from the mayor and the DA's office almost every day," he said. "They want answers."

"We'll give them answers as soon as we get them," I said.

"When we get enough clues, we'll solve this case, just like we always do," Danny said.

"Clues are never easy to find," I said to Danny, "but they're everywhere."

"What do you mean?" Danny said.

"A good investigator needs to be perceptive enough to recognize a clue when he sees one," I said. "If he misses a clue, then that clue doesn't exist, and it's of no value to him or his investigation."

"What is this, police academy 101?" Briggs said. "I need answers."

"We're getting answers," I said.

"And when we get enough answers," Danny said. "We'll call a press conference and give them a headline we can shove down their throats."

Briggs liked what Danny had said. He gave him a big smile.

***

The screwdriver that was used to kill Father Faynor was similar to the one used on Father Conlon, a round shaft Phillips head. There were no prints found on it. The investigation, thus far, found nothing untoward in Father Faynor's room. According to the coroner, Father Faynor had died from a single stab wound, which punctured his aorta. Essentially, he bled to death. Father Conlon was inflicted with multiple stab wounds to numerous organs, which resulted in his death.

There was nothing similar between the murders of Father Conlon and Father Faynor, other than they were men of the church, and both were killed with a screwdriver.

I was keeping, confidential, what Father Sidletski had revealed to me about the relationship between Father Conlon and Father Faynor until I could be satisfied with proof of their association. Other than Danny Nolan, no one else was aware of the information. I had to be careful. If Briggs found out I was keeping relative information from him, he'd have my ass.

I decided to dig further into Father Faynor's life. Perhaps he had an enemy from his past or someone that might have carried enough animus to contemplate doing him harm. There may even have been a link between the murders of Father Conlon and Father Faynor. I began by asking Monsignor Belducci for Father Faynor's file. It would be chock full of details about his early life, personal and academic. The Monsignor was hesitant about giving up the file, but when I suggested I could obtain a subpoena, he acquiesced.

I sat at my desk and studied the file for nearly two hours.

Jonathan Faynor was born and raised in a rural Ohio town to Irish Catholic parents. He had one sister, Margaret. His childhood was uneventful. He attended grade school and graduated from High school where he played Basketball until his father's job promotion necessitated a transfer to the big apple. The family moved to Queens and lived a peaceful, productive life. It was during his time at college that young Jonathan decided to devote his life to God. After attending seminary school, he entered the priesthood and was assigned to St. Trinity in New York City. He had arrived there a year after Father Conlon had. His record at St. Trinity was exemplary. He served Mass, taught catechism, and coached basketball on weekends with the CYO. There was nothing in the file that was not innocuous.

I checked with the coroner for the address of the Faynor's in Queens, New York, but he had none; although he was able to give me the name and address of Margaret Faynor-Blake, Father Faynor's sister, currently married and living in Norwalk, Connecticut who had been the next of kin notification. I needed to interview Father Faynor's sister. I was sure she could give me a better insight into her brother than what was in the file.

Father Faynor was laid to rest that weekend in the church cemetery, which was the custom regarding all resident priests. The funeral mass was as large as Father Conlon's. Monsignor Belducci offered the eulogy. Margaret Faynor-Blake, naturally, attended her brother's funeral. It saved me the drive to Norwalk. It's always a delicate situation, interviewing someone who is grieving a loss, but I had done it before and understood enough to be professional, yet, compassionate.

***

Margaret Faynor had taken a room at the Roosevelt Hotel on 45th Street in Midtown. When I phoned and asked her for the interview, she was more than willing to help in any way, find her brother's killer.

"Sorry for your loss," I said. I showed her my ID.

"Thank you," she said, without looking at it. "Please sit."

She was a small woman, unlike her brother. Her hair was a deep brown, pulled back into a modest bun. She wore a deep purple, almost black dress, with a white collar. She appeared to be close in age to her brother.

We sat on a sofa. The room was spacious and immaculately kept. On the coffee table in front of us, I couldn't help noticing several framed photographs. The top one displayed Margaret and Father Faynor arm in arm, smiling into the camera. She saw me noticing the photos and said, "Photos we'd displayed at the wake. I need to bring them back home."

"Of course," I said.

"I have always been close to my brother. He was a good person."

"I'm sure," I said, "and devoted to the church."

She sat up on the sofa, smoothed the wrinkles out of her dress, and said, "Now detective, how can I help you find my brother's murderer?"

"I was hoping you could give me a detailed insight into your brother's life," I said, "his recent history: friends, acquaintances, and activities, anything that would help formulate a motive for the crime. I read his file from St. Trinity but if you could supply any more, it would be helpful."

She removed a flowered handkerchief from her dress sleeve, dabbed her moist eyes once, then began. "My brother's life was an open book," she said. "What one saw was what one got. At the risk of sounding like I'm trying to make him a martyr, a saint even. I can only say good things about him."

"I understand," I said. "And I'm sure what you say is true. But I'm more interested in the particulars of his life: people that he knew along the way, friends, relatives, employers, girlfriends."

She lowered her chin to her chest and removed her handkerchief again. She wiped her eyes and then looked up at me. Her eyes were sad.

"Detective," she said. "I afraid, under the circumstance, I must reveal a dark secret concerning my brother's life, one that had been kept by him and by me alone. But now, if it will help find Jonathan's killer, it can no longer remain a secret."

She stood and walked to the window and looked down onto 45th Street. "Since Jonathan was a teenager," she began, "he has been struggling with sin, a personal sin within himself. Even when he gave his heart to the Lord, he carried the weight of perdition. It was a constant battle within his mind and soul, behavior contrary to the laws of God. A sin he could not repent. He asked forgiveness many times, but the sin prevailed. In time, he accepted his burden and tried to make up for it by giving more to the Lord and his fellow man. But the effort was futile. The burden was his forever."

I was beginning to see a picture. The words of Father Sidletski came to mind. Margaret Faynor's words sounded ominously familiar. I sat quietly and waited for the bombshell.

She turned away from the window and walked back to the sofa, but did not sit. I stood up as she approached me. She looked at me with a hard face, as if trying to muster the courage to say what she knew she had to say.

"Since a very early age," she said. "My brother has had a marked propensity towards—"

She stopped suddenly, dropped her face into her hands, and sobbed quietly. I stood and placed a comforting arm around her shoulder. There were no words for me to say.

Chapter 22

"Troy Conlon arrived on the eighteenth of August via Delta Airlines," I said. "Father Conlon was murdered on the twenty-second."

"That makes your theory feasible," Briggs said.

"That's not all," I said. "I contacted LAPD about Conlon and they faxed me a rap sheet as long as your arm; mostly misdemeanors, but this guy is no choir boy, no pun intended."

I handed the printed rap sheet to Briggs. He looked it over, then put it in his desk drawer.

"I want to go out there," I said.

"To L.A.?" Briggs said. "To what purpose?"

"Find out what I can on this guy. That rap sheet puts him in a different perspective."

Briggs leaned back in his chair and began to stroke his mustache with his thumb and index finger. He was contemplating whether my proposal was viable and how he'd convince the Mayor and the council members it was essential.

"You think this guy could be our man?"

"Even though he's a degenerate character, I have no valid reason to make him a killer, right now. Digging deeper might prove otherwise."

"When do you want to do this?"

"The sooner the better. I'll only need a day or two."

Briggs thought for a moment longer. "I'll have to get travel expenses approved by finances," he said.

"If it becomes a problem," I said, "I'll pay for my lodgings, it's worth the expense to me to find Andy Conlon's killer."

The next morning, I was in my apartment packing an overnight bag. Sandy was helping me. I rolled up several pairs of underwear into a ball and placed them into the bag; Sandy took them out, folded each one, and put them back, neatly.

"There's no need to fold underwear," I said.

"Neatness counts," she said.

I balled up a couple of pairs of socks and tossed them on top of the underwear. Sandy took them out, folded them, and laid them carefully side by side. I did not comment. If it made her happy, it made me happy.

Briggs had gotten approval for the flight expense. I was to pick up my ticket at the Jet Blue ticket counter at Newark Liberty airport. He had also secured the proper permits, allowing me to carry my gun in my overnight bag. I wrapped the gun in one of my socks and slid a box of cartridges in the middle of it all. My flight to Los Angeles was scheduled to depart at 11:45 a.m. I had called on my own and booked a room at a motel not far from the Los Angeles police department, on West 1st. Street. I had parked and locked my Chevy Nova at the curb in front of my apartment. Mrs. Jankowski assured me it would be safe and that she would "keep an eye on it."

"If I drive you to the airport in your car," Sandy said. "It'll make it a lot easier."

"Thanks," I said, "but it's not necessary, and safer for you. I'll be worried about you until you get home. I'll take a cab." Sandy called me a cab while I finished packing.

It was almost 10:00 a.m. when the cab arrived. It would take nearly an hour to get to the airport from my apartment. I was dressed comfortably in a pair of Dockers and a short-sleeve shirt. I knew it would be warm when I arrived at L.A.

Sandy walked downstairs with me to the waiting cab. I gave her a long kiss and hug.

"Send me a postcard," she said.

"I'll be back before you receive it," I said.

"I'll be waiting," she said.

I tossed my bag into the back seat and slid into the front seat.

Sandy leaned into the open window and gave me another kiss on my cheek.

I took it to L.A. with me.

***

My flight departed on time. I stuffed my overnight bag in the compartment above my head and took my seat by a window. The weather was good, visibility clear. The weatherman in L.A. was calling for a comfortable day.

A short while into the flight, the attendants rolled the food cart out. I wasn't sure if it was breakfast or lunch, considering the time, so I had pancakes, a cup of fruit, coffee, and a bottle of beer. The guy in the seat next to me ordered a bowl of Oatmeal garnished with strawberries and a large glass of milk. He had to be over six feet tall and looked to weigh at least two-sixty. Every time he put a spoonful of Oatmeal up to his mouth, he jabbed me in my shoulder with his elbow. He responded each time by telling me he was "sorry", but the practice continued just the same. I tried to scrunch myself closer to the window. It didn't help.

After I ate, I stretched out with my paperback book. I knew we'd be in the air at least five hours, which would allow me to read at least half of the novel I'd been trying to finish for the past two months.

I fell asleep.

When I woke up, my seat partner was asleep with his head on my shoulder. The only person that had ever slept with their head on my shoulder was Sandy. I had to use both of my hands to push his fat head over to the other side of the seat. When I did, he woke up startled, rubbed his eyes, and said, "Are we there?"

I said, "Where?"

"I'm going to L.A.," he said.

"We're all going to L.A.," I said.

"Oh," he said.

Satisfied, he leaned his head back on the seat and snored himself back to sleep. I opened my book and tried to read again. We landed at LAX around 5:30 p.m. I walked off the plane with the usual stiffness in my legs that I endured every time I took a flight. I carried my bag through the main terminal, following the signs and arrows, until I found the TSA checkpoint. After I showed the agents my ID, shield, and permits, I was cleared to start looking for a cab stand. My legs began to loosen up by the time I stepped through the sliding doors into the bright sunshine where there was a line of cabs waiting for fares. A yellow cab pulled up in front of me. I opened the door before anyone else could, threw my bag into the back seat, and got in the front seat. The driver was a young kid wearing a Dodger's ball cap and a sleeveless shirt. I told him where I wanted to go. He drove off without a word.

We rode for forty minutes through the streets of L.A. Traffic was heavy and reminded me of the streets of Manhattan. My driver hadn't said a word until I said, "This traffic reminds me of New York City; that's where I'm from. Even with public transportation, Manhattan ranks number one in car ownership per capita."

He seemed uninterested in my statistic, and simply said, "It's always like this."

Twenty minutes later we reached my motel. It was a low four-story building with a flat roof and lots of balconies. The grounds were meticulously landscaped and there was a pool surrounded by palm trees in the center of a courtyard.

I got out of the cab, retrieved my bag, and paid the driver. Although he was less than hospitable, I tipped him a ten, anyway. He didn't thank me.

Check-in was uneventful. My room was ready. The desk clerk handed me my key and assured me I would "enjoy the stay." There was no elevator in the lobby, so I trekked up four flights of stairs to begin "enjoying my stay."

My room overlooked the center courtyard. It consisted of a king-size bed, two night tables, a large flat-screen TV mounted on a wall, one chest of drawers, and an adjourning bathroom. I didn't bother to unpack my overnight bag since I hadn't planned on staying more than a day or two.

I was hungry.

I changed my shirt, which was damp and clammy from the plane ride, slid my overnight bag under the bed, clipped my gun to my right hip, and went down to the first floor where there was a small cafeteria. I ate a large dinner and went back to my room. It was still early, so I decided to call Sandy. It was one o'clock in the morning back east, but she'd insisted I call her regardless of the time. Briggs could wait until morning.

"This is the lonely traveler," I said when Sandy answered her phone.

"I miss you already," she said.

"Did I wake you?"

"Of course," she said. "How'd it go?"

"Uneventful," I said. "I just had dinner and I'm planning on turning in early. I'm beat."

"Next time I'm going with you," she said. "I've never been to Los Angeles."

"I wish you were here now," I said. "I'm lying here in this double bed, thinking about making passionate love to you with the California sunshine streaming through my window."

"Don't tease," she said. "It's dark and drizzly here right now."

"It's warm and cozy where I am," I said. "Call me tomorrow," she said. "And be careful."

"First chance I get," I said.

She blew me a kiss through the phone. I blew her one back and ended the call. Then I took a cold shower and went to bed.

Chapter 23

I hadn't set my cell phone alarm but didn't need to. The sun streaming through a side window in my room woke me. I got up, took a shower, and made myself presentable. I pulled my bag out from under the bed and put on the one suit I had taken with me. It was a single-breasted, cream-colored suit. I wore a white shirt with no tie. I kept the collar open. I looked, "Hollywood." I clipped my gun and holster to my belt; with the suit jacket on you couldn't tell it was there. I went downstairs for breakfast.

The "free" breakfast buffet was located in a room off the lobby. It was a simple setup, which appeared to offer everything one would want in a delicious breakfast. I collected the necessary accouterments and headed for the coffee urn. I filled my mug with ten ounces of coffee and made my way to the scrambled eggs and bacon. Upon closer examination, the eggs I scooped up looked as dry as confetti, and the bacon strips appeared to have a greenish tint to them. Or was it the lighting? I moved further down the table and opted for a buttered croissant and a jelly doughnut. The croissant looked brittle, but the jelly doughnut seemed okay. I found a seat by a window and sat down to "enjoy my stay." At least the coffee was good.

When I got back to my room, I called Chief Briggs and Danny Nolan and updated them on what had happened so far, which wasn't much. Then I called Captain Wells of the LAPD homicide division. Wells said he could meet me at any time. I asked if right now was good. He said that was fine. I said I'd be right over. I took a cab to Police headquarters on 1st Street and was escorted to Wells' office on the second floor.

Captain Wells was a tall man with a dark complexion and curly black hair. He was wearing a gray three-piece suit, with a bright white shirt and navy-blue tie. He appeared to be in his forties.

"Detective, Graham," he said, "welcome to L.A."

He extended his hand. I took it. He had a good grip. In the interest of protocol and respect for the office, I removed my shield and ID from my pocket and showed them to him. He glanced at it, then waved for me to put it away. He knew who I was. Like a seasoned cop, he had, no doubt, checked me out before acquiescing to my requests.

Wells' office was very impressive; done in warm mahogany. The floor was carpeted in deep blue. On the wall behind his desk were several framed documents and awards attesting to his achievements in police work and public service. A gun case with a glass front hung on the wall just left of his desk. It held several Winchester rifles and a Smith & Wesson pump-action shotgun. An assortment of handguns was displayed on hooks just below the long guns.

Wells walked behind a large glass top desk and gestured for me to sit in one of his guest chairs. He opened his desk drawer and removed a small notepad. He flipped it open to the first page and said, "You're here to find out what you can about Troy Conlon."

"I am," I said. "He's a possible suspect in my murder investigation."

He offered no comment as he tore the top sheet from the pad and handed it to me. "That's his pertinent info," he said. "You should be able to follow it easily. If you require any assistance, of course, you can notify me. Other than the rap sheet I faxed to you, there isn't any more information I can give you about this guy."

"Thank you," I said. I folded the paper and slid it into my pocket.

"You said he was a suspect in your murder investigation."

"Possible suspect," I said. "From what you know of him, do you think he's capable of murder?"

Wells took a seat in the leather armchair behind his desk and said, "I believe anyone can commit murder, and those who think they're incapable of it can be driven to it by circumstance. Troy Conlon has had run-ins with the law for as long as I've been in this position. He's committed a broad spectrum of crimes: public drunkenness, B&E, disorderly conduct, vagrancy. Most of his charges were misdemeanors, that were dismissed. If you're asking me if he's capable of committing murder, I couldn't fathom a guess. I suppose it would depend on the circumstance."

"Why were his charges dismissed?"

"Insufficient evidence, liberal judges with soft hearts for petty criminals."

"Every system has its bias," I said.

I thanked Wells for his cooperation and left the police station. It was almost 11:00 a.m. when I got outside the building, I removed the paper from my pocket that Wells had given me and read it. It listed Troy Conlon's address, the name and location of his favorite bar, and the name and address of a former girlfriend. It was a good start. I'd begin by trying to gain access to Conlon's rented room.

I called a cab from my cell phone and had to wait almost thirty minutes. The cabby was an older guy with a full white beard and a silver earring in his right ear. I gave him the address where Conlon rented his room. Unlike the first cabby I'd had, he was amiable and talkative. As he drove, he described the famous sights of the city whenever we passed one. His descriptions eventually morphed into a dissertation on the History of Los Angeles. I sat listening, only slightly interested. I tried to ask a question or two, for the sake of sociability, but his incessant rambling made it difficult for me to get a word in; this guy's mouth ran faster than his meter.

Although the ride was entertaining, I was glad when it was over. I wasn't sure whether I'd enjoyed it or not. When I got out, I tipped him a ten, anyway. I figured he deserved it for his effort.

Troy Conlon was renting a room in a boardinghouse on La Brea Ave. It was a low whitewashed building, fairly well kept but in need of a new roof. I wanted to get into Conlon's room but wasn't sure how I could accomplish that. I walked up to the front door and pressed the door buzzer. After a few more tries, a young girl came to the door. She looked about, fifteen. She was listening to music through a pair of headphones and didn't bother to turn the music down while she spoke to me.

"Yea?" she said.

I took out my ID and showed it to her. She glanced at it and said, "Whattaya want?"

"Is this where Troy Conlon lives?" I said.

"What?" she said.

"Troy Conlon, does he live here?"

She looked at me, annoyed and indifferent. I reached out and turned down the volume knob on her headphones. She scowled.

"I'm looking for Troy Conlon," I said.

"He ain't here."

"I need to see his room."

"My parents won't be home until later."

"I didn't ask to see your parents."

"I ain't supposed to let nobody in when they ain't home," she said.

"I'm the police," I said.

She thought about that for a second, then held the door open for me. I stepped into a small vestibule. She pointed down a long, dark hallway. "His room's at the end of the hall on the left," she said, "but it's locked until he comes back."

She closed the front door, turned the volume back up on her headphones, and walked away without any further interest in me.

I made my way down the hallway to Conlon's room. The door was locked, as the girl had said. There were no additional locks, just a simple doorknob lock with a keyhole. I removed my credit card from my wallet and slid it between the doorjamb and the lock. It was unethical, but it had helped me solve a few cases in the past. When I turned the doorknob and maneuvered the credit card in just the right way, the door opened. If you did it enough times, you got good at it.

I pushed the door back and stepped into a darkened room. I was immediately hit with the acrid odor of stale beer and cigarette smoke. I turned on the light switch by the door. The room was untidy, as I'd expected. There was a single bed shoved into a corner, in addition to a dresser and a small desk. Several crumpled packs of cigarettes and an ashtray mound with cigarette butts sat on a night table beside the bed. A half-empty bottle of Dewar's Scotch lay on its side next to the ashtray.

I closed the door and walked further into the room. The dull white walls were decorated with posters of rock bands and horror movies. I started with the dresser and opened the drawers one at a time; three were empty and one contained a pair of black socks and a pair of patterned boxer shorts. I went to the only closet in the room and opened the door. It was empty, but for some wooden clothes hangers. Conlon must have taken every bit of his wardrobe with him when he left. When I opened the one small drawer in the night table, I found a package of rolling paper and several "girlie" magazines, but nothing else. The desktop was littered with scrap paper, a bunch of scattered photos, and a large ceramic ashtray, which held a single Bic lighter. When I pulled on the top drawer of the desk, it was locked, which told me it was the drawer I needed to look into. I took out my pocketknife and jimmied the lock. I found one large manila folder in the drawer. I laid it on the desk and opened it. Inside were many photos, large and small, of no particular interest: a group of young people sitting at a table wearing party hats, a middle-aged man leaning against the fender of a Chevrolet Corvette, and a young boy peddling a red scooter.

Buried below this collection of memories was an eight-by-ten photo. When I slipped it out from beneath the others, I immediately recognized a full-face portrait of Father Conlon, taken from his waist up. He was wearing his Cossack robe and smiling into the camera. Draped over his folded hands was a set of rosary beads. I picked up the photo and looked at it with disturbing curiosity. Andy Conlon's face had a large X placed over it with a red marker. Also, there was a crudely drawn knife protruding from his chest with a depiction of blood dripping from an opened knife wound. The photo was an obvious display of hatred for Father Conlon. Was this a creative attempt by Troy Conlon to vent hatred for his brother, or had he obtained the photo by some other means and hidden it in a folder out of sight?

I took a picture of the photo with my cell phone camera and placed the photo back into the folder. I put the folder back into the drawer and left the room.

I had seen enough.

I made my way down the hallway toward the front door. The house was quiet. I didn't see my young hostess. I closed the front door gently as I left and started walking several blocks in the direction of a busy commercial street. It was 1:00 p.m.

As I walked, I looked over the paper Captain Wells had given me and noted the address of Troy Conlon's favorite bar hangout; a place within walking distance of his rented room.

I walked two blocks to the main thoroughfare heavy with traffic. The area was littered with bars, fast-food joints, a tattoo parlor, a car wash, and a movie theater. I found "Pugly's Bar" situated between a barbershop and a Chinese laundry. It was a rundown structure with peeling red paint and a large cracked window on one side of the entrance door. A sign, hanging above the door, was missing the letter "P", so that it read, "ugly's" Bar. I smiled to myself and wondered what the proprietor looked like.

A group of men was hanging around the front door as I approached. A few stared at me like I had two heads. Two were pitching pennies against the building.

"I smell cop," I heard one say.

I ignored the remark and walked through them. As I did, one of the penny pitchers, a kid about sixteen, stepped in front of me, blocking my way. "Where ya goin', Pop?" he said. He was wearing tight black pants and a tight black muscle shirt. His glossy black hair was spiked in the center and his right nostril had been pierced to accommodate a silver ring.

"I'm not your Pop," I said. "And if you don't get outta my way, I'll teach you a lesson your Pop should have."

"Whoa, tough guy," he said.

He looked over at his partner expecting moral support but was offered none. Before he had a chance to say another word, I reached out and grabbed the ring in his nose, and pulled him out of my way. He screwed up his face in agony and let out a few yelps like an injured puppy. He had no choice but to follow my lead. When I turned him loose, he fell against the building and stayed there massaging his nose.

"You learned a valuable lesson today, kid," I said. "Don't talk to strangers."

I heard his partner laughing at him as I opened the door to the bar and walked in.

I let the front door close behind me and stood until my eyes adjusted to the smoky darkness. Music was blaring from a jukebox. A bar to my left ran the entire length of the place. It was filled with men and women, drinking, laughing, arguing, and shouting over the noise of the music in a futile effort to communicate with each other. Although it was midafternoon, the place was packed. The main floor was dotted with round tables, most occupied with patrons, either drunk or halfway there. A large moose head hung on a distant wall between the restrooms marked: *His* and Hers. A placard behind the bar announced in bold letters: TIPPING IS PATRIOTIC.

At the bar, I ordered a beer. A young lady seated on a stool in front of me turned and gave me a look. I said, "Hello," in a loud voice. She offered a quick smile, then turned back to her drink. She had blonde hair down to her shoulders, and a ton of makeup caked on her face. Her lips were painted deep red and looked inordinately wider than they should have. Without all that makeup, she might have been attractive. She was wearing very tight jeans and a light blue blouse; its top buttons opened enough to expose plenty of cleavage.

The bartender brought my beer. The beer felt good going down. I hadn't had any lunch and wondered if they offered food, then thought better of it. I'd eat when I got back to my motel.

In a place as crowded as this, there had to be a good amount of people that were familiar with Troy Conlon, especially since this was his usual watering hole. I could arbitrarily take my pick and come away with an abundance of information. I started with the girl on the stool, who had flashed me a smile. I finished my beer and set my glass down on the bar. "Excuse me," I said. She slid off her stool and stood next to me. "It's okay, honey," she said. "I'm leaving anyway."

"Do you know, Troy Conlon?" I said before she had a chance to walk away.

She touched her ear, indicating she hadn't heard me due to the loud music.

"Troy Conlon," I said. "I'm trying to locate him."

She kept her hand to her ear and said, "Sorry, honey, can't hear you over the noise."

I took a ten out of my wallet and handed it to her; she took it without reservation and shoved it into the front pocket of her jeans. "Who wants to know?" she said.

"An old friend," I said.

"Honey, don't bullshit a bullshitter. I know a cop when I see one."

"Okay," I said, "but I'm still a friend of Troy's."

She sat down again on her stool and ordered another drink. I put a twenty on the bar and ordered the same drink for myself. The bartender brought the drinks and my change and placed them on the bar in front of her. I waited while she downed half of her drink.

"I haven't seen Troy in a while," she said, wiping her lips with the back of her hand; "and I don't want to."

"Are you his girlfriend?"

"Hell, no," she said. "We met here one night and spent time drinking together. He didn't seem like a bad guy until he got me jammed up with the cops."

I offered her a, "Wow" and said, "What happened?"

She picked up my change from the bar, her drink, and mine, and indicated for me to follow her to a table. We found an abandoned table in a corner where the music wasn't so loud. She set the glasses down and spread the bills on the table between us. She finished her drink and signaled to the bartender for another. I drank some of mine.

"How were you in trouble with the law?" I said.

"Troy and I were having drinks at a table when this big guy walks over and he and Troy start arguing. They were both shitfaced. I was okay."

"What were they arguing about?"

"Don't know. It was hard to hear."

The bartender brought her drink and she continued. "Next thing I know. They're swinging at each other. I'm screaming for them to stop, but they don't listen. The big guy grabs me and tries to choke the shit outta me. Troy grabs the guy's neck and starts hoking' him. People in the place are screaming' but nobody tries to stop it. The big guy pushes me to the floor. When I look up, I see two cops standing over me. I get up fast and try to get even with the big guy, but wind up hitting a cop by mistake. The cop puts me in a headlock and cuffs me. His partner cuffs Troy and the big guy and they take us out. I did thirty days for assaulting a cop."

"You got off easy," I said. "What happened to Troy?"

"Thirty days for drunk and disorderly."

"Did you see Troy after that incident?"

"No, I want nothing to do with that bastard," she said. "I should have never got involved with him."

"Seems to me, you put yourself in harm's way by even associating yourself with him in the first place."

"He seemed like a nice guy in the beginning, 'til he started drinking."

"What you see isn't always what you get," I said, sounding very philosophical.

"If he didn't act like a jerk that night, I wouldn't o' got jammed up. Now I got a record."

I was satisfied that I had gotten all the information I needed from this young lady, so I got up and pushed in my chair. When I did, she reached out and took my hand. "Do you have to leave already?" she said. "My apartment's not far from here."

"Thanks," I said, "but I promised my wife I'd help her with the groceries."

She pulled her hand away feeling only half indignant and downed the rest of her drink. I smiled at her and walked out.

I was getting the same information about Troy Conlon from everyone I had interviewed, east or west coast. He was a degenerate jerk. So far, I hadn't found anything that would convince me he was a murderer. The photo I had found in his desk drawer certainly was incriminating, but there could be multiple meanings behind it, especially coming from someone with Troy Conlon's habits and disposition.

I had one more name on the list Captain Wells had given me, which might prove to be significant, a former girlfriend of Troy Conlon's. I had to take a cab since the address was on the other side of town.

The ride took nearly a half-hour. We rode down Beverly Blvd. until we arrived at Rosewood Ave. Troy Conlon's ex lived in a four-story rental complex. I paid the cabbie and walked up the long walkway to the front entrance. There was the possibility that she might not be home since it was two in the afternoon and it was a Tuesday. I opened the front door and stepped into a small vestibule. On the wall, to my right, was a bank of mailboxes with handwritten name tags taped to them. I looked for Emily Atwood. I pressed the small button on the mailbox and waited. When there was no answer, I pressed it again… still no answer. I turned and was about to leave when I heard a voice say, "Who is it?"

"I'm looking for Emily Atwood," I said.

"Who's looking for Emily Atwood?" the voice said.

"My name is Max Graham," I said. "I'm a friend of Troy Conlon's."

"Didn't know he had friends," the voice said. "What do you want?"

OTHER MEN'S SINS

"I'm trying to locate Troy," I said. "I haven't seen him in a while."

"Neither have I," the voice said. "What do you want with me?"

"I thought you might help me locate him."

"Is he in trouble?"

"He might be," I said.

"I'm not surprised," the voice said. "Are you a cop?"

"From New York City," I said.

"I don't want to get involved if you're a cop."

"I'm just trying to find Troy," I said with the sincerest inflection in my voice I could muster.

There was a half-minute of silence before the electric door lock buzzed. I opened the door and stepped into a large hallway. I looked for an elevator, but there was none. I had no choice but to take the stairs directly in front of me. I challenged myself by taking two steps at a time just to see how my legs handled it. I made it to the second-floor landing with no problem, but once there, I had to stop to catch my breath. I decided to take the rest of the steps, one at a time.

What was I trying to prove?

On the fourth floor, I walked down a brightly lit hallway, reading each red-painted door number until I found 4-B.

I knocked.

I heard the security change jangle on the other side of the door, and then the door opened. An attractive dark-haired woman looked out at me through the few inches of the door opening.

"What did you say your name was?" she said.

"Maxwell Graham," I said.

"Show me a badge," she said.

I showed her my ID and shield. She opened the door.

I was looking at an attractive woman, perhaps in her thirties. Although she wasn't wearing makeup, her natural beauty precluded it. Her skin was of a caramel creaminess, and her eyes were a mesmerizing emerald green. She was wearing a knee-length white satin robe and matching bedroom slippers.

OTHER MEN'S SINS

"Thanks," I said. I walked into a small living room, sparsely furnished but neatly kept. A leather sofa sat beneath a pair of windows that looked out to the street. There was a small desk in one corner, and a large screen TV hung from a wall bracket opposite the sofa. A potted floor plant completed the furnishings.

She closed the door and reattached the security chain.

"You can't trust anyone these days," she said, "especially in this neighborhood. But I'm well protected."

I wasn't sure just what she meant by "well-protected". A woman living alone in a bad area, in a building with scant security, and a single door secured only with the addition of a chain lock, didn't seem well protected to me; especially one as attractive as her.

"I apologies if this is a bad time," I said.

"It's okay," she said. "I work nights."

"Are you a dancer?" I said.

She laughed. "Do I look like a dancer?"

I had put my foot in my mouth. Even thru the robe she was wearing, I could tell she had the right figure for a dancer and great legs. I stood for a moment, not knowing what to say.

She made a quick pirouette to further mock my assumption as she made her way to the desk. She removed something from the top drawer, and when she turned back to face me, she was holding a nickel-plated Colt 1911 with ivory grips. She held the gun with the barrel pointed at the ceiling and waved it about threateningly. The nickel reflected the light like a well-polished gem.

"See, well-protected," she said.

I stepped back and put my hands in the air.

She laughed as she walked closer to me. "Relax," she said. "I'm a Los Angeles police officer." She removed her shield and ID from the pocket of her robe and held it up for me to see.

I put my hands down.

This could make things easier or harder, I thought.

"I'm sorry," I said.

"Don't be sorry," she said. "I'm flattered. Have a seat."

I remained standing. "I won't take much of your time," I said.

As she returned the gun to the desk drawer, she said, "What's your interest in Troy Conlon?"

"I'm in the middle of a murder investigation," I said. "He may be a suspect."

"I'm not surprised," she said.

"I suppose you're pretty familiar with Conlon."

"What L. A. cop isn't?"

"The info I received, lists you as his 'girlfriend'."

"Ex," she said. "It was a long time ago before I joined the police force. We'd met at an employment agency. I had just lost my job."

"Troy was employed there?"

"No, he was looking for work, too. He was always in and out of a job, always broke."

"Did you have a steady relationship with him?"

"For about three months, until I made it onto the police force. It was just as well."

"How so?"

"His drinking got out of hand. I couldn't take it any longer. I dumped him."

"How did he take that?"

"Not very well, he couldn't accept it. He stalked me for a while and threatened me."

"Were you afraid for your life?"

"I wasn't sure what he was capable of when he was drinking. But I wasn't afraid of him. I can take care of myself."

"By the way you handled that cannon, I believe you."

She was amused at that and gave me a big smile.

"His rap sheet is pretty extensive," I said, "but nothing that comes close to murder."

"It could be just a matter of time with Conlon," she said. "The guy's a wacko when he's boozed up."

That was something I already knew. I hoped she would tell me something I didn't know.

"I haven't seen him in a while," she said, "maybe he turned over a new leaf."

"He's in New York City," I said. "His brother was murdered; he flew in for his part of the inheritance."

"He's a suspect in his own brother's murder?"

"One of several," I said, "but the more I dig up on him, the higher up on my list he moves."

"The guy's a pathetic asshole," she said.

"I've heard those adjectives applied to him before," I said. "Can you tell me anything more that might be helpful?"

"I don't know what more I can tell you," she said. "You seem to have him pinned down pretty well. The hard part for you comes now," she said.

"What's that?" I said.

"Proving beyond a reasonable doubt that he's your murderer."

Chapter 24

I had gotten everything I could on Troy Conlon. My trip wasn't as fruitful as I'd hoped it would be, other than I'd found that disturbing photograph in Troy Conlon's desk. At least that would justify my trip to Briggs.

My flight landed at Newark Liberty at 10:15 p.m. The push and shove through the airport terminal was a nightmare. Waiting in one line or another was incessant agony. It reaffirmed to me why I disliked air travel.

I took a cab back to my apartment. The drive on Route 78 took an hour, and I nodded off twice. When I got home, I tossed my bag onto my bed, stripped down to my skivvies, and dropped onto the bed next to it. I text Sandy to let her know I'd gotten back safely. Then I fell asleep.

It was raining lightly when I woke up. My night table clock read: 8:30 a.m. I felt like I had a hangover. Maybe I had what some people called "jetlag". I wasn't sure since I hadn't had enough experience with long flights to know.

I missed hearing Sandy's voice but knew she couldn't answer her cell phone because, at this time of the morning, she'd be tied up in court. So, I text her and told her I'd call her later that afternoon when I got a chance.

I put on my bathrobe and fuzzy slippers and went downstairs to my mailbox. I found my mail piled neatly on the small table, secured with a rubber band. Before I went back upstairs, I knocked on Mrs. Jankowski's door. I could hear her using her vacuum cleaner. I knocked again until she shouted out over the sound of her vacuum. "I'm not interested."

"It's not a salesman, Mrs. Jankowski," I yelled through the door. "It's me. I just wanted to let you know I'm home."

"Your mail is on the front table," she shouted back.

"Thank you," I said, "I've got it."

Back at my kitchen table, I sorted through my mail: a water bill, an electric bill, two magazines that I'd never subscribed to, and one legal-size envelope with no stamp or postmark. It had a single sloppily handwritten word on it: "Graham".

The envelope flap had been tucked in, not glued. When I slid it back, I found a single folded sheet of paper inside. I unfolded the paper by its corners and read the typewritten words. There were plenty of typos and misspellings as if the writer were grammatically inept or was unfamiliar with the use of a typewriter, or both. At the bottom of the page, was presumably David Crockett's scrawled signature. It didn't take me long to realized Crockett was confessing to the murder of Father Conlon. He gave his reason as a deep hatred toward the father for destroying his relationship with the only girl he had ever loved, Eileen Conlon. He said he was sorry and knew what he had done was wrong and hoped God would forgive him. "Don't try to find me," he wrote. "I'll keep running until I get away or I'm caught."

Above the signature were the words, *"Tell Eileen, I love her."*

I went to my kitchen drawer and got a Ziploc bag and placed the letter and envelope inside. If we could prove this letter to be genuine; it could be the beginning of the end of this case.

I called Briggs to let him know I was back. I didn't mention the letter or offer any info about my trip. He said he wanted to see me right away.

My morning shower felt great. I finished it up by letting cold water stream down over me for almost five minutes. It brought me back to life.

I scrambled a few eggs, seared two sausage links, and drank two ten-ounce cups of coffee. I put some "Doo Wop Gold" in my disc player and listened to my favorite music while I ate breakfast. It was therapeutic. It felt good to wind down and sit alone quietly for a change. The only thing I liked better than having breakfast alone was having breakfast with Sandy.

I put on a pair of khakis, a long sleeve shirt, and my corduroy jacket. I put Crockett's letter in my inside jacket pocket along with my cell phone. I shut off the disc player, clipped my gun to my belt, and went downstairs to the Chevy.

The rain had stopped, and the sun was warming the day quickly. I took a long deep breath of the cool morning air, which felt good after having endured the oppressive air on the west coast.

My Chevy Nova was parked where I'd left it, undisturbed; other than a mosaic of bird droppings, which had obliterated the windshield. I hiked back upstairs and got some spray window cleaner and a roll of paper towels and spent the next ten minutes clearing the window. When I was finished, I tossed the cleaning supplies in the back seat and got in behind the wheel. I hoped the Chevy would start after having sat for two full days. If it didn't, I'd have to get the jumper cables off the back floor and ask Mrs. Jankowski for a jump from her Volkswagen Beetle.

I'm not superstitious, but I mentally crossed my fingers and turned the key. There was a short rumbling of the motor, then a hesitation. I waited and then turned the key again. After a loud pop and a groan, she started with her usual billow of blue smoke. I smiled and patted her dashboard as a token of my gratitude and drove away.

***

Briggs was at the water cooler getting a drink when I walked into his office. His suit jacket was draped over the back of his desk chair, and his tie was loose. His shirt sleeves were rolled up to his elbows. "Want a drink, Graham?" he said.

It wasn't a good sign when he referred to me by my last name.

"No, thanks," I said.

Briggs downed his water, then crushed the cup and tossed it into the wastebasket. Back at his chair, he sat upright and looked at me. "I hope you've got good news," he said. "City Hall is up my ass and I need to tell the mayor something viable."

I sat down in his guest chair and took my cell phone out of my pocket. I brought up the picture I had taken of the photo I'd found in Troy Conlon's desk drawer. I handed the phone to Briggs. He looked at it.

"The hell is this?" he said.

"That's a picture I took of a photo I found in Troy Conlon's desk drawer in his room," I said.

"Did he draw that sick shit on it?"

"Probably," I said.

"But why does he have it and why is he keeping it?" Briggs said.

"It indicates hatred and a desire to do his brother bodily harm," I said.

"Obviously," Briggs said.

He studied the photo for a few more beats, and then said, "This guy's our man. Why don't you make the arrest?"

I took Crockett's alleged confession letter out of my pocket, removed it from the envelope, and slid it across the desk to Briggs.

"It hasn't been to the lab yet," I said.

Briggs opened it by its corners and began to read.

"It was in my pile of mail when I got home," I said. "No postmark or stamp. Somebody probably hand-delivered it to my box."

"If somebody was clever enough to put it in your mailbox without getting caught," Briggs said, "You can bet we won't find prints on it."

He finished reading the letter, then looked at me. "You think this is genuine?"

"I have my doubts," I said.

"Seems contrived to me."

"I agree," I said. "Not many people *use* or even *have* access to a typewriter these days. Most printing is done on a computer."

"We can trace the paper," Briggs said. "Find out where it was purchased and then follow up on it?"

"Could be a thousand places that sell that paper," I said, "It's common stock. It would take forever."

Briggs looked down at the letter again and said, "I don't believe this crap. This guy's on the run and trying to take the heat off himself."

"Maybe," I said, "but I'm not sure Crockett killed anybody. I don't have a shred of evidence that substantiates it."

"Then why's he telling us he did?"

"Maybe he's not," I said. "Maybe somebody else is telling us he did."

"The hell are you talking about, Max?"

We were back on a first-name basis again.

"Maybe somebody else is trying to take the heat off themself by setting up Crockett."

"This is getting more convoluted every day," Briggs said. "What am I gonna tell the mayor that makes sense?"

I stood, and retrieved my phone and the letter, and put them back into my pocket. "I've got a working hypothesis that might solve this case if I can tie a few ends together," I said.

"If you know more than I know, Max, you better tell me now. I need info."

"It's just an idea," I said. "If I'm right, it'll close this case. Meanwhile, you can tell the Mayor and council members about the photo and the letter."

"And what else do I tell them?"

"Tell 'em Graham's on the case," I said.

Chapter 25

The following morning Danny and I were having breakfast at "Snookie's Diner" on 8th avenue across from the Port Authority Bus Terminal. It was a place we frequented often. I liked their breakfast menu. Danny liked their waitresses.

He was working on a six egg omelet, a double order of rye toast, orange juice, and coffee. A customary white napkin was tucked neatly into his collar by his tie like a bib. Danny was meticulous in his dress and a single speck of food arbitrarily landing on any part of his day attire would be a catastrophic occurrence to him.

We sat in a booth by the window and watched the hustle and bustle of vehicular and pedestrian traffic. It didn't matter what hour of the day it was; the maelstrom of midtown was always the same, part of the charm and character of New York City.

"Sandy bought me two framed prints," I said. "She said they were copies of priceless original paintings, a Pollock and a Picasso. One looked like a ball of string that had come undone, and the other looked like a blue alien creature with two eyes on one side of its head. She had me hang them on my bedroom wall where she said they would go perfectly with the wall color. I didn't know what to say to her except, 'thanks'." Danny dunked a piece of toast in his coffee and smiled. "You need to be more understanding," he said.

"I am," I said, "but I don't need a blue alien staring down at me whenever I climb into bed at night. And it might put a damper on things when we're making love."

"Turn out the light," Danny said.

I scraped the rest of my oatmeal from the bottom of my bowl and downed the rest of my coffee. As I did, I heard Danny's fork drop on his plate. When I looked, he was staring out the window; his eyes intense on whatever he was searching for.

"What is it?" I said.

"Crockett!" he said. "I'm sure I saw him go into the terminal." He yanked the napkin from his collar and slid out of the booth in a hurry. I fumbled in my pocket, found a twenty, and dropped it on the table. I slid out of the booth and hurried after Danny.

When I caught up with Danny, he was dodging his way through midtown traffic, heading for the front entrance of the bus terminal. I maneuvered my way between cars and trucks, trying not to get crushed to keep up with him. I wasn't as young as Danny, but my arms and legs were still adequately agile, due to my days of running track at college.

When we finally made our way into the terminal front lobby, Danny looked hard in every direction.

"Are you sure it was him?" I said.

"It was him," Danny said. Then he pointed across the lobby at the escalators, on the lower level. "There he goes," he said.

Danny had been right, Crockett had seen us and was on the escalator, taking two steps at a time, trying to get away. Danny started after him, I started after Danny.

From the top of the escalator, we saw Crockett jump off the steps at the bottom and disappear. When we reached the bottom, we looked around but didn't see Crockett.

"Come on," Danny said.

We made a left at the bottom of the escalators and hurried through a wall of open glass doors. I followed Danny's lead, trusting his instinct. There were people everywhere, and it was difficult to maneuver around them and still keep up a good pace.

We stopped at the second set of escalators, which lead to an upper and lower level. Crockett might have continued on this level or jumped the escalators to go up or down. We had three choices.

"Whattaya think?" Danny said.

"I'm for up," I said. "I think he'd try to double back."

We stepped on the escalator and rode it to the top.

An endless string of retail stores populated both sides of the promenade. Crockett could have ducked into any one of them and vanished. It was like searching for the proverbial "needle in a haystack".

"Let's split up," I said. "You take that side. I'll work this one. Keep in sight of each other in case we spot him. Keep surveying the crowd and glancing into the stores. It's all we can do."

Danny zigzagged his way through the crowd to the other side of the promenade. There had to be a million places Crockett could've used to secure his escape: retail outlets, public washrooms, utility closets, and a forest of cylindrical supporting pillars that reached from floor to ceiling that he could've easily hidden behind and kept in motion while making good his escape, and of course, escalators, and more escalators.

I walked along the storefronts, keeping close to their facades, concentrating on the crowd, and looking into the stores as I went. It wasn't long before my eyes began to ache, and the crowd began to blend into one endless mosaic of colors and shapes. I was sure my chances of spotting Crockett were slim to none. I was relying more on Danny at this point.

I searched through the crowd and found Danny standing in front of a newsstand. He was waving his arms at me and pointing to a set of escalators that lead to an upper level. Danny jumped on the escalator and rode it up. When I came up behind him, he said, "He's up ahead I saw him go up."

From the bottom of the escalator, we spotted Crockett at the same time he spotted us.

Crockett started running.

Danny started running.

I started running.

Crockett wasn't far ahead. I was sure we were gaining on him. He made a left into a smaller promenade. There were fewer people here, which made it easier for Crockett to put on some speed. Danny was holding his own, although it wasn't easy running in a three-piece suit and dress shoes. I used a breathing technique I had learned during my track running days, which allowed me to keep up with Danny.

Crockett made another left and then vaulted over a low metal fence that partitioned an area that led to a new set of escalators. Danny negotiated the fence without breaking stride. I paused and climbed over it one leg at a time.

We weren't far behind Crockett now, and I was sure we would have him at any moment. That's when I saw the custodian rolling a pail of dirty water across the floor in front of us.

Danny didn't.

Danny's foot caught the pail.

The pail spilled over.

Danny fell.

I fell on top of Danny.

The custodian fell on top of both of us.

We had a "hell of a time" trying to untangle ourselves from each other, slipping and sliding in the murky water. When Danny and I finally got to our feet, we helped the custodian up; then, we turned and continued our run without offering an apology, leaving the man in shock and disbelief.

We sprinted a short distance, hindered by slippery shoes on a wet tile floor until we stopped at a large pillar. We scanned the area for Crockett. He was nowhere to be found. We stood by a glass railing at the escalators feeling exhausted and defeated, until Danny said, "There he goes."

He pointed to the lower level. When I looked over the rail, I saw Crockett scurrying through the crowd. Danny and I watched helplessly as Crockett hurried out a door onto 8th avenue and vanished. We were both breathing hard, tired, wet, and mad as hell.

"That's the second time I chased that guy, and he got away," I said.

Chapter 26

The following morning, I was at my desk when my phone rang. Caller ID told me it was Lieutenant Sean McCaffrey. I wasn't eager to take his call.

McCaffrey and I had worked the streets together for several years before he made rank and was transferred to the 32nd. At the time, he considered the advancement proceeding as a personal rivalry between him and me. I had never been a part of that mindset. The proceedings were as fair as they had always been and based strictly on merit. When he made rank, I congratulated him with a handshake. Although he was transferred uptown, he continued to hold on to an unwarranted dislike for me. I had nothing personal against McCaffrey, other than the baseless animosity he exhibited toward me whenever I was in his presence. In my opinion, he was a mediocre cop at best, with a propensity for displaying an abundance of arrogance. At times, he could be the epitome of professional ineptitude. Although he was a pretty good street cop when we'd worked together, I think the responsibilities of rank were, quite often, beyond his abilities. Making the wrong choices in this job could get someone killed. There had been no love lost between us over the years, and I'd tolerated him only for the sake of professional courtesy.

When I picked up the phone, he said, "McCaffrey here."
I said, "Good morning, Lieutenant."
"Graham," he said. "I've got your man."
"Which man?" I said.
"Your APB, Crockett."
"In lockup?" I said.

"He's holed up in a warehouse surrounded by my men. You better get your ass over here if you want him."

McCaffrey wouldn't think twice about taking the credit for arresting Crockett and sealing up a case I'd worked hard and long on. I wasn't about to let that happen. I wrote down the address he gave me and hung up without thanking him.

I called Danny on the road and told him to pick me up at headquarters. I explained to him about McCaffrey's call and what was going down while we headed uptown.

The address McCaffrey had given me was in the midst of a neighborhood of row houses located in East Harlem. Several blocks had been cordoned off in every direction with patrol units and yellow tape. I parked by a hydrant, and Danny and I got out. The tableau was one of organized confusion. At the center of it all was a metal warehouse. It consisted of a large overhead door and a small entrance door to the right of it. Several spotlights flooded the front of the structure. Officers with their guns at the ready were crouched behind their cars, respectively. Red and blue strobe light flashed everywhere. There were an ambulance and a SWAT armored vehicle parked in the middle of the street.

I spotted McCaffrey standing with his hands on his hips talking to several officers beside an unmarked unit. He was in full uniform with the brim of his hat pushed back on his head, revealing his wiry red hair and freckled face. He hadn't changed much since I'd last seen him, other than he looked like he had gained a few pounds, but I was sure his attitude toward me hadn't changed. When Danny and I walked up to him, he continued his conversation with his officers without acknowledging our presence. When he was through, he turned to us. I took it as a deliberate move of disrespect just to agitate me.

"Graham," he said.

"Lieutenant," I said and made a gesture toward Danny. "My partner, Detective, Nolan."

McCaffrey offered a dismissive nod.

"What's the status?" I said.

"Patrols spotted your man coming out of a liquor store down the block. When they approached him, he pulled out a gun and ran. They chased him into that empty warehouse."

"What makes you think, he's my man?" I said.

"Fits your APB description, and he didn't run for nothing."

Two quick shots rang out from inside the warehouse. Everybody ducked. There was a small window in the entrance door. The shooter had broken the glass and was randomly firing shots at the police.

"My orders are to hold fire," McCaffrey said. "We've been trying to talk to this guy, but he only answers with gunfire. I ordered an evacuation of the residences on this block and the one behind it. I'm getting to the point where I'll have to employ my SWAT team."

I was thinking, if this was Crockett, he must have lost his mind completely, or had killed Father Conlon and was desperate for escape, if he were willing to shoot at and possibly kill police officers.

One of McCaffrey's men was standing behind a unit closer to the warehouse. He was wearing a helmet and a vest and held a megaphone in his hand. Periodically he would raise it to his mouth and, ostensibly, use his negotiating skills to reason with whoever was inside the warehouse doing the shooting, hoping to persuade him to come out with his hands up. Each time he completed his carefully rehearsed soliloquy, his words were answered by a burst of gunfire, which sent him and the rest of us crouching for cover.

"See what I mean. Every time we try to talk to this guy, he shoots back," McCaffrey said. "You got any ideas, Graham? Maybe your boy will listen to you."

"I don't know, yet that it is 'my boy'," I said.

"Hey, Graham," McCaffrey said. "I gave you a courtesy call."

McCaffrey was asking for my help but didn't want to use the words.

I looked at Danny.

"Your call," he said.

I took a moment to contemplate my next move. Danny knew what it would be, so did McCaffrey, he said. "You want a vest?"

I had no special negotiating skills but figured I couldn't do any worse than the professional negotiator had done. Besides, if that was Crockett inside the warehouse, he just might deal with me.

I took off my jacket and handed it to Danny. McCaffrey removed a vest from the trunk of his vehicle and tossed it to me. "Watch your ass," he said. "I don't wanna get blamed because you were dumb enough to catch a bullet. I got enough paperwork."

McCaffrey was true to his game, concerned more for himself than the wellbeing of his fellow officers.

I put on the vest. I crouched low behind several units and made my way to the officer with the megaphone. He handed me the megaphone and moved away, a bit too quickly I thought, leaving me alone behind a single unit.

It had been quiet inside the warehouse since the last round of shots. The small window was dark and I could see no movement behind it. The time seemed right. I raised the megaphone and said, "Inside the building. It's Detective, Graham. Be smart and give it up. We'll talk."

My attempt at reasoning was answered by a succession of gunshots. I hit the ground and waited for the barrage to end. In the ensuing silence, I got to my feet cautiously and brought the megaphone up again. "Don't get yourself in any deeper," I said. "We can work—"

Shots rang out a second time, one pinged off the fender of the patrol car in front of me. I dropped and covered my head.

My meager negotiating skills had proved fruitless. That last shot was too close for comfort. I left the megaphone on the ground and hurried back to Danny and McCaffrey.

McCaffrey said, "Son of a bitch is crazy. I'm sending in the team."

"Sure you wanna do that?" I said.

"He's giving me no choice."

I handed the vest back to McCaffrey and put on my jacket. As Danny and I walked back to our unmarked unit, he said, "If it was me, I'd sweat the guy out before rushing in."

Although I agreed with Danny, I didn't offer a response.

We sat in the unmarked and watched the proceedings. Danny said," If that's Crockett, he's gone wacko."

"We'll find out quick enough, who it is," I said as I saw McCaffrey give the signal for the SWAT team to move in.

The six-man team, wearing heavy armor and carrying state-of-the-art assault weapons, stepped into formation and moved silently toward the front door of the warehouse. Danny and I watched as they split formation. One of them covered the side windows while another moved to the rear of the building. The four remaining team members stood at the ready by the front door. When the signal was given, the lead member, carrying a battering ram, swung it against the front door, once, then twice. On the second swing, the door shattered with the sound of splintering wood and crunching metal. The team rushed into the darkness. There was rapid gunfire, then a short pause, and a second round of fire, and then silence.

"Lots of firepower," Danny said.

We got out of our vehicle and walked over to McCaffrey.

An officer came to the front door and gave an all-clear to McCaffrey. Several uniformed police entered the warehouse to secure the scene. At the same time, an EMT vehicle pulled up to the front door. Two medical techs climbed out, slid a gurney out of the rear door, and rolled it inside.

"Sometimes it doesn't end well," McCaffrey said.

"Depends how it's played," Danny said.

McCaffrey gave Danny a disapproving look.

We walked to the ambulance and waited until the EMTs brought the perp out on the gurney. He was in a black vinyl body bag. McCaffrey put one hand up, indicating for them to stop. He asked them to unzip the bag. When they did, I looked at the deceased, so did Danny. McCaffrey didn't bother; his lack of self-awareness and his high degree of arrogance precluded the idea that he could ever make a mistake.

"Guess you can wrap your case up, Graham," McCaffrey said. "You can thank me later."

I looked at McCaffrey and said, "Thank you for nothing. That's not Crockett."

McCaffrey looked like he was about to become apoplectic. His face almost turned the color of his hair. He looked at Danny for confirmation of what I had said. Danny shook his head.

"You sure?" he said. "The guy fits your description."

"A lot of people could've fit that description," I said. "I'm surprised at you, Lieutenant."

McCaffrey's sergeant walked up to us and handed McCaffery the dead man's wallet.

"No ID," the sergeant said. "When they print him, we'll find out who this guy is."

I saw an opportunity to make McCaffrey sweat a little.

"A rush to judgment," I said. "You might've shot the wrong guy."

McCaffrey tried to conceal the uncertainty in his face.

"Well, he ran from us, didn't he? He must be wanted for something."

"Hard to justify one guy being shot to death by a six-man SWAT team. He might've had a pile of parking tickets he didn't want to pay."

"He had a gun and fired at my men."

I shrugged my shoulders and said, "It's your show."

McCaffrey examined the dead man's wallet, hoping to find something to justify his actions, then said, "Well... anyway, I got this one off the street."

"You're my hero," I said.

"Looks like your boy is still your problem," McCaffrey said with a snide expression.

"Yeah," I said. "But the dead guy in the bag is your problem."

Danny and I turned and left.

McCaffrey was still the asshole I'd known him to be.

Chapter 27

I had the testimony I needed to corroborate Monsignor Belducci's disclosure about Father Conlon and Father Faynor. What Margaret Faynor had revealed to me erased all doubt in my mind. This presented a new path, a new picture, but at least I had a direction. The new question was: Why were two men murdered, both of whom just happen to be priests and homosexuals? What was the connection?

My desk phone rang. It was Eileen Conlon.

"Detective, Graham," she said, "David Crockett has been to see me."

"Where and when?" I said.

"Not more than an hour ago," she said. "He forced his way into my home. He had a gun."

"Did he hurt you?"

"No. He threatened me if I didn't help him. He made me give him the keys to my car and took it without my permission. He also took whatever money I had in my purse."

"Where is Troy?"

"I don't know. He's wasn't home when David showed up. I'm glad he wasn't here. He might have had an encounter with David and gotten himself or David hurt trying to defend me."

"Lock your doors and stay put," I said. "I'll send a patrol car to sit in front of your house. You'll be okay. I don't think he'll be back. Don't open the door for anyone but Troy. And wait there until I get there. Give me the make and model of your car and the license plate number."

"It's a white Lexus SUV," she said. "I don't know the plate number. I'll look it up. Hold on."

I waited until she came back with the tag number. I jotted it down, then ended the call.

I put the vehicle information on the air immediately. If Crockett were trying to get away in Eileen Conlon's car, there would be a good chance patrols would spot it quickly in the metro area traffic.

I made it to the Conlon home in good time. When I got there the house was dark. I parked on the street and walked quietly up the driveway. At the front door, I listened but heard nothing inside. I rang the bell. No answer. I looked through the front window, but the interior was too dark for me to discern anything.

I was contemplating forcing the front lock when I perceived someone approaching from behind me. I turned to see Troy Conlon coming up the walkway.

"What's wrong?" he said.

"How long have you been away?"

"Couple of hours. What's happening?"

"Where've you been?"

"I was at the 'Red Hen'. Why the third degree?"

"Your sister's inside. She might be hurt. I couldn't get a response when I rang the doorbell. I'll explain inside."

Troy Conlon removed his key ring from his pocket and unlocked the front door. When he flipped on the light switch in the living room, we saw Eileen Conlon lying on the sofa. Her eyes were closed and there was blood flowing down her cheek from a wound on her left temple. She appeared to be unconscious but opened her eyes quickly as I helped her into a sitting position. Troy Conlon stood there looking at his sister with indifferent, listless eyes.

"Get her something cold to drink," I said.

Troy went to the kitchen and brought back a glass of tap water.

Eileen Conlon took a moment to regain herself, then took a drink from the glass. When she was through, I pressed my handkerchief against her wound.

"How'd this happen?" I said.

"He hit me," she said.

"Who?" Troy said.

"Crockett," I said to Troy Conlon. "He forced his way into the house and tried to coerce your sister into helping him get away."

"He took the Lexus," she said.

Troy Conlon removed a cigarette from the crumpled pack in his breast pocket, lit it, took a long drag, and blew the smoke out casually before he said, "How are you involved with this guy?"

"I'm not," she said. "I thought we were friends, but I guess after tonight, we're not."

"Crockett's running from the law," I said. "He might be a suspect in the killing of your brother."

"*Might be?*" Troy Conlon said.

"We haven't had anything feasible to charge him with, before tonight anyway. At the very least, now we've got: B&E, assault, armed robbery, and grand theft auto, all felonies."

"Are we in any danger?"

"*We*", I thought. This guy seems to be more concerned about himself than his sister.

"I don't think so," I said. "Crockett got the wrong idea that your sister would help him, but she nixed that. I doubt he has any reason to bother her again. We'll have the patrols give extra attention to your house for a while."

"You'd better take care of that cut," Troy said.

"I have a medical kit in the bathroom," she said. "I'll dress it and then go right to bed."

"You know how to reach me," I said to Eileen Conlon.

She nodded and walked out of the room as Troy Conlon walked with me to the front door.

After Troy opened the door, I said, "If you were here with your sister tonight, this might not have happened." "I'm not her babysitter," he said.

"I'm talking about someone who might have killed your sister. Your lack of concern is surprising."

He didn't respond to that, but said, "I won't be going out anymore tonight. She'll be okay with me here."

"If Crockett comes back, don't do anything stupid. Call the police."

"I will," he said, then closed the door without thanking me. I was surprised by the attentiveness he'd suddenly exhibited for his sister. Maybe my short rebuke had brought it on. I wasn't sure it was genuine.

***

The "Red Hen" was a bar on 39th Street. It was one of those subterranean places where one had to walk down several stairs to get into the place. I navigated the cracked concrete steps and pushed open the front door. After my eyes adjusted to the darkness, I made my way to the short bar along the left wall. The place was small but neat. There were tables scattered about in no particular order, draped with white linen tablecloths. A small stage was in a far corner; there were instruments on it but no musicians. A jukebox, flashing bright colors, was playing a country song. Behind the bar hung a huge cardboard caricature of a red hen with the name: "Mollie" printed in large red letters beneath it.

I'd decided to do some checking of my own on Troy Conlon. There was something about this guy that I didn't like, right from the "get-go". His attitude concerning his sister's encounter with Crockett seemed less than genuine. I had too many unanswered questions about him that I wanted to be answered.

It was just passed two in the afternoon, and the place was already crowded. Most of the patrons were at the bar. I slid onto a stool as the barkeep approached me. He was a burly guy with a salt and pepper mustache and goatee. I ordered a beer. When he brought the beer to me, I said, "I'm looking for a friend of mine. He comes in here often, name o' Troy Conlon."

"You a cop?"

"A friend. Haven't seen him in a while," I said. "Trying to catch up with him."

OTHER MEN'S SINS

This guy knew I wasn't telling him the truth. He knew a cop when he saw one. "Get a new line," he said. "Every nosey cop uses that one." Then he said. "Try the guy at the end of the bar with the cowboy hat. He's here just about every night, name's Harlan."

I grabbed my beer mug and walked down to the end of the bar and slid onto the empty stool next to Harlan. Harlan was wearing jeans, a sweatshirt, and sported a dark handlebar mustache. His eyes were glassy when he turned to look at me.

"Harlan?" I said.

"Who wants to know?"

"I'm a friend of Troy Conlon. The bartender says you might know him."

"You a cop?"

"A friend, we served together. I'm trying to catch up with him."

Harlan didn't believe me. either. I watched him take a long draw from his bottle of beer, while he thought about whether he wanted to talk to me.

"I know the guy," he said. "Don't know nothin' about him outside this bar, though. Comes in and drinks a few times a week. Some other guys know him too."

I took a sip of beer. "Wow," I said. "I'm glad, at least, I found somebody that knows him. Wondering how things turned out for him. Can you tell me where to find him?"

Harlan drained his bottle, then turned on his stool to face me. "Look, mister," he said. "I don't like the guy; I don't have nothin' to say about him that you would like to hear."

I finished my beer and ordered another and a bottle for Harlan.

"Anything you can tell me, good or bad would be helpful," I said.

He took a draw from his bottle. "You look like a cop," she said.

"A friend," I said.

Harlan smiled at me, took a cigarette from a pack in his shirt pocket, lit it, and then pulled an ashtray closer to him. He blew out the smoke comfortably, before he said, "The guys a jerk. Gets a few drinks in him and thinks he's Superman. He's never happy; complains about everything."

He stopped and looked at me for a reaction.

"I'm telling ya like it is," he said. "You asked me."

"What's he complain about?"

"Last week he shot his mouth off about his family. How he hated his brother and his sister. I told him it's not my business. I didn't what to hear it. He was pissin' me off, but he was half in the bag so I let him talk. Carl don't like no trouble in here."

"Did he say why he dislikes his siblings?"

"His what?"

"His brother and sister."

"He said his brother died recently and his sister got most of the inheritance. Pissed him off caused things should have been split equally. He was upset about that. He said they always gave him the "shit end" of the stick. I told him it was only money."

He finished his beer, and said, "That's all I know, mister, just what he talks about in here. I don't wanna get involved with the guy."

I gave Harlan another, "Wow" and said, "He was a nice guy when I knew him. Hope things haven't gone downhill for him."

Harlan shrugged his shoulders in a sign of indifference. "If you wanna know more, check with Regan there, he's done some drinking with your boy."

When I looked in the direction Harlan had indicated, I spotted Arnie Regan seated at a table with two of his working buddies. I took a ten-spot from my wallet and slid it in front of Harlan. He picked it up and put it in his shirt pocket without a word. I slid off my stool and headed for Arnie Regan.

Regan was doing shots with two of his friends when I approached the table. There were two bottles of whiskey on the table, one for Arnie and one for his friends. When he saw me, he said, "Man, I can't keep my ass away from you."

"Everything's cool, Arnie," I said. "Just want to ask you a few questions."

"Ain't I answered enough of your questions?"

"This is different," I said. "I'd appreciate it."

One of Regan's drinking partners stood up. He swayed a bit from trying to keep the amount of alcohol he had sloshing around in his head from knocking him off balance. He was fat, bloated and red-faced, and reeked of liquor. His partner, a guy with hair down passed his shoulders, had his face buried in the tabletop. He looked like he was long gone.

"This guy lookin' for trouble?" the red face guy said to Regan. He gave me what he thought was a threatening look, and said, "Whatta you want, mister, an ass-kickin'?"

I let it go and took a five out of my wallet and tossed it on the table. "Take your girlfriend and buy her a drink," I said. The guy took the time to focus on the five and then picked it up. Without a word, he helped his partner up from the table and they staggered toward the bar. I took a seat opposite Regan.

"I don't want any more trouble," Regan said.

"No trouble," I said. "What do you know about Troy Conlon?"

"Sure, I know Conlon," he said, "the priest's brother. So what?"

"How well do you know him?"

"We drink together sometime when he comes in here. He drinks too much, shoots his mouth off. Not a good guy to be around."

"What does he talk about?"

"Bitches all the time, never happy. He thinks he's the only guy in the world that's got problems. I can't listen to him after a while. I try to avoid him."

I hadn't gotten much from Regan, other than he had substantiated most of what Harlan had told me about Troy Conlon.

I stood and said, "Have you seen Crockett, lately?"

He shook his head. Arnie was being honest with me. He'd learned his lesson and didn't want to invoke my wrath.

"How's Kevin?" I said.

"Happy with his mother."

"He needs his father," I said.

He filled his shot glass with whiskey and didn't answer.

"Instead of sitting here saturating yourself, why don't you visit your son?"

"I need permission to see him," he said.

"Get permission."

"Don't you think I want to be with my son?"

"I know you do," I said.

"They won't let me spend the time with him that I want to."

"Try cleaning up your act, and being a father," I said.

"Does Kevin enjoy being with you?"

"We get along fine."

"Then get the permission you need and go see him, Arnie."

He downed the shot and said, "They won't let me."

I took a ten out of my wallet, dropped it on the table, and walked out.

Chapter 28

Sandy and I spent Friday together. Sandy was free, and it was a regular day off for me. In the evening, we took in a movie, ate dinner at Branigan's, and afterward went back to her apartment for dessert, and to watch, "West Side Story" on TV; which she said was her favorite musical. Sandy had baked cupcakes earlier in the day, chocolate with white icing. I ate three while watching the movie and washed them down with a large glass of cold milk. Sandy had one with a cup of green tea.

I wanted to stop thinking about the Conlon case for a while, clear my mind and begin anew when I went back to work, with a fresh perspective of what I had already accomplished. I had made some positive strides, but there were still some questions unanswered.

We were sitting on the sofa in front of the TV with just the light from the screen filling the room. Sandy had fallen asleep beside me. I was contemplating whether I should have another cupcake when my cell phone rang.

"Detective Graham," a voice said, "this is Gwen Regan."

"Is there a problem?" I said.

"I'm not sure. I almost feel foolish calling you, but I'm concerned, and somewhat frightened."

"What is it?"

"Arnie came to see me this morning."

"With permission?"

"Yes. He phoned me earlier and asked if he could visit with Kevin. I said he could if he decently presented himself. He said he would. When he showed up an hour later, I was surprised by his appearance. He was clean-shaven and dressed in jeans and a freshly pressed shirt. His hair had been cut short and cut neatly. His boots were even polished.

"And the problem is?"

"I could see that Kevin was glad to see his father. They gave each other a hug and Arnie asked if Kevin would like to go to the park and maybe do some fishing at the lake. 'If it's okay with Mom,' he'd said. I didn't object. There was something about Arnie that made me feel everything would be all right. Kevin was excited and wanted to go." "No problem, yet," I said.

"Arnie promised to return with Kevin by 5:00 p.m.," she said.

I looked at the clock on the TV box. It read 7:50 p.m. I guessed now there was a problem.

"And they haven't returned yet?" I said.

"Exactly," she said. "I haven't heard from Arnie since they walked out the door. I supposed there might have been a delay in their plans, but when it got this late, I started to panic. I'm afraid Arnie might have taken Kevin away from me."

Her voice was shaky. I could tell she was about to break down.

"Calm yourself," I said. "We don't know if that's the case. Were you able to contact, Arnie?"

"I don't know how I would. He doesn't have a cell phone. They could be anywhere. I've been upset since five o'clock. I thought of calling the police but decided to phone you."

"You did the right thing," I said. "Do you have any idea where they might have gone? Maybe they visited someone."

"There is no one," she said. "I have a sister that lives across town, but Arnie and her don't get along. Arnie's father lives alone on a couple of acres in North Jersey, but I don't know what Arnie's present relationship is with him. They've had unkind words for each other in the past."

"I suggest you wait a while longer, if Arnie and Kevin come home, call me. I'm sure Arnie will have a satisfactory explanation for their delay. They're probably having such a good time they lost track of time. If you don't hear from Arnie in the next hour, call the police."

"I don't want to involve the police," she said, "that's why I phoned you."

"Then you have no choice but to wait. If you don't hear from them before morning, call me back."

I ended the call and looked over at Sandy. She was still asleep. I clicked off the TV and sat in the dark. The TV box clock read, 8:05. I knew I wouldn't fall asleep waiting for a possible second phone call from Gwen Regan.

I hoped Arnie hadn't done something stupid, kidnapping is a felony, which carries a severe penalty, even if it's your own child. Gwen Regan said Arnie looked like a new man. Maybe my advice had somehow gotten through to him. Gwen Regan was, no doubt, in a panic state, but was handling the situation well. I like to think she found solace and strength in the knowledge that I was empathetic to her problem and was willing to help. She had learned to handle crisis well, after all she had been through with her marriage to Arnie. But, when it comes to the welfare of one's only child, "concern" is a word inadequately used.

***

The ringing phone jolted me out of a deep sleep. I sat up quickly. When my eyes adjusted to the bright sunlight streaming through the front window, I realized I was still on Sandy's sofa. There was a blanket covering me, but I didn't see Sandy anywhere. I picked up my cell phone and said, "Hello". As I did, I glanced at the TV clock, it read, 7:40 a.m.

"He took my child!" Gwen Regan screamed. "Arnie kidnapped Kevin!"

Her frantic scream shot up my adrenalin. I took a deep breath and cleared my head before I said, "Calm yourself and tell me what happened."

I could hear strong erratic breathing, which told me she was in panic mode. There was a short pause while she composed herself.

"I waited until midnight," she said, "but they didn't come back. I—I must have fallen asleep on the sofa. When I woke up a few minutes ago, I realized Arnie and Kevin never returned. I know he has taken Kevin from me. What are we to do?"

"Did you notify the police?" I said.

"I phoned you," she said. "Please, help me find Kevin."

"I'll be there as soon as I can," I said. "Stay put and keep your door locked. If Arnie shows up before I get there, call me."

"Okay, please hurry," she said.

I ended the call just as Sandy appeared at the doorway, rubbing sleep from her eyes.

"What is it?" she said.

"Gwen Regan's got trouble. She believes her husband has taken her son from her."

"As in kidnap?"

"I'm going to see what I can do."

The majority of child abductions in the United States are parental kidnappings, where one parent takes a child without the knowledge or consent of another parent. I certainly had no intention of imparting those statistics to Gwen Regan.

It was inconceivable to me that Arnie Regan had kidnapped his son, intending to keep him away from his mother, permanently. He didn't have the financial means to support himself and his son. I had known Arnie to do some stupid things, but nothing as daring or criminal as this. I hoped my presumption was correct.

I climbed the stairs to Gwen Regan's apartment and knocked. When she opened the door, I was looking at a woman I had not seen before. The stress she had endured for the past twelve hours showed mercilessly on her face. I closed the door behind me and brought her to the sofa. I sat beside her. I could see a tinge of panic in her eyes. I said, "The first thing we need to do is calm you down." I took her trembling hands and rubbed them between mine. I wasn't sure what that was supposed to do, but I'd seen it on TV. I watched tears roll down her cheeks.

"I don't know what to do," she said. "I'm so frightened."

I used my thumb to wipe the tears from her face. She smiled.

"I need you to pull yourself together," I said, "We need to work together to find Kevin."

She got up and went into the bathroom. I heard the water running. When she returned, she looked calmer and more refreshed. "Thank you," she said. "Can I get you something?"

I shook my head.

She went to the kitchen counter and started the single cup, coffee maker. When she finished preparing her cup, she brought it to the kitchen table. I took a seat beside her.

"Do you have any idea where your husband might have taken Kevin?"

She took a large gulp of coffee before she said, "He said they were going to the park."

"Central Park?"

"Yes. He said they might do some fishing at the lake. And that he had fishing gear in his truck."

"Was Kevin willing to go with his father?"

"He was excited about it."

"Can you think of any place where Arnie might hide out with Kevin?"

"Hide out," she said. "Oh, my God."

"I mean someplace where he might be with Kevin."

She put her coffee cup down, lowered her head into her hands, and closed her eyes. I thought she was about to break into tears again but, instead, she said, "Arnie's father lives alone in North Western New Jersey since his wife died three years ago."

When she raised her head, the stress had returned to her face.

"He and Arnie were never on the best of terms. Arnie might've taken Kevin there since it's a rural, out of the way place. Then she added, "It's just a guess."

"It's a good start," I said. "What's his name?"

"Frank," she said, "Franklin Regan."

"Can you think of any other place where they might have gone?"

"That's the only possibility," she said. "Of course, they could be anywhere."

Gwen Regan was right. Arnie could have been driving his pickup truck across state lines as we spoke, transporting Kevin to places unknown. It was a viable scenario, but one I didn't lend much credence to. I certainly didn't mention it to Gwen Regan.

"Do you have a recent photo of Kevin?"

"I have a school photo from last year."

"That'll do."

She went into the bedroom and brought back a wallet size photo of Kevin. "What will you do with the photo?" she said.

"I'm hoping, nothing," I said. "I won't have trouble identifying Kevin or your husband."

"Identifying?" she said.

I had made her uncomfortable with my choice of words and quickly said: "When I find them."

"You're going to do this on your own?"

"I don't think Arnie has done anything drastic," I said. "I'd like to cut him one more break to help him get his family back. If I can keep the police out of it, we might be able to settle this to the benefit of both of you. I'm sure you would want that."

"I do," she said. "How can I help?"

"Stay calm and close to the phone. If you hear from Arnie, call my cell."

I left Gwen Regan with my instructions and headed back to my apartment. I called Sandy to update her on what was happening, and then I called Danny at headquarters. I asked him to search for Franklin Regan in one of the counties in North Western New Jersey.

I took a shower and got dressed. I put on a pair of jeans, a black sweatshirt, clipped my gun to my belt, and laced up my Rockport boots. I wasn't sure just what I was getting into, but I wanted to be prepared. By the time I took my shower and finished dressing, Danny had called back with an address.

As usual, Danny was very efficient.

Chapter 29

Arnie Regan could have taken his son anywhere. There were countless possibilities. My cynicism dictated I had little chance of finding either of them. I'd give it my best effort for Gwen Regan's sake. The most logical place for me to start looking was also the most *illogical*—Arnie Regan's apartment. It wasn't reasonable to think Arnie would've taken his son there if he intended to keep him away from his mother and the authorities; but then, I wasn't sure, at this point, what Arnie Regan's intentions were.

I arrived at Regan's apartment on Rivington Street and parked in front of his building. I didn't see his green pickup truck parked on the street, anywhere. I entered the building and climbed the three flights of stairs to his apartment. When I reached the top, I walked past several doors until I came to Arnie's number. I leaned close to the door and listened. There were no sounds inside, and no light showing under the door.

I waited. After a full minute of silence. I knocked.

There was no response. I knocked again.

I slipped my old credit card between the doorframe and the lock and with a little hand magic, gained access easily. It was dark inside the apartment other than daylight streaming through a dirty front window. I gave the living room a cursory look; everything seemed in its place. I checked the bedroom and the bathroom but found nothing unusual. The entire apartment appeared as it should be. I didn't expect to find Arnie here, but I couldn't leave this stone unturned. My next logical move would be to drive to the senior Regan's residence.

***

Franklin Regan lived in rural Sussex County, New Jersey. I relied on the GPS on my cell phone to get me to the address. The ride would take at least an hour. I headed west on Rt. 22 with the Chevy doing a steady sixty; she rode like a Cadillac when she was in cruise speed.

Just over an hour later, I found myself in Greenwich Township in Warren County. The GPS took me over the main road through the township's main commercial shopping area and then directed me to several secondary roads through a more rural setting. I found myself in open country where farmlands and cornfields were populating the landscape. As I drove an unpaved road, the countryside became more desolate with almost no manmade structures. There were acres of trees and expanses of open fields with no signs of human or animal life.

I was negotiating a curve on a dirt road, which made its way up a grassy hillside, when at the crest; there appeared in the distance, a large rustic-looking house and a nearby barn. I surveyed the area through my windshield. The two-story house was painted dark brown, its wooden roof singles were weather-worn and loose. A large stone chimney rose from one gable end, but there wasn't a trace of smoke rising from it. A split-rail fence ran the length of the property as far as I could see. I couldn't detect any movement. The house and grounds seemed to be abandoned. The barn was in disrepair, and the house had been equally neglected. The possibility existed that I had somehow screwed up, and sent myself on a "wild goose chase". I wondered if my GPS had taken me in the wrong direction until it told me I had "arrived at my destination".

I pulled the Chevy behind a small thicket near the opened gate and cut the engine. I didn't see a sign or mailbox indicating this was the residence of Franklin Regan. My dashboard clock read: 2:15 p.m. I decided to sit and watch for any signs of life. There were no lights behind the front windows of the house, and I saw no movement inside the house. If Arnie Regan was in there with Kevin; I certainly didn't see any evidence of it. I had no choice at this point, but to approach the house.

My only option was to walk across the open field toward the house. I wasn't comfortable with the idea of being out in the open, unconcealed. My best bet was to make my way to the barn, then move around the back of the barn toward the house.

I exited the Chevy and closed the door quietly. The stand of trees would conceal me, part of the way, but once I'd passed them, I'd be in the open until I reached the barn. If someone in the house wanted to take a shot at me, I'd be an easy target.

I moved through the trees, keeping an eye on the house and the barn for any movement. Once I passed the trees, I picked up my pace but didn't run. The house was quiet and still. When I reached the side of the barn, I peered through a small window; the barn appeared empty other than an array of rusted farming tools and an older pickup truck parked along one wall. I continued along the back wall until I reached the corner of the barn. From my position, I was about twenty yards from the house and able to see more detail now. Through the side window, I could see the usual furnishings in what appeared to be a large living area, but still no movement inside. The front door was opened behind a dirty screen, and the stairs leading up to the small porch were in dire need of repair. At this point, I wasn't sure how to proceed. I couldn't knock on the front door and expect Arnie Regan to greet me with a smile and open arms. I wasn't even sure if Arnie or Kevin were inside the house, or if I'd be confronted by a hostile stranger.

I was contemplating my next move when I sensed someone or something behind me. Before I could turn, I felt the cold steel of a double-barreled shotgun against the back of my neck. "Don't turn around," I heard a coarse voice say.

I didn't.

"Who are ya?" the voice said.

"My name is Max Graham," I said.

"Didn't you see the sign?"

"I didn't see a sign," I said.

"It says: 'No trespassin'."

"My bad," I said.

"Turned around, slow."

When I turned, I was facing an older guy wearing soiled overalls and a tattered wide-brimmed hat. He sported a full gray beard and reeked of stale tobacco. He stepped back but kept the shotgun pointed at my chest.

"By rights, I can shoot ya right now," he said.

He cocked both barrels of the gun and raised it to my face. My heart began to pound as I watched his shaky finger tighten around the trigger. I thought I had run into a deranged mountain man who was about to kill me for no justifiable reason.

Deliverance came to mind.

I was about to make a move before I became a dead man, when he said, "What do ya want here?"

"I came to see Arnie."

"What business ya got with, Arnie?"

"I want to help him."

"You a cop?"

"I am, but I'm also his friend."

He scrunched his face up in an expression of skepticism and said, "Why should I believe ya."

"I can show you my badge if you want. It's in my side pocket."

"Take it out, slow."

I took my ID out of my pocket and opened it for him to see. He gave it a quick look, and said, "You here to arrest Arnie?"

"No, I said I wanna help him."

"Arnie don't need no help."

"I think he does."

He uncocked the shotgun and said, "Let's go up to the house."

He kept the shotgun against my back as he followed me to the house. When we reached the front porch, he shouted through the screen door, "Arnie, git out here."

Arnie Regan appeared at the front door. He didn't look surprised to see me. "Graham," he said. "I knew it would be just a matter of time."

He let the screen door slam behind him as he stepped out onto the porch. I couldn't detect the usual anger in Arnie's face; his demeanor was calm and non-confrontational, totally out of character for the Arnie Regan I knew. Gwen Regan was right, Arnie looked different. He was dressed in jeans and an open-collar shirt. He was clean-shaven, and his hair had been combed neatly and parted to one side.

He turned to the old man and said, "It's okay, pop. I know this guy."

"Can ya trust him?" the old man said.

"No, but it's okay anyway."

The old man half-heartedly lowered the shotgun to his side and walked to the front door and into the cabin, keeping a wary eye on me as he did. "I'll be right inside if ya need me," he said through the screen door.

"Okay, Pop," Arnie said.

When the old man disappeared inside, I said to Arnie, "What are you up to, Arnie?"

Regan hesitated before he said, "Spending time with my son."

"Did your wife agree to this?"

"Yeah, she did."

"About coming here?"

He didn't answer.

"Your wife is near hysteria," I said.

"It's the only way, Graham, don't make thing difficult for me."

"I want to help," I said.

"I've asked for your help before," he said. "You can help me by leaving us alone."

"You can't do this alone," I said. "There are laws and courts. You'll only make things worse for yourself and Kevin. Kidnapping is a federal offense. You could spend a long time in prison."

"Kevin is my son," he said.

"It makes no difference; the law still applies. Come back with me and we'll work this out."

"I tried it your way. It didn't work."

"Now you have someone who'll help make it work," I said.

He said nothing, but I could tell he was considering my offer.

"For Kevin's sake," I said.

"What guarantee do I have that I won't be arrested and wind up in jail?"

"The police don't know about this," I said. "It's between you, me, and Gwen. I can keep it that way if you're willing to cooperate. I know Gwen is willing to try to make things work again. If that's what you want?"

"I want to help my boy grow up. That's all I want."

"Then come back with me. We can make it happen."

"I heard that before."

"Where is Kevin?"

"Inside."

"Can I see him?"

Arnie thought for a moment, then said, "Be careful what you say to him."

"Of course," I said.

He turned and opened the screen door, then pointed to the stairs and said, "Watch your step."

The cabin consisted of one large living room area and a small kitchen at the rear. A set of stairs led up to the second floor. At one end of the living room were a sofa, a coffee table, and a flat-screen TV. Lying on the floor in front of the TV was Kevin Regan. He was on his belly with his hands holding up his chin, engrossed in a series of animated videos. When he laughed aloud at the colorful antics on the screen, Arnie looked at Kevin, and let out a short laugh himself, then turned to me and smiled. I smiled back.

Paternal pride.

I had never seen Arnie that way. He was like a man I didn't know. I wondered if my meager efforts had anything to do with his transition.

"Kevin," Arnie said, "come meet someone."

Kevin turned his head and looked up at us. He had that wonderful boyish innocence inherent in a well-raised ten-year-old. Being the father of two girls whom I loved dearly; I had never experienced the pleasure of a father-son relationship.

Kevin jumped up and walked over to his father. Arnie put a caring arm around his son's shoulder. "I want you to meet, Mr. Graham," he said.

Kevin looked up at me with inquisitive eyes and said, "I know you."

"We've met before," I said. "At the rec center."

"That's right," I said.

"Mr. Graham is here to take us back to mama," he said.

"I miss, mama," Kevin said.

Arnie Regan looked at me, then back at his son. "Then we'll start back right away," he said.

***

I closed the apartment door after Arnie and I stepped inside with Kevin. Gwen Regan rushed to her son and put her arms around him. She squeezed him tightly and kissed both of his cheeks. "Are you all right?" she said. She ran her hands over his shoulders and down to his hips as if to see if he had suffered any injuries.

"I'm okay, mama," Kevin said.

She shot a look of anger at Arnie, then looked back at her son with an expression of love and understanding only a mother can have. It was the same look I had seen Marlene give our girls many times. Gwen Regan kissed her son on his forehead and said, "Go in and wash up, then go to your room and change. I'll be in, in a bit."

Kevin started for his room, then turned and said, "I had fun Dad. Can we do it again?"

Arnie smiled and said, "sure." "Goodbye, Mr. Graham," Kevin said.

I gave him a big smile.

After Kevin had gone to his room, Gwen Regan looked at Arnie and said, "How could you have done this?"

Arnie seemed contrite when he said, "He's my son, too."

Gwen Regan thought for a moment, then said, in a gentle indulgent way, "Of course he is."

She took on a sympathetic manner as she approached Arnie and took his hand in hers. "We have to work on things," she said, "if you want to be a family again."

"I do," Arnie said.

I was beginning to feel like an intruder. I wasn't a marriage counselor and felt that I had done all I could, for now, to help bring this family back together. The rest was up to them.

My concern was for Kevin. My daughters had gone through a trying time when Marlene and I went through our divorce proceedings, and I knew, firsthand, how such a situation can adversely affect young minds. I didn't want that to happen to Kevin.

I turned and opened the door behind me. "I think my work here is done," I said.

Gwen Regan shook my hand and said, "Thank you."

I looked at Arnie. "Kevin was in good hands," I said.

"We have some work ahead of us," Gwen Regan said.

Arnie looked at me but didn't say a word. I could see the gratitude in his eyes. I gave him a nod and closed the door.

On the ride back to my apartment, I felt satisfied that I had done all I could. I believed both Arnie and Gwen Regan wanted to resolve their differences for the sake of their son. Marlene and I had held those same sentiments for the benefit of our daughters after our contentious divorce. We had made it work. I believed the Regan's could too.

Chapter 30

Saturday afternoon was unusually quiet, so I asked Danny to drop me off at the "Midtown Tonsorial" so I could get my hair cut. He waited for me in the Impala while "Rocco", my favorite barber, gave me my usual trim cut and head massage. When I returned to the Impala, Danny wrinkled his nose. "You smell like a French whore," he said. He opened the driver's window to mitigate, what he believed, was an offensive smell.

"It's pomade," I said, coquettishly. "See how it augments my brown highlights."

Danny wasn't amused.

"It gives a soft hold, not too much sheen, and it smells—"

"Like a whore's crotch," Danny said.

I was about to remind him of the "axle grease" he ran through his hair every morning when I was interrupted by the car radio.

Patrols had spotted Eileen Conlon's white SUV weaving through traffic on 7th Avenue. Crockett was in the driver's seat. Several units were following closely, so as not to lose him, as per my instructions. Danny pulled the Impala away from the curb and we headed in that direction. Before we got to 7th Avenue, the radio reported Crockett had turned east onto 42nd street. Danny and I were traveling west. Traffic was heavy for a Saturday, making it difficult to spot Eileen Conlon's car. The patrol vehicles were easier to spot. There were three units following Crockett. We couldn't turn around in traffic, so Danny drove around the block and entered back onto 42nd Street, and headed east.

I picked up the radio mic: "Secure suspect with as little force as possible," I said.

Patrols responded in the affirmative.

We could see the patrol vehicles several blocks ahead of us, but we couldn't see Eileen Conlon's white SUV. After driving several more blocks, the SUV came into view. Crockett was pulling into a gas station. I picked up the mic and ordered the patrols to stay put and keep a distance.

Danny parked the Impala across the street. We watched and waited.

Crockett got out of the SUV and stood by the driver's door and waited for an attendant. In less than a minute, an attendant came out of the small office and approached Crockett. They exchanged words, and then the attendant went back into the office. There was no one else in the station, which presented the ideal time to take Crockett.

I picked up the mic, and gave the order to, "Move in."

The patrols descended on Crockett "like a duck on a June bug." Two patrol cars moved in at an angle to prevent Crockett's vehicle from leaving the station. Crockett was quick. He turned and ran behind the building that housed the station's small shopping mart.

"He's running," Danny said.

"Let them handle it," I said. "He won't get far."

Four officers jumped out of their cars and started after Crockett. They ran around the back of the building where Crockett had run. Danny and I leaned forward to get a better look.

We saw Crockett emerge from the rear of the building, and attempt to climb a chain-link fence at the perimeter of the station. He scrambled up, slipped back down, and scrambled back up again. The officers came from behind the building, and before he could get over the fence, one reached up and yanked him down by the seat of his pants. He hit the ground hard. When they lifted him off the ground, he wisely put his hands in the air; not resisting was the smartest thing he had done for himself since getting involved with the police. An officer patted him down while another cuffed him. They led him back to a patrol car, put him into the back seat, and closed the door. The scene was secured, and Crockett was escorted away. Eileen Conlon's car would be impounded as part of the investigation.

Danny drove back to headquarters where we awaited Crockett's arrival. He was to be brought to me at the bureau as per my directive.

We were waiting at my desk when they brought Crockett in. I intended to be as fair as was possible with him. Find out what I needed to know, once and for all. Crockett had the answers.

Crockett looked tired. His hair was disheveled, and it looked like he'd been wearing the same clothes for a week. Whatever he'd been running from had worn him down.

Two officers escorted him to a chair beside my desk. I asked them to remove the handcuffs. They did. I thanked them, and they left. Danny Nolan sat on the edge of my desk and waited. I got right to the point.

"Why are you running?" I said to Crockett.

"Because I don't wanna go to jail," he said.

"Have you done something that might put you in jail?"

"No," he said.

"Then you're running for nothing," I said.

I removed a printed sheet from my top drawer and laid it on my desk. "I have an affidavit here from Eileen Conlon, claiming you broke into her home and held her at gunpoint."

"Not true," he said. "This is what I mean. I'm being accused of something I didn't do."

"She claims you threatened her life if she wouldn't help you. Said you took her money and her car against her will."

"That's a bunch o' crap," he said. "She was more than willing to help me."

"Then you don't deny being at her house?"

"I was there," he said. "I went to ask her for some cash. She offered me her car, and the money to help me get away. I didn't have to threaten her."

I picked up the affidavit and held it up to give him a closer look. "I have her signed affidavit here that states otherwise," I said.

"She's lying," he said.

"Why would she lie?"

"I don't know, but I'm telling you the truth."

"She had a pretty good knock on her head when we found her," Danny said. "You do that to her."

"No," he said. "I told you, she was helping me. Why would I do that?"

"Why did you keep running?" I said. "If you're innocent, the smart move would have been to face the questioning and clear yourself."

"I know how the system works," Crockett said. "Too much evidence against me: the screwdriver, the overalls they found, and my DNA. I've heard stories about innocent people going to jail. I took my chances."

"The DNA in the overalls didn't match your DNA," Danny said.

Crockett tried not to look surprised. "Lucky me," he said.

"How well do you know Arnie Regan?" I said.

Crockett thought for a second. "Worked a few construction jobs with him," he said. "Had a few drinks together a couple o' times. I haven't seen him in months."

"He claims you paid him three hundred dollars to work me over," I said, "get me to drop the case."

"That's crazy. I don't know what you're talking about."

Danny got up from my desk and walked around to the other side of the chair where Crockett was sitting. "Now's the time for you to come clean," he said. "You've got several charges against you, but, so far, one of them is *not* murder."

"I told you why I ran," he said. "I was scared. Maybe it was stupid, but I was scared."

"If Eileen Conlon was helping you, why would she claim you broke into her house and threatened her with a gun?" I said.

"I don't know," he said. "Eileen and I had a thing going back a while ago. It lasted a few months until I ended it. She took it hard. We hadn't seen each other for a while until she showed at the church just before Father Conlon died. She was receptive and friendly, so I hooked up with her again. You saw us at the shore house."

"Where did you get the gun?" Danny said.

"I don't own a gun."

It was the first definitive lie Crockett had told during the questioning.

"Come, clean," Danny said. "Obstructing a murder investigation is a felony."

"I gun was found in your dresser drawer in your room at the rectory," I said.

"What right have you got to go through my things," he said. "Don't you need a warrant or something?"

"No," I said.

Crockett accepted that and said, "Okay. I had a gun. It was illegal, so I threw it in the Hudson. I didn't want anything more to incriminate me."

"When was that?"

"A few days after Father Conlon was killed. I don't remember exactly."

Crockett's story was weak but feasible, the murder weapon of choice was not a gun, and owning an illegal gun didn't incriminate him in any way with this crime.

If Eileen Conlon's story was untrue, why would she go to such lengths to devise such a story? Why would she want to make Crockett look guilty? I was holding off, showing Crockett the letter I'd found in my mailbox. I'm sure he would deny having written it, after all he had told us.

"What's your relationship with Troy Conlon?"

"Don't know him."

"He's Eileen Conlon's brother."

"She never mentioned she had a brother, other than Father Conlon."

"Then you never met him?" I said.

"I don't know him. I keep telling you the truth but it comes out sounding like a lie."

"I believe you," I said.

OTHER MEN'S SINS

Crockett seemed relieved by what I'd said, almost grateful.
"Am I under arrest?" he said.
"Yes," I said. "Until you can clear yourself or this case proves otherwise. You have multiple charges against you. You'll have to stay downtown unless you can make bail if there *is* bail?"
"Do you have a lawyer?" Danny said.
"Can't afford one," he said. "We'll need an affidavit from you stating everything you just told us here today. Are you willing to submit one?"
"Sure," he said. "I'm not hiding anything."
He leaned forward in his chair closer to me and said, "I swear, Graham, I didn't kill Father Conlon. Why would I? He was almost like a father to me. You got to believe me."
He sat back in his chair again, looking almost defeated. "I read about Father Faynor in the papers," he said. "Am I a suspect in that one too?"
"Not at the moment," I said.
Crockett stood and raised his hands in the air, "Man, now you know why I ran," he said. "The more I co-operate with you guys, the deeper into trouble I get."
"No one is accusing you of that," I said. "You asked a question, and I answered it."
"Somebody's not telling the truth here," Danny said. "The evidence will either exonerate you or put you away for a long time. Obstructing justice is a serious crime. The same applies to Eileen Conlon if she broke the law."
I had gotten all I wanted from Crockett. The officers came back, cuffed him again, and took him downtown to lockup.
"We need to talk to Eileen Conlon," Danny said. "Somebody's lying here."
"I don't like being lied to," I said.
"How could I forget," Danny said.
"We still have no evidence that points to Crockett murdering Father Conlon," I said.
"Doesn't mean he didn't," Danny said.

213

"Why would Eileen Conlon fabricate a story to make Crockett look guilty? Why did she pay Martin Denman to spy on me and rough me up?"

"Reasons unknown," Danny said. "Let's lean on her a little."

We asked Eileen Conlon to come in for an interview. We informed her that Crockett had been arrested and that we needed to clear up a few things regarding her affidavit.

She showed up at the bureau later that afternoon. She was modestly dressed in low heel shoes and a white, one-piece dress that reached down almost to her ankles. She had changed her hairstyle since I'd last seen her. It was cut short now, neatly set with bangs delicately adorning her forehead. She wore no make-up. Around her neck, she hung her polished silver crucifix. She seemed a bit too pious to me. There was a small bandage on her left temple.

"Thank you for coming," I said.

She sat in the same chair Crockett had sat in.

"Can I get you something?" Danny said. "Coffee?"

"No, thank you," she said. "I no longer drink coffee. But I will take a glass of cold water." Danny went to the cooler and brought back a cup half-filled with water and gave it to her. She drank some, then looked around for a place to set the cup down on my desk.

"Do you have a coaster?" she said.

I tore off a sheet of paper from the small notepad on my desk and slid it over to her. She delicately placed the cup on top of it.

"We've asked you here to clear up a conflict in your affidavit," I said.

"A conflict?" she said. "What conflict could there be? Now that you've caught the killer of my brother, he'll be brought to justice and we can all get on with our lives."

"It's true, David Crockett has been arrested, but he hasn't been charged with the murder of Father Conlon."

"Why not?" She seemed suddenly annoyed, almost indignant.

"We have no conclusive evidence that proves so," I said.

"It's apparent," she said. "He ran away. Doesn't that imply guilt?"

"Yes, it does," I said.

Danny said. "Cases don't get solved by implication."

Danny was beginning to get tough with her. I let him.

"What would you like me to tell you that I haven't already told you?" she said.

She took another sip from the cup, then placed it back on the paper.

"For one," I said. "Why did you pay Martin Denman to rough me up?"

Her eyes widened. She wasn't ready for that one.

"I have no idea what you mean," she said. "I hired Mr. Denman's services to help find who murdered my brother. He was thoroughly vetted."

"Vetted how?" I said.

Danny wasted no time hitting her hard. "He's a phony," he said. "You know that as well as we do. We checked him out."

"Why would you accuse me of that?"

"Because Denman told us as such," Danny said.

"And you believed him?"

"Under the circumstances, at the time, he was in no position to lie," I said.

She kissed the crucifix hanging from her neck, then removed a handkerchief from her purse and began to dab the perspiration forming on her cheeks and forehead.

"Oh, my Lord," she said. "I suddenly feel like I'm being persecuted for trying to find who took my beloved brother's life. Christ was persecuted for his innocence also," she said.

I wasn't buying the "holier-than-thou" attitude.

"Why didn't you tell us you had a relationship with Crockett earlier?" Danny said. "He said the two of you were together for a while and then had a breakup."

"It's true," she said. "We were together until he turned into his true evil self. Using swear words that repulsed me, drinking too much. Lying to me to the point where I couldn't believe a word he said. He eventually showed his true colors, just like most evil men do. I prayed that he would, but the Lord saw fit to have me find my way. I left him."

"Then why did the two of you hook up again?" Danny said.

"'Hate the sin, not the sinner'," she said. "When I saw him doing such menial work at the church and living alone with no companionship; the Lord told me I should offer him comfort, the way all sinners need to be comforted. We developed a mutual understanding and became friendly again. Things were good for a short while until he returned to his iniquitous ways. When my brother was killed, I was sure this evil man had committed the deed. He had enough of the Devil in him to do so."

"Why would you believe that?" I said.

"He never liked my brother, only pretended to. Andrew was not happy with David seeing me, and he told David so. David told him to mind his own business. I tried to tell Andrew it was like bringing someone back into the fold, but he was not having it."

Danny walked around in front of Eileen Conlon and let the hammer drop. "Why did you sign an affidavit stating that David Crockett broke into your home at gunpoint and coerced you into helping him escape? Perjury is a felony in this state."

"It is the absolute truth," she said, "I have the wound to prove it. See where he hit me with his gun." She reached up and touched the bandage on her temple.

"Looks ugly," I said.

"It is," she said. "This whole ordeal was ugly." "Do you have an attorney?" I said.

"Do I need one?"

"It might be a good idea for you to retain one now," I said.

She stood up and moved away from her chair. "I'll leave it in the Lord's, hands for now," she said. "Is there anything else?"

"No," I said. "Thank you for your time."

She turned without a word and walked out of the bureau.

"She's lying," I said.

Before I could say a word, Danny said, "I know—you don't like being lied to."

She had left her water cup on my desk. I picked it up by its rim and placed it inside an evidence bag. I handed it to Danny.

"DNA and prints," I said.

Chapter 31

I opened the envelope that was sent up to me from the lab. Danny waited by my desk. I read the short-printed paragraphs, then looked up at Danny. "The unidentified prints on the crucifix match Eileen Conlon's prints," I said.

"Puts her in a bad place," Danny said, "enough to secure an arrest and charge her with murder. You wanna bring her in?"

"Let's hold off," I said. "We still haven't concluded motive. Maybe we can clear this whole thing up if we play our cards right. Let's pay Eileen Conlon an unexpected visit."

We took the Chevy to Eileen Conlon's Long Island home. It was late afternoon when we arrived. The house was quiet. I rang the doorbell and waited. Eileen Conlon opened the door quickly. She was excited.

"Detective Graham," she said. "I was about to call. Come in."

We entered the living room where she continued. "Troy is in a rage," she said. "We had a huge argument. He demanded I tell him everything that was going on. I didn't know what he wanted me to tell him. He said he was tired of protecting me for no reason and didn't want to be left in the dark any longer."

"Had he been drinking?" I said. "Some," she said, "but he wasn't drunk. We were having a late lunch when the conversation began. He didn't seem to believe anything I told him. Demanded that I tell him the truth or he would get the truth from somewhere else."

"What did he mean by that?"

"I don't know," she said. "I got scared when he went upstairs and got the gun, then left in a hurry."

"You keep a gun in your house?"

"It was my father's; he kept it for years for home protection."

"Do you have any idea where Troy might have gone?" Danny said.

"No. He was angry and determined, and he took my car. I was about to phone you when you arrived, but God sent you to me in time."

"Stay in the house until you hear from me," I said.

I played a hunch and drove to the "Red Hen". I wasn't sure what Troy Conlon wanted to know or where he thought he would find it, but the "Red Hen" was a good place to start.

When we got to the "Red Hen" it was almost five o'clock. We walked into the usual noise and smoke. The place was crowded. It was "happy hour". Danny and I made our way to the bar and looked down the length of it. We didn't see Troy Conlon. The stage was occupied by musicians playing country songs. The volume of music was deafening. I ordered two beers, then I tapped Danny on his shoulder and indicated for us to take a table. We sat at one in the center of the room and began to drink our beers. It was dark and smoky.

I was watching several couples dance to a slower-paced country song when thru the haze of cigarette smoke, I saw Troy Conlon emerge from a dark corner with Arnie Regan. I indicated with a nod of my head in their direction. Danny turned and looked. Troy Conlon kept his hand pressed against Arnie Regan's back. I was sure he was holding a gun. Danny looked back at me and made an instinctive move to get up from his chair. I reached over and put my hand on his arm and shook my head, "no".

We watched as Troy Conlon prodded Regan out the back door. We waited until they were out of sight, then we went to the door and peered through a small window into the rear parking lot.

Troy Conlon was pointing the gun at Regan and ordering him into the driver's seat of Eileen Conlon's car. Regan got in and Troy slid into the passenger's seat.

"What's up with that?" Danny said.

"Come on," I said

We headed toward the front door, maneuvering around dancing couples and pushing our way through the crowd. Outside, we got into the Chevy and waited. It wasn't long before Eileen Conlon's SUV pulled out of the parking lot and into the street. Regan was driving. I started the Chevy and followed them.

We had no idea where we were, or where we were going. The landscape transformed from city streets to suburban roads to rural highways. After thirty minutes of highway travel, Regan pulled the SUV over. I pulled the Chevy to the side of the highway about a half-mile behind them. We watched them get out of the SUV. Troy Conlon walked behind Regan with the gun at his back and they disappeared into the roadside trees.

"What now?" Danny said.

"Now we play Daniel Boone," I said.

Danny looked confused, then he smiled and said. "Oh, I get it. Daniel Boone, Davy Crockett."

I hadn't meant it to be funny, but it was. "No," I said. "What I mean is, now we go trekking through the woods looking for these guys."

"What's Troy gonna do with Regan out here?" Danny said.

"Let's find out," I said.

We got out of the car and made our way into the trees.

The woods were damp but cool. The sun was beginning to set, making it tough to see between the trees. There were flying bugs everywhere. We walked about a half-mile over a pine needle floor, stepping over fallen twigs and branches, which made the trek feel more like five miles. My legs were aching by the time we came upon Troy and Regan standing in a small clearing, well in from the roadside. Regan had his back against a large tree. Troy kept his gun pointed at Regan. We moved in a little closer so we could hear the dialogue.

"How are you involved with my sister?" Troy said.

He brought the gun up closer to Regan's face. Regan looked scared.

"She paid me to rough up that detective."

"Why?" Troy said.

"I didn't ask. It was easy money."

"How is Crockett involved in this?"

"She paid me an extra hundred to say Crockett was the one who hired me."

"And you obliged her?" Troy said.

"Easy money," Regan repeated.

What Regan was saying corroborated Crockett's testimony. No one had paid Crockett to rough me up. It was Eileen Conlon who paid Regan and offered him an extra hundred dollars to say it was Crockett who hired Regan. Why?

"You put my sister in a lot of danger," Troy said.

"She came to me," Regan said.

"Where is Crockett?"

"I don't know," Regan said.

Troy pushed his gun against Regan's forehead. "Don't lie to me or I'll do you right now," he said.

"That's all I know," Regan said.

"I swear you better tell me something." Troy Conlon shouted back. "Or I'll waste you right here and bury you in these woods."

I wasn't sure what Troy Conlon was capable of, but when it looked like he was about to waste Regan, Danny and I stepped into the clearing, guns drawn.

"Hold it, Troy," I said. "Put the weapon down."

Troy Conlon hesitated. He kept his gun pressed firmly against Regan's forehead. Regan's eyes widened, panic causing his face to quiver. No one spoke. We waited in an intense moment, the silence broken only by the incessant sounds from birds and insects. Danny stood motionless; his gun hand steady; his sharp eyes watching Troy Conlon's every move. I was hoping Troy wouldn't make the wrong choice. My gun hand was sweating. My finger was on the trigger. If I had to shoot Troy Conlon to saved Regan's life, I would. I knew Danny would, too. It wouldn't be a pretty picture.

"Drop the gun," Danny said, "before you get into real trouble."

We waited again. I saw Danny's hand tighten around his gun when Troy Conlon's eyes darted from us to Regan and then back to us.

"Do it now!" I said.

There was an intense moment between us until Troy's face softened and he lowered his gun and let it drop to the ground. I removed my finger from the trigger. Danny lowered his gun to his side. Troy was smart enough to make the right choice.

Regan wasn't as smart.

He snatched up Troy Conlon's gun, then turned and ran into the foliage. Instinctively, I started after him while Danny kept Troy Conlon at gunpoint. I pushed my way through tree limbs and shrubbery, but quickly lost sight of Regan. The sun was almost down and the woods were getting darker. I wasn't sure which way Regan was running, but I took my chance and continued straight ahead. I tried to employ my meager talent for tracking someone by looking for signs of broken limbs or footprints on recently crushed leaves, indicating Regan had gone in the direction I was heading. I saw none.

I removed my handkerchief from my rear pocket and wiped the sweat from my face and forehead. The woods were cool but humid, making it difficult to breathe.

I put my gun away. I didn't want to shoot Regan and believed he didn't want to shoot me. I stopped and listened. Among a symphony of chirping birds and a chorus of insect sounds, I could discern the occasional sound of running feet on dried leave ahead of me. Unless there was a man-size animal in the woods or a Bigfoot, those footfalls had to be Regan's. I wondered where he thought he was going.

My breathing came hard, but I pushed myself to move on. When I looked behind me, I couldn't see the clearing where I had left Danny and Troy Conlon. Finding my way back would be another challenge.

I came upon a second clearing. This one was dotted with tree stumps as if the area had been assaulted by an army of lumberjacks. I stepped to the edge of the woods and looked out. In the distance, I found Regan sitting on the ground behind a tree stump. He wasn't doing a very good job at concealing himself. He looked tired. He was sitting with his back to me with Troy Conlon's gun in his lap. The grass was high here, which made it easy for me to approach him without him detecting my presence. I removed my gun from its holster and stepped out into the clearing, keeping a sharp eye on Regan's every move. I was less than ten feet from him when he sensed my presence. He jumped up and pointed his gun at me. I stopped and raised my gun hand over my head

"Put the gun down, Arnie. You're not going to shoot me."

He kept the gun pointed at me. His hand was trembling. I was sure he wished he hadn't put himself in this situation.

"Where you headed, Arnie?" I said.

"Away from you," he said, "and that crazy Conlon. He wanted to kill me."

"It's okay now," I said. "You can come back with me."

"I don't think so."

"We only want to find out what's going on here."

"I'm not going with you. If I go to jail, I'll never see my son."

"You're not going to jail, Arnie. You're the victim here."

"What do I have to go back to? They won't let me have Kevin. I'm tired of fighting."

I moved a step closer to him. He raised his gun to my face.

"I mean it, Graham," he said. "Stay away from me. I got nothin' to lose."

"You've got everything to lose," I said, "including Kevin."

I raised my other hand over my head to present myself as less of a threat. This guy was scared and unsure of himself. I didn't know what he was about to do.

"Use your head," I said. "You're lucky if you can find your way out of these woods, there are animals. You'll probably get eaten before you get out."

He didn't respond. I could see he was unsure of what to do next.
I tried to create a diversion by looking quickly to my left. It was one of the oldest tricks in the book, and it usually worked. Regan fell for it.
When he followed my look, I slapped the gun from his hand. He dove for it, but I got there first. He scrambled to his feet, stepped back, and raised his hands. I holstered my gun and put the gun Troy Conlon had used on Regan in my pocket. "Put your hands down," I said.
Regan looked at me with a pathetic sorrowful look as he lowered his arms. "Gimme a break, Graham," he said. "I only want my boy back."
I struggled for an instant, separating my emotions from my professional ethics. I was willing to help Regan, but I couldn't help him if he wasn't willing to help himself.
I offered no reply, but turned and started walking back to where I'd left Danny and Troy Conlon. When I looked behind me, Regan was following like an obedient puppy.
Although the woods were dark and lighted only by a partial moon, we found our way back to the clearing with no trouble. Danny had cuffed Troy Conlon and was leaning against a tree, waiting. "I knew Daniel Boone could find his way back," he said.
I instructed Danny to remove Troy Conlon's cuffs.
"What did you think you were gonna do here?" I said to Troy.
"I just wanted to scare him. I'm tryin' to help my sister," he said.
"By kidnapping and threatening someone's life?" Danny said.
"I want answers," Troy said. "I had to take things into my own hands for Eileen's sake."
"Are we under arrest?" Regan said.
"You're being detained," I said.
Danny walked back to the Chevy and drove it back to where we were. I put Regan in the Chevy with me. Danny put Troy Conlon in Eileen Conlon's car with him.

Before we drove off, I said to Arnie, "I'm tired of seeing you, Arnie."

"I'm tired of seeing you too, Graham. But you keep popping up in my life."

"That may be a good thing for you," I said.

"What does that mean?"

"You might have a friend you don't know you have," I said.

I wasn't sure he understood what I meant. If he could get his act together, I'd be willing to use my meager influence to help him get his family back.

"How are things with Kevin?"

"We're getting along."

"I'm sure Gwen is willing to work with you."

"We're making it work, for Kevin's sake."

"Where do you want me to take you?" I said.

"I'm not under arrest?"

"You're the victim here, Arnie. You almost got yourself killed. Stay out of harm's way. And stay away from the Red Hen. Spend more time with your family."

He sat silently for a moment, then said, "Will you take me to Gwen's? I want to see Kevin. After what I went through today, I'm lucky I'm alive."

"About time you realized it," I said.

I started the Chevy and drove away; hoping Arnie had put himself on the right track.

***

After I left Arnie Regan at his wife's apartment, I drove to the Conlon home. Danny had already arrived with Troy Conlon. Eileen Conlon answered the door. She was wearing a long pink lounge robe and bedroom slippers. The same silver crucifix was around her neck that she had worn the day she came into the bureau for questioning. She still had a bandage on her temple. She didn't say a word as I followed her to the living room where Danny and Troy were sitting on the sofa. Troy was holding an ashtray in one hand while he puffed on a cigarette like a freight train. He was angry and frustrated. I sat down at the far end of the sofa beside Eileen Conlon. I removed her gun from my pocket and handed it to her. I handed her the clip separately.

"I suggest you lock these in a secure place if you intend to keep them," I said.

She took the gun and clip and put them in the pocket of her robe.

I pointed a finger at Troy and said, "And you need to stop playing detective. If there're any questions to be asked, I'll ask them."

Troy crushed his cigarette out and placed his ashtray on the coffee table. He leaned back against the sofa back, closed his eyes, and began rubbing his temples.

I hadn't seen anything criminal in Troy Conlon. Other than he had tried to help his sister foolishly. I was sure he wasn't involved in any part of something he shouldn't be. He was not a likable guy in his demeanor and appearance, but that only made him guilty of being a degenerate "jerk". His behavior had been erratic, at first, showing indifference toward his sister, then becoming a concerned brother. Maybe his sentiments toward his sister were genuine, maybe not.

"You could be arrested and charged for the dumb thing you did today," Danny said.

"You're lucky Arnie Regan doesn't press charges," I said. "Kidnapping's a serious offense."

"I'd keep an eye on him if I were you," he said, "and that Crockett, too."

He got up and walked to the bar and poured himself a drink.

"I'm sick of this whole business," he said. "I just wanna get my money and get away from here."

Eileen Conlon stood suddenly. "If you're in such a hurry to leave, I'll write you a check from my account in the amount you are to receive," she said. "Then you can be on your way. Will that make you happy?"

"Very," he said. "I didn't come here to be involved with these people."

Troy drained his glass and walked closer to Eileen Conlon. "Your life might be in danger," he said. "Someone brutally killed your brother, and no one knows why. Did it ever occur to you that you might be next?"

Troy had a point, but no evidence had presented itself to suggest that. As far as I was concerned, Eileen Conlon was my prime suspect in the murder of her brother.

Chapter 32

Sandy and I were having dinner at "Chen's Garden" in midtown. I was having chicken and broccoli, while Sandy enjoyed her beloved Beef chow mien. I broke open a fortune cookie and read it to Sandy. I said, "Man who fart in church, must sit in own pew."

Sandy didn't laugh. "That one's older than you," she said. "Get some new material."

"The old ones are the best ones," I said. "Funny is funny."

She offered me a false smile, which quickly disappeared when she took a forkful of chow mien. I poured some wine into Sandy's glass and filled mine. Sandy wiped her mouth with her napkin, and said, "The Father Conlon case is finally coming to a close?"

"Very perceptive, counselor," I said.

"I can always tell when you're about to solve a case," she said. "Your demeanor changes when you're with me, from determining preoccupation to pensive thoughtfulness."

"Not true," I said. "You're always the first thought in my mind."

She took another forkful and waited for me to continue.

"Danny and I have chiseled away several suspects," I said.

"Have you brought charges?"

"No. We want to establish a motive before we make an arrest."

"Smart," she said. "I've seen many cases where the judge declared a mistrial because of improperly obtained or insufficient evidence."

"My dear," I said. "You are talking to a fine-tuned, seasoned detective, with years of experience. I resent the implication of professional incompetence."

She stuck her tongue out at me and went back to attacking her chow mien.

***

I had a crazy idea of why Eileen Conlon might want to kill her brother. It was a bit "far-fetched" even for me, something I had been contemplating for weeks, but had kept to myself. Unless she was being framed, which was unlikely, those prints on the crucifix made her guilty. I had to justify the motive before I could prove it.

A week had passed since my encounter with Troy Conlon at the Conlon home, and I had nothing to add to substantiate Eileen Conlon's guilt. I was looking for a motive.

I didn't believe Troy Conlon killed his brother. He, no doubt, had drawn that depiction of a knife in his brother's heart in the photo I'd found, probably while in a semi-drunken stupor. It was evident that he held an unwarranted animosity toward his brother and always felt like the family, "black sheep", but that didn't make him a murderer.

I drove to the Conlon home alone, unannounced. I knew what I was trying to do, but had no idea how to do it.

When I rang the bell, Eileen Conlon answered the door with a surprised look on her face. She looked like she had been crying. Her hair was in disarray, and she wore no makeup. She was dressed in black sweatpants and a matching black sweatshirt and navy blue Adidas running shoes. The silver crucifix around her neck shone brightly against the black cloth.

Dark circles beneath her eyes confirmed to me she had been losing sleep.

"We need to talk," I said.

"Of course," she said. "Come in."

We went to the living room and sat on the leather sofa.

"Can I get you something?" she said.

"I'm okay," I said.

I could see she was uncomfortable with my being there, by the way she kept rubbing the crucifix between her thumb and forefinger and fidgeting on the sofa like she couldn't find a satisfactory sitting position. There were several moments of awkward silence between us, until she said, "Are you any closer to finding Andy's killer?"

"I may be," I said, "if I can tie up a few ends."

"I've been tying up a few loose ends myself," she said. "I gave Troy his money. He promised he would leave for places unknown by the end of the week. I'll probably never see him again."

"I've been praying to the Lord for guidance," she said. "There is so much sin. *There is sin everywhere, in the good as well as the bad.* There is obvious sin, and there is hidden sin. Hidden sin is the worst kind," she said. "It must be brought to light and eradicated. It must not be allowed to exist." "Do you see sin in Troy?" I said.

"Troy is an imprudent individual," she said. "He sinned himself, not the Lord."

"And Father Conlon," I said. "Did you find sin in him, as well?"

She became anxious when she heard the question. She walked to the piano, removed a tissue from the box there, and pretended to wipe her moist eyes.

"I loved my brother Andrew dearly," she said. "He was closer to God than I had ever been. But he succumbed to the devil."

"Your brother loved," I said. "What sin is there in love?"

"He did not love the way God intended one to love," she said.

"Love is love," I said, "regardless of how it's expressed."

"There was no love there," she said, "only carnal pleasure."

"Andrew struggled and resisted against his secret sin. He knew it was wrong. He knew he was offending God, but the devil won. I could not help him. No one could help him. He could not help himself. I had to stop the evil influence. I had to remove Satan from within him."

"Without the Lord's help, how did you accomplish that?"

"Prayer did not work," she said. "Confession did not help. There was no other way."

"But to end your brother's life," I said.

"Yes!" she said. "He was on the road to perdition. I couldn't let it happen. The Lord answered my prayer, told me what had to be done, I was simply the instrument of his wishes."

Her emotions were building now, bordering on hysteria. I stood, not knowing what to expect when I saw her remove the gun from the pocket of her sweatpants. She pointed it at me. Her hand was shaking. I kept silent while watching her every move.

"You were the one that would not allow it to happen," she said. She held her arm out straight and pointed the gun directly at my face. "You wouldn't let Andrew ascend to the Lord in peace. You would not let me accomplish the work the Lord had assigned to me. For your sin, you must answer to the Lord."

Instinctively, I knew she was about to pull the trigger when a voice came from the open doorway. "Put the gun down Eileen!"

I looked to see Troy Conlon entering the room. Eileen Conlon kept her gun pointed at me but turned to look at her brother. "Why did you come back?" she said.

"Put the gun away," he said. "This isn't the right thing to do."

"It is all part of his plan," she said.

There was a moment of intense silence between us. I waited to see who would make the next move. I couldn't reach for my gun without eliciting a dangerous reaction, so I broke the stalemate by saying, "I guess I was wrong about you, Troy. You're just as guilty of killing your brother as she is."

"I came here with *money* on my mind, not *murder,*" he said.

"Yet, you let yourself get tangled in a web of murder," I said.

"When my brother made his will, he left the pie to my sister and the crumbs to me. The wayward, prodigal brother didn't deserve what was rightfully his; not an admirable way to think for a priest who is supposed to demonstrate compassion. I never had much love for my brother, and I suppose he never loved me. But the crumbs he left me were an insult. I was broke, couldn't find work. I even had to borrow money for my flight here."

"You're breaking my heart," I said.

"You have about as much compassion as my brother had," he said.

"I have little compassion for criminals," I said.

"The Lord shows his compassion," Eileen Conlon said.

"Did you know she was the one who killed your brother?"

"Not until a few days after I arrived. She confided in me, wanted me to help her make it look like David Crockett had killed my brother. She said she would split her part of the inheritance with me."

I was watching Eileen Conlon. Her gun hand was shaking. Her eyes kept darting from me to Troy and then back to me. Her face was glistening with perspiration. I paid close attention to her trigger finger.

"Half of her inheritance was a lot more than the crumbs I was left with," Troy Conlon was saying.

"You are a part of God's plan as well as I am," Eileen Conlon said.

"When you found out what she had done, why didn't you go to the police?"

"The idea of getting all that money sounded good to me."

"Accessory after the fact makes you as guilty as her," I said.

"Maybe," he said. "But I can't let her commit another murder. You heard her twisted reasoning for committing these crimes. She needs help."

"The Lord is my shepherd," Eileen Conlon said.

"She also killed Father Faynor," I said.

"When I saw it on the news, I knew she was the one. The connection was obvious. I knew she would be caught eventually, all I had to do was keep my mouth shut and wait."

"And with her in jail, the entire inheritance would be yours."

"I deserve it more than her," he said.

"You're blinded by greed."

"Guess I am," he said, "but I'm not a murderer."

"You should not have come back," Eileen Conlon said. "You have interfered with God's design. When Troy Conlon stepped closer to her, she stopped him with, "Stay where you are, Troy. I have the Lord on my side. I don't need you anymore."

He extended his hand to her. "Give me the gun," he said. "We will ask the Lord to forgive us."

"There is nothing to forgive," she said. " 'Thy *will* be done'."

She turned the gun suddenly and pointed it at her brother. Troy Conlon put his hands out in front of him. "Wait, Eileen," he said. "I'm here to help you."

"You should not have come back," she said again, and then she pulled the trigger—twice!

The sound of gunshots reverberated within the room with a deafening explosion. Both rounds hit Troy Conlon in his chest. Webs of blood exploded on his white shirt as he grabbed himself and fell to the floor.

Eileen Conlon swung her gun back in my direction. I didn't wait for her to fire again. I dove to the floor and rolled behind the end of the sofa. She squeezed off another round that whizzed by my head, spraying plaster out of the wall behind me. I pulled out my gun and waited. I wasn't sure what her next move would be or where it would come from. My finger was tight on the trigger.

The room was quiet. I peered over the top of the sofa's arm. Eileen Conlon was rushing out of the living room. I watched her hurry through the kitchen and out the back door.

I got up and walked to where Troy Conlon was lying. Blood had saturated the front of his shirt and was spilling onto the carpet. Although his eyes were open, I was sure he was dead. When you see it enough, you just know.

A mental picture of Father Conlon lying on the carpeted floor in his office came back to me. The horrific stab wounds, the blood trailing down his white shirt and pooling on the carpet,

OTHER MEN'S SINS

and the look on his face, similar to Troy Conlon's. I shook the image out of my mind and hurried to the back door.

When I looked through the screen door, I saw several acres of manicured lawn and shrubbery, and a large kidney-shaped pool, and a pool house close by. The area was meticulously kept. There were several poolside tables with umbrellas poking from the middle of them. Scattered around the pool were several cushioned lounge chairs. There was a glass, and metal bar, and a stone barbecue grill. At one end of the pool was a diving board.

Eileen Conlon came into view, suddenly. I watched her run past the pool and continue along a hedgerow at the perimeter of the property grounds. She was headed for what looked like an intricately designed rose garden in the distance. From where I stood, I could see a low picket fence surrounding some elaborately configured rose bushes. The giant bushes were comingled with concrete statues of various Roman figures and an occasional wrought-iron bench.

I pushed open the screen door and moved along the same hedgerow she had. As I did, I watched her disappear into the rose garden. I didn't know if she knew where she was going, but I had to stay close or I'd lose her.

When I reached the rose garden, I crouched low and hugged the hedgerow to make myself less of a target. She was still carrying her gun. I was not familiar with the grounds and didn't know if she had an escape route or if she was playing "hide and seek" with me, or I was being sucked into a trap.

I stepped over the low fence and took cover behind a life-size statue of a man wearing a toga. He had wings and a halo sculptured in concrete and looked out with pious majesty over the Conlon estate.

The grounds were quiet, save for the occasional chirping of birds and an occasional breeze rustling the nearby tree branches.

I waited.

I couldn't see or hear movement. I kept low with my gun at my side. The garden was of substantial size, and as I moved deeper into it, I began to feel like I was navigating a maze. I didn't see Eileen Conlon, but startled myself more than once, each time I turned a corner and ran into another of my concrete friends.

Not far ahead, I came upon a small opening amongst the rose bushes; it appeared to be a circular area designed for meditation or prayer. At its circumference, there were several wrought-iron benches; at the center, on a pedestal, stood a larger-than-life statue of Mother Mary.

I stepped out into the opening. The area was serene and comforting, much like the interior of a chapel. A gentle breeze swayed the surrounding roses, disseminating their fragrance in the air, while the tranquility was disturbed only by the muted chirping of birds.

A gunshot rang out! A round passed close by my head and lodged in the Holy Mother's chest, spitting fragments of concrete into the air. I hit the dirt. When I looked up, I saw where the shot had been fired from by the lingering smoke encircling the area. I fired off three quick shots in the direction of the smoke, to discourage any additional shots that might be coming my way. I scrambled to my feet and maneuvered around the edge of the circle until I got to where the shot had been fired. I could smell gun powder but saw no one. At the base of a bush, I noticed a spent casing reflecting sunlight. I picked it up. It was still warm. Eileen Conlon was desperate to get away, and I knew now, for sure, if it meant killing me to accomplish it, she would. She was somewhere within the maze of this rose garden. I had to be careful, or I'd wind up as cold as one of these statues.

As I continued toward the front of the rose garden, Eileen Conlon burst out of a bush and darted across the lawn in the direction of the pool house. I holstered my gun, vaulted the low fence, and put on a good pace after her. When I was close enough, I reached out and grabbed her shoulder, pulling her back and off-balance. She tumbled to the ground. I went down with her. She tried to bring her gun up. I grabbed hold of it and tried to twist it from her. That's when my body exploded with pain as she drove her knee into my crotch. I rolled over onto the grass, convulsing in agony. When I looked up, she was running across the lawn toward the pool house. I wondered why she hadn't taken the opportunity to kill me.

I laid in the grass, waiting for the fire between my legs to subside, as I watched her open the pool house door and disappear inside. I struggled painfully to my feet and hobbled across the lawn toward the pool house. I felt vulnerable in the open space of the yard until I reached the pool area where I was able to conceal myself behind the furniture. I kept low and moved from table to lounge chair, to table.

Outside the pool house, I hunkered behind one of the arborvitae scrubs that surrounded it. The door of the pool house had a small window in it. I looked through the window, but it was too dark inside to see anything. Eileen Conlon had entered the pool house. Why did she run in there?

Opening the door and walking into the darkness would set me up as too much of a target. I walked around the building and found no additional windows or doors, which meant Eileen Conlon was still inside. I decided to wait her out. I walked back around to the front of the building, concealed myself between the shrubbery, and removed my gun from my holster, and waited.

There was silence other than the low humming of the filter in the pool behind me.

After I had given her enough time, I crawled closer to the door, reached up, and turned the knob. As I pulled the door open, a shot splintered the wood of the doorframe near my head. I slammed the door and threw myself back into the shrubbery. As I did, Eileen Conlon pushed the door open and rushed past me. She was carrying a large overnight bag as she ran toward the front of the house. She was still carrying the gun at her side. I waited for her to disappear around the front corner of the house and then got to my feet.

I inched my way along the side of the house, hoping she wouldn't jump out from the corner and start firing at me. When I reach the front of the house, I peered around the corner. From my position, I heard the humming of the electric garage door opener, which told me she was attempting to get away in her car. I moved along the front of the house until I reached the garage door. It was in a fully open position. I had to think fast. I couldn't let her back the car out of the garage and make good her escape. I didn't want to shoot her, and I didn't want to get shot.

I waited, expecting to hear the car's engine start. When it didn't, I stepped into the garage opening behind the car and pointed my gun at the car interior through the back window.

"Eileen," I said. "Don't try to run."

The inside of the garage was dark. The only light visible was the car's dim interior light. The car's engine still hadn't, so I moved along the driver's side of the car. The driver's door was ajar. Through a side window, I saw Eileen Conlon in the driver's seat, staring through the windshield, her eyes wide and empty. She appeared to be looking at nothing as if she were in a stupor. I opened the car door carefully. She was holding the gun on her lap. I reached in and slipped it from her fingers and put it in my pocket.

"Eileen," I said.

She didn't respond.

"Eileen, it's time to come with me," I said.

I looked closer to see if she had harmed herself. There were no signs of injury. I could see motion in her chest, due to her heavy erratic breathing. I waved my hand in front of her face. She remained static, not a twitch of a muscle or a blink of an eye. She was entirely inanimate. I felt like I was looking at a store mannequin.

My eye caught movement at the curb out front. Danny Nolan had parked the Impala at the curb and was getting out. When he saw me, he walked into the garage. He assessed the scene quickly. He saw Eileen Conlon seated in the car, and my gun in my hand.

"You okay?" he said.

I nodded.

"Garcia told me you'd be here."

"Troy Conlon is on the floor in the house with a bullet in his chest," I said. "He's dead."

"Did you shoot him?"

"She did," I said.

Danny peered through the car's rear window at Eileen Conlon sitting motionless. "Is she—?

I shook my head, "no".

"I'll call it in," he said.

As he turned and walked out of the garage, I looked back at Eileen Conlon. She was lifeless, a prisoner in her world, unaware of her surroundings.

I called her name again.

She didn't react.

I shook her shoulder, gently, and said, "Eileen... Eileen...."

No response.

Chapter 33

Sandy and I were sitting at my kitchen table enjoying a Saturday breakfast. She had whipped up a batter and made a dozen golden brown silver dollar pancakes. We divided them with a number she considered fair; eight for me, four for her. She sprinkled some strawberry syrup on hers, while I drowned mine with my favorite, Maple flavor. Sandy poured some coffee in her cup and filled mine from a carafe on the table.

It had been a week since the Conlon trial had ended and I was feeling myself again, although my heart ached at the loss of Andy Conlon. It would be some time before I got over that, if ever.

"What was Eileen Conlon's motive for killing her brother?" Sandy said.

"She'd become a victim of her twisted mind," I said. "She could not accept her brother's way of life. She struggled with it herself for many years, keeping her brother's secret and hating every second of it. Eventually, it distorted her way of thinking to the point that she believed the only way to free her brother from his burden was to send him to 'a better place'. In essence, she believed she was helping him, liberating him from sin."

"Why did she kill Troy?"

"Anger, outrage, indignation. In the name of God, she killed both of her brothers."

"And Father Faynor?"

"She discovered he was her brother's enabler and believed he was the catalyst that perpetuated her brothers sinning. He needed to go to 'a better place' too."

"Why'd she implicate Crockett?"

"At one time she'd been very fond of Crockett, probably thought she loved him. But after he broke up with her, she held a deep animus toward him. When she planned her brother's murder, she intended to make it look like Crockett did the deed. Thus taking her revenge on him, for what she believed, was his unwarranted mistreatment of her. He was a set-up, a patsy. She even paid Regan to hire some thugs to work me over and put the blame on Crockett."

"Which Regan accomplished very convincingly."

"I believed Regan at the time; had no reason not to."

"Or, maybe you wanted to believe him," Sandy said.

"I guess I did," I said.

"If Eileen Conlon hated Crockett, why did she get back together with him?"

"She wanted to keep him close, make it easy for her to manipulate him into making himself unwittingly, look guilty."

"For someone with a deranged mind, she designed a fairly elaborately plan," Sandy said.

"Even to the degree of obtaining a screwdriver and a pair of old work overalls," I said, "and saturating the overalls with her victim's blood. Thus, further incriminating Crockett, the custodian who wore work overalls and used hand tools."

"And she typed that phony letter about Crockett to solidify his looking guilty," Sandy said. "And went so far as to hide the overalls and screwdriver in a nearby trash bin where she knew they would be easily found."

"Clever," I said, "but a banal attempt to deceive the police."

Sandy waited while I took a mouthful of pancake and washed it down with coffee.

"As careful as she was in her planning, she made one mistake," I said. "She left her fingerprints on the crucifix."

"A slip of the lip..." Sandy said.

"As close as we can figure, she went to her brother's office and when his back was turned, struck him with a heavy brass crucifix, causing him to lose consciousness and fall to the floor, and then—here comes the sick part—she jumped on him and strangled him in a rage until he was dead. Then, in a sustained rage, she used the screwdriver and proceeded to stab him multiple times, thus, releasing him from sin... in her mind."

I had one pancake left on my dish. Sandy had been sticking her fork in the two she had left without eating them.

"Are you gonna eat those?" I said.

She slid her dish over to me and said, "Why did Crockett run if he knew he was innocent?"

"Fear, ignorance, mistrust of the system," I said.

I soaked the pancakes with syrup and went to work on them. I washed them down with more coffee before I said, "In any event, he's been exonerated of any wrongdoing, even got his job back at the rectory. Monsignor Belducci said he had nothing to forgive Crockett for."

"I feel sorry for the Regan kid," she said.

"Arnie Regan wants to be with his son. That's what almost got him in trouble with the law, fighting for his son the wrong way. I think he's learned that the way to go, is respecting his ex-wife and child. It might generate a mutual desire to rekindle their love for each other again. I'm doing what I can to help them become a family again."

"What happens to Eileen Conlon now?" Sandy said.

"Eileen Conlon will spend the rest of her life behind bars, whether in prison or a state mental institution. A judge will make that determination based on testimony from psychiatric professionals. Either way, it's not likely she'll ever be released."

"I'm sure, in her own way, she'll find solace with the Lord," Sandy said.

I finished my coffee, got up and walked to the front window, and looked down at the activity on Bigelow Street. The morning was fresh and clean; tree limbs, wet from an overnight rain glistened in the morning sun. The street was busy for an early morning. People were driving and people were walking on their way to wherever they needed to go, to get on with their lives. There were people from every walk of life, every faith, and every color, sharing the same ideas, hopes, dreams, and despairs. Men and women existing together in an assemblage known as humankind.

Sandy came up beside me. She slid her arm around my waist. "What is it?" she said.

I continued to look down at the street. "I can't help feeling empathy for Eileen Conlon," I said. "She had once been a loyal servant of the Lord, but through her own misguided belief, became a victim of self-destruction."

I looked at Sandy. "Eileen Conlon was right," I said. "There is sin everywhere, in the good as well as the bad."